DRAGONS
OF THE
THAUMATURGIC REALM

Dragons
OF THE
Thaumaturgic Realm

Revolt

KYLEEN VALLEAUX

Dragons of the
Thaumaturgic Realm:
Revolt

ISBN-13: 978-1-944895-05-1

www.thaumaturgicrealm.com

Published by Fusion Graphics
P.O. Box 13284
Lansing, MI 48901-3284
www.fusiongraphics.org

Printed in U.S.A

To Alex- who was the first reader of this adventure, many years ago, and who is also the best child a mother could ever wish for.

Love and Kissies.

ACKNOWLEDGEMENTS:

First, my family, small as it is, they are why I keep going.

My editor, Michelle Dunbar, made this story shine. Without her, and her encouragement, I'm not sure this book would have ever seen the light of day.

My cover artist, Anika Willmanns, took a stick figure pencil sketch and made my vision a reality.

And my friends, many as you are, both in "real life" and social media platforms, your belief in me makes me keep going when fear and panic make me want to quit.

Thank you.

Table of Contents

MAY DAY AT THE KEEP

"Hooray! Hooray! It's the first of May!" rang a chorus of young male voices from beyond the walled courtyard of Sebastian's keep. The revelers had started early this year. Maug's lips twisted into a brief smile, knowing the rest of the rhyme, but his attention returned to the laptop on the small ornate metal table. This side garden was one of the few spots in the Thaumaturgic Realm that guaranteed an internet connection to the Geotic Realm. With trading in New York ending in a matter of minutes, there was little time to get his last two transactions in.

"Ah!"

Maug lifted his eyes from the screen with a twinge of annoyance. *Turis? Ugh.*

"I should have known you'd be hiding out here, Maug."

The other man was taller with broad shoulders; his features were sharp and handsome. His black hair hung long and straight around his neck. Turis didn't wait for an invitation but pulled up a chair and sat across the table from Maug, watching him with a glint of amusement. Maug ignored him. He finished his transaction and closed the laptop, cocking his head in the older dragon's direction.

Turis, Dragon Lord of the North, had almost three hundred years on Maug, who hadn't yet reached his half-centennial. Turis was in his prime. His true form was a huge black dragon, whereas Maug's was a smaller red dragon, the only dragon lord that didn't have his horns yet. Maug had the advantage in that he'd studied more advanced magics and was a true mage, but Turis was an unstoppable warrior, and the one dragon lord Maug couldn't be certain of taking in a head-on fight.

"I'm not hiding," Maug said. His human form was that of a young man, with a slimmer frame than Turis. His bright red hair was clipped short, with his bangs pushed away from his face. His fine features were sharp; more from his dam, he'd been told, than his sire. "I had business to attend to."

"You and your hobbies," Turis mocked. Maug let it go. Turis, while openly teasing, had never seriously challenged him. He was an annoying old bastard, but not a threat. "How is your aunt?"

"Aunt Maggie?" Maug smiled. "She's fine. Stay away from her."

"Oh, ho!" Turis offered a wide predatory smile. "Defending her honor?"

"Like I'd have to. Charles would skin you and gift her your hide."

"Ah, yes." Turis leaned back, and his smile eased. Charles Tampton was one of the few humans Turis actually liked, probably due to the Advocate of Ridges Hollow being every bit as powerful as a dragon lord. "I heard the advocate would be in attendance. Will the lady be joining him?"

Maug shook his head, glad that Turis was using the native language of dragons rather than the human English the fairy court favored. Charles had made it clear from the moment he and Aunt Maggie wed that neither the Fairy King or Queen was to know he had taken a dragon for his wife. "You know better than to ask that. Charles is here to talk to the Advocate of Spoons Forge about the border trouble we've been having, that's all."

"We?" Turis arched an eyebrow. "You're not still on that folly to be advocate after Charles Tampton, are you?"

Maug worked to keep his temper and his tongue still. He'd had this argument with the full Council of the Dragon Lords more than once. They felt him being an advocate would split his loyalties and Maug strongly disagreed. Neither he nor they had come to a satisfactory resolution of the issue.

"What are you doing at Court, anyway?" Maug turned the conversation away from himself. Turis cleared his features and arched an eyebrow.

"I drew the short stick. You know well that King Oberon demands at least one of us dance attendance at these events. Had I known you'd be here, I wouldn't have bothered."

Maug met Turis's pale grey eyes with his own dark ones. "You're lying."

Turis offered a hint of a smile. "Prove it."

Maug shook his head and stood, picking up his laptop with one hand. If it didn't affect him, Charles, or Ridges Hollow, it wasn't worth pursuing. The older black was canny and kept his own counsel. "I don't care to."

"Good day, Lord Dragon." Turis gave a small smirk as Maug turned away.

~ ~ ~

Turis watched Maug as he crossed the small side patio and left by a small gate. He caught a familiar scent and snorted.

"Tell me, wolf." He moved to stand. "Does the boy know you shadow his steps?"

He caught the wolf shaman's movement as she shimmered into human form. She was tall for a female but slight, with long white hair and golden eyes simmering with wild ferocity. Her command of magic inside the fairy stronghold impressed him. Here, working a spell was like swimming in mud due to the wards set by King Oberon's powerful inhuman mages.

"As if I'd let you be alone with him." Her soft voice held menace. The wolves were loyal to their pack and suspicious of outsiders. Maug's father, the black dragon mage Mugan, had been the wolf woman's pack "brother." From what Turis could gather, she'd helped raise the young red after he'd been orphaned. "And he is no boy. He is a dragon lord."

"As am I, so watch yourself, bitch."

Laru's lip curled to bare her teeth. He put up a hand. "I am no threat to your pup, woman. You should know that by now."

"Then why are you here, Lord Turis?" She folded her arms in front of her. "I know it's because Lord Maug is. If not to spy, then what?"

The wolf appeared to know more about the political scenery of the realm than the lad.

"We don't come to the Keep unless there are at least two of us these days, but better three or four. Jaka and Giet will arrive this afternoon," Turis said. Laru's nose wrinkled with a hint of curiosity. "Tell me Laru-baba, why doesn't your Lord know more about what is going on? Why have you kept him from the truth?"

"The truth?" That earned him a small wolfish grin. "Oh, good Lord Turis. The truth is a very fickle thing. And besides, my Lord is hotheaded and rash. Charles and I believe it best that he learns his own truth. We see no reason to push him into an ill-conceived action."

Turis weighed her words and had to agree. The boy, while he favored his mother in appearance, was far more his father's son than any hatchling had a right to be. Young Maug's black eyes flashed with Mugan's arrogance and temper.

"The others"—Turis switched to the language of dragons, suspecting the wolf understood it all too well— "don't know who the boy will stand with when it's time. They worry that Oberon has sunk his claws deep into the fledgling."

"My Lord will stand with the dragons," Laru replied in the same clipped tongue, confirming his suspicion. "However, it is in his best interest, and those of the Dragon Lords, that it doesn't come to pass until all are ready to act."

She inclined her head and shifted into her wolf form, and trotted out of the patio with her tail held high. Turis turned her words over in his mind. When the wolf spoke, you heard the truth… but, as she had mentioned, the truth was a very fickle thing.

~ ~ ~

"Hey," Bobby said, pulling at Katrin's sleeve and pointing. "Did you see that dress?"

As they rounded a corner in the long stone hallway, they had nearly collided with a woman close to their age, who met them with a stony glare of indignation. Clasping their hands together, they scurried away, laughing. They had gotten lost exploring Sebastian's Keep, but were hopefully making their way back to the rooms afforded to Bobby's grandfather.

It's more Ren Faire than Royal Court, Bobby thought with humor. That dress would have been popular in the 1500s, with its long sleeves and a bright yellow brocade stitched in green. She and Katrin wore jeans and light t-shirts, common in the Geotic Realm. It hadn't occurred to them that their attire would make them stand out among the denizens of Sebastian's Keep.

"You would look better in it," Katrin said, eyeing Bobby's jeans. A year older than Bobby, taller, and with more curves, she was also the one people noticed. Her long brown hair curled naturally into ringlets, and her bright leaf-green eyes seemed to glow when she spoke. Her bronzed skin and classical features attracted far more attention than Bobby's short black hair ever would, and while not completely boyish, Bobby didn't have Katrin's feminine shape.

"We should go back and change," Bobby said. "Granddad said he had some business to take care of though."

Coming to Sebastian's Keep for the May festival was like stepping into a dream. She'd spent her summers at Spoons Forge since fifth grade. Her grandfather, Ezra Parks, was the advocate for the region, or constabulary as they called it in this place. He'd steadfastly told Bobby that until she turned twenty-one, she was too young to go to the Keep. With her birthday a mere two months away, she had campaigned to attend the May Day festivities since Easter. Granddad had finally relented, but only if she promised to stay out of the way when he had meetings with the other advocates. She'd assured him she would, and dragged her best friend, Katrin, along with her too.

Katrin's mother was from the Thaumaturgic Realm, though she had died when Katrin was a child. Katrin was a dragon too, which made her a mid-powered magic user, but she was born in the Geotic Realm. Ezra Parks had found the orphan an adoptive home not far from where Roberta lived with her parents. They had been best friends for as long as Bobby could remember. She was one of the few people in her life who even knew about the Thaumaturgic Realm. Bobby couldn't remember a trip here that didn't involve Katrin in one way or the other.

Sebastian's Keep was home to the immortal Fairy King and Queen. And while they didn't rule the entire realm, Spoons Forge was located inside their kingdom.

They had to turn around twice, but finally found their way back to the heavy wooden door that would lead to where they were staying. Bobby paused outside, putting a finger to her lips and Katrin nodded.

"We'll be quiet as field mice," Katrin whispered. "Ezra won't even know we're there."

They tried to enter quietly, but the door betrayed them with a loud *creak*. They stilled, leaning on it, doubled over in silent laughter.

The main room was long and narrow with a fireplace at the far end. A long table ran along the front of it, clearly the better position during the colder months. But right now, the warmth of spring made a fire unnecessary.

Bobby's grandfather conferred with two other men, a large map spread out in front of them. One was older, but not as old as her grandfather, his blond hair dusted with grey. The other man was much younger, around her age, and looked utterly bored. He was slim and tall and had the brightest red hair she'd ever seen. Katrin gasped and put her hand over her mouth.

"What?" Bobby hissed at her. It drew the young man's attention. His dark eyes flicked over Katrin with a slightly raised brow, and then settled on Bobby with a gaze sharp enough to cut glass. She colored up to her ears. He eased into a friendly smile.

"Oh? Roberta?" Ezra turned towards their direction. "Did you have a good tour of the Keep?"

Bobby cleared her throat and shook her head, stepping forward. "It's huge, Granddad," she said. "We didn't know where to start."

Katrin found her voice. "The maids kept directing us toward the kitchens." She motioned to what they were wearing. "They thought we were drudges."

"Ah, well." Ezra chuckled. "It's better than getting lost. Charles, this is my granddaughter, Roberta Parks, and her friend Katrin. They begged to come to Court for the May festival. Roberta, Charles and I still have work to do, but I'll try and show you around later…"

Charles stood up and moved forward, extending his hand, friendly and warm. Bobby smiled at him, and he returned the gesture.

"Your grandfather speaks well of you, Miss Parks. This is Maug; he's my second at Ridges Hollow."

"Ladies." The red-haired man inclined his head with a hand on his chest. He followed Charles over, and Bobby got a better look at him. He had to be over six-foot-tall. Bobby's head only came up to his chin. "I think you look fine, but it's true what they say, the Thaumaturgic Realm fashion trends are at least five hundred years behind the times."

"You're from the Geotic too?"

Maug offered her a rueful half smile. "I split my time, thanks to Charles." Maug threw a grin of affection toward the older man. "He made me go to school there. It was barbaric."

"Oh? Where did you go?"

"Harvard. Terrible place. Absolutely wretched."

Bobby giggled.

Charles nodded to Ezra Parks. "Why doesn't Maug show the ladies around?"

Ezra hesitated, as if uncertain of the offer. Bobby felt her heart leap in her chest. She turned to her grandfather with a nod, hoping he would say yes.

"You can keep the ladies out of mischief, can't you, son? He knows the inappropriate places to avoid."

The young man perked up. Bobby wondered if he was bored out of his mind waiting attendance on the older men.

"I'd be happy to." He offered them a wide smile that seemed genuine. "And perhaps I could escort the ladies to the ball this evening? It should be fun. I hear they are getting a Maypole out to dance around."

"Ah, gods." Bobby's grandfather rolled his eyes. "That's all we need. They will be fornicating in the roses again."

"Probably," Charles agreed. Then he nodded. "Maug, no fornicating in the roses."

Maug grinned. "You take all the fun out of it, Charles."

"W-we need to change," Katrin stammered. She grabbed Bobby's arm and dragged her into the side room they were sharing.

"Oh, my god," Katrin whispered, leaning against the door after it closed. Her face drained of color.

"What?"

"That's one of the Dragon Lords," she hissed. "I wasn't sure until they called him by his name. Oh, gods."

"What does that mean?" Bobby had heard about the seven standing Dragon Lords but didn't know who they were, or what they did. Obviously, they were dragons. Other than that, she guessed they were fierce warriors. She had heard they held the wild territories away from the kingdom, fending off invaders from the darkest parts of the realm. Her granddad hadn't elaborated on who or what they were, so everything she knew was hearsay and guesswork.

Katrin locked eyes with Bobby. "It means he has better things to do than play chaperone to us." She pushed away from the door and went to the large window overlooking an expansive courtyard below. Bobby hopped on the bed, perplexed by Katrin's odd behavior.

Bobby smiled. "He's pretty hot."

"Well, I don't like him. And don't think I do and try to set me up. It's not happening."

Bobby cocked her head to one side with concern. She had never seen Katrin so visibly shaken before. "If you say so."

"It'll be okay." Katrin drew a deep breath. "What they said is true. Lord Maug spent half his childhood in the Geotic Realm. Charles Tampton is his foster father."

Bobby nodded. She could sense the affection between Charles Tampton and Maug.

Katrin rubbed her palms on her legs. "He's not like the others," she told Bobby. "We'll be safer with him than anyone else."

"What are you worried about?" Bobby asked. Katrin looked at her with stricken eyes then closed them, turning her face away.

"It's nothing," Katrin said, giving her a weak smile. Bobby wasn't convinced. She thought Katrin would have been interested in meeting a handsome young dragon, but that didn't seem to be the case. Katrin turned and crossed the chamber, opening the doors of the wide wooden wardrobe. "Why don't we see what we have to wear tonight?"

~ ~ ~

Maug turned back to Ezra Caleb Parks. "Who's the green?"

The old man paled. "No one my Lord Dragon need be concerned with."

Maug flicked his eyes to his own advocate, who offered a small shrug. Charles didn't know either? Curious.

"I wasn't aware of any dragon owing allegiance to Spoons Forge," Maug mused.

"She's an orphan," Ezra Parks replied. "Much like yourself."

Maug turned his attention back to his foster father. "I thought I was out of the last clutch known to have hatched."

"That's true from everything we know," Charles said. "At least in the Thaumaturgic Realm."

"Wait." Maug moved back to the table. Parks was going over the maps of where he had raiders attacking his holdings. Spoons Forge and Ridges Hollow held a long border, so attacks from outside forces concerned both constabularies. "Advocate, that girl is younger than me, I am sure, and her power is minimal, even for a green. Are you saying this girl… Katrin… wasn't hatched in the Thaumaturgic Realm?"

"The girl is none of your concern."

"Are you serious?" Maug took a step towards Ezra Parks, fists clenched at his side. "When a dragon hasn't laid a clutch in the last forty years? And yet this child exists, from somewhere? Are there more? Who are her parents? Why is she living in the Geotic Realm? As a dragon, I'd say this is absolutely my concern!"

"Maug." Charles's tone was quiet but full of warning. Maug snapped his mouth shut. He seethed at the gall of the human's interference. Charles? Yes, Charles could interfere. Not only was he the only father he had ever known, he had married Maug's blood aunt. Charles and Maggie had their own children and they carried the blood of dragons in them. Something Charles worked very hard to keep concealed.

There was a reason for his secrecy, one that Charles didn't care to share with the young dragon. But it had to be the reason not one dragon had laid a clutch.

Not one.

"I'll take the ladies out," Maug said. He drew a deep breath and worked to relax his stance. "And I'll keep them from mischief. Which will be a challenge in its own right. You are aware I am not the only dragon in the Keep for the festival? And from what I heard from Lord Turis today, I won't be the only dragon lord in attendance either."

"I am certain"—Ezra Parks forced a small tight smile—"that Lord Maug is capable of keeping two young women from harm at the most civilized place in the Thaumaturgic Realm. Queen Titania—"

"Titania?" Maug exploded.

Charles laid a hand on his shoulder and leaned close to his ear. "We don't want this fight," he said lightly.

Maug glared at Charles. He trusted the man with his life, but although Spoons was important to Ridges, Maug would have no hesitation in breaking off their ties should Ezra continue with his "most civilized place in the realm" bullshit. The young dragon lord inclined his head, silently fuming as he left the chamber to get ready for the evening's adventure.

~ ~ ~

The festivities were in high swing by the time Turis stepped into the Crimson Ballroom. Its blood-red marble walls and floor had given the venue its name. One of three ceremonial halls, each had its own unique decor. The other two was used exclusively by Queen Titania or King Oberon. The two fairies were more often at odds with each other than not, so they each held separate courts.

But the Blood Hall, the Crimson Ballroom's unofficial name, was where both fairies held court. It was considered "neutral" ground in the never-ending marital battle that often spilled into their respective courts.

Turis was not an official member of either court. Out of all the Dragon Lords, only Maug and old Lord Tsui belonged to one, and that was Oberon's; a fact that made Turis's brethren uneasy. Neither the King nor Queen was in current attendance, which suited the black dragon. It took work not to show open contempt for either of them.

Lord Giet caught his eye and tapped his companion's arm. Turis recognized the other as Jaka, Dragon Lord of the Northwest. Turis noted they, like he, were wearing richly embroidered tunics rather than their typical day-to-day armor. Both moved purposefully in his direction and offered a polite nod.

Like Turis, Giet, who held the south, was a black dragon. His dark hair was clipped tight to his head.

Compared to the other two dragons, Lord Jaka, a purple dragon, was shorter and of a slighter build, with dusty brown hair and vivid purple eyes. He had been Oberon's choice when his predecessor was killed in a challenge against Lord Maug's sire. Mugan had no use for the Dragon Lords and refused to take on the role of Dragon Lord of the Northeast. Eager to fill their ranks with a weakling, Oberon offered the title to Jaka, a favorite of Queen Titania's court at the time. Little did the Fairy King realize that he had put one of dragon-kind's greatest minds into their ranks. While he wasn't as powerful as the rest, the standing Dragon Lords respected his keen intellect and considered him their equal.

"Turis," Giet said with a slight incline of his head. "Have you seen our fledgling?"

They spoke in the language of dragons, drawing sneers from those nearby. Oberon had made it quite clear that he considered dragons an inferior, barbaric race, and had long decreed that no dragon could reveal its true form, ever, at the Keep. And while he couldn't ban their language, its use was frowned upon.

"Briefly," Turis answered. "Earlier. Use caution, the wolf is shadowing him."

"When is she not?" Giet snorted. "No, I meant this evening. He's escorting two females."

"Two," Jaka confirmed as he held up two fingers with a wink. "Oh, to be young and foolish, again."

"It's of little interest," Turis said, having already made plans of his own. Trin, the daughter of the eldest Dragon Lord, Tsui, had flirted for his favor. A yellow, she was ardent in bed. Tsui had hopes of Lord Turis taking her as a mate. Turis, however, was not of a mind to keep her. Nevertheless, the black dragon didn't plan on sleeping alone. It was May Day after all.

"Oh, not true." Giet's mouth twisted into a smile. He had a reputation for being polite and affable, and for that, he led their council. But he could be a wicked bastard in a fight and had a vicious, mean temper. "You should get a closer look."

"Why?" Turis scanned the room to see if he could spot the young red. Ah, there. Maug stood near a set of patio doors in one corner of the marble hall, just off the rose garden. He was with a small knot of younglings. No surprise. Maug enjoyed the company of his peers, most of whom spent as much time in the Geotic Realm as he did. Another habit that irked the Dragon Lords, but as long as the red didn't neglect his responsibilities in the Thaumaturgic Realm, they had no call to challenge him.

"Because I tried to get close, and he threw a glare hot enough to scorch. I have no interest in fighting a challenge with the little bastard." Giet grinned. Turis smirked, knowing that Giet was likely still smarting from the beating Maug had given him when he claimed his title. Out of all the Dragon Lords, only Giet had called challenge after Maug became Lord of the West. Since it had been Giet's sire Maug killed for that title, it was almost required that the Lord of the South demand the fight. Maug had shown more maturity than any of them expected when he spared Giet's life at the end of it.

"So you want me to irritate him?" Turis let out a short, humorless laugh.

"He's not stupid enough to take you on," Giet said.

"You give him too much credit," Turis replied. But his curiosity was piqued, so he nodded politely and made his way toward Lord Maug and his female companions. He paused when he caught an intoxicating scent. It set him on edge; he felt a stir of excitement in his gut.

What had started as a curiosity became intent and he moved with more purpose. Maug jerked his head up and caught Turis's eyes. The red narrowed his gaze and tightened his jaw.

"Ladies." Maug excused himself and moved to head off the black dragon's approach. Turis stood half a head taller than the red and met him with a frown. Maug dropped his voice to a bare whisper, knowing Turis's sharp ears would hear. "Don't."

The word held both warning and menace. Turis felt a hot flash of temper and met the young one's glare.

"Who is that?" Turis's eyes narrowed on the young green in human form. She wore a bright green spring dress, her brown curls pulled away from her face. She kept her gaze on the floor, as if aware of his scrutiny. Her face flushed with heat, and it took nearly all his self-control not to move to her side. Her scent directed his actions more than any amount of common sense did. He felt a light shove as Maug pushed him back. He met the red's eyes with a snarl.

"She is not your concern, Dragon Lord," Maug said in a low voice. "And she is under my protection."

"Ascribed to your house?" Turis silently weighed the option of challenging the young red for her.

Maug shook his head. "No," he said. "She is out of Spoons. Charles asked that I keep the ladies out of trouble for the evening. Do you understand, Turis?"

Turis tightened his jaw. He returned his attention to the green and nodded. For the moment, the female was protected by the Dragon Lord of the West. Young as he was, Maug took these things seriously. And while Turis felt sure he could take the young red in a challenge, he didn't doubt he would suffer heavy damage in doing so.

Not worth it for a bed warmer; at least, not at the moment.

"I understand." Turis turned his attention back to Maug. "But understand, youngling, this isn't over."

~ ~ ~

Bobby heard Maug muttering a curse as he returned to their side. He looked troubled, and she leaned forward to get a better look at the man he'd spoken to. He was large, dark-haired, and she got the impression he might be a dragon too. Although there was no sure way of knowing, Katrin had been trembling since his approach.

"Who is that?" she asked.

Maug cleared his features and offered a half smile. "Lord Turis of the North. But he's not your worry. Tell me more about your job in the copy center? What do you do there?"

"It's not that interesting." Bobby rolled her eyes. "But the customers can be. Last week, we had this guy—"

"Bobby, Bobby!" a shrill, excitable voice called out. There was a blur of white as a young man barreled into her. "I knew I'd find you here. I just knew it!"

"F-Farni?" Bobby stammered. Maug collared the boy, yanking him away from Bobby, and then held him, so he teetered on his toes. For his part, the lad wasn't fearful at all. He turned his large blue eyes and bright smile on the dragon lord.

"Hi," the boy said brightly, "I'm Farni. Who are you?"

"Ugh." Maug snorted and dropped the boy. "A unicorn?"

"Mmmm!" Farni nodded. "Ezra wanted me to stay in our rooms, but that's no fun!"

"Parks obviously has more common sense than you," Maug remarked.

"Don't be mean." Bobby gave the dragon lord a flirtatious push; he grinned and her heart skipped.

She liked him—a lot. He was her age. He knew about the Thaumaturgic Realm but had spent enough time in the Geotic that they had a lot in common.

"Only for you," Maug teased. She offered him a bright smile. The music started, and the floor cleared as couples started to dance.

"Oh, Oh, I know this one," Farni squealed. "Dance with me, Bobby! Plllleeeaaase!"

"Well, um…" Bobby hesitated and looked at Maug.

He touched her arm lightly, leaning over to speak into her ear. "It's your first ball. Enjoy it. But I expect the next dance."

His soft, deep voice made her melt inside. She paused, met his eyes, and nodded.

"All right," she agreed.

"Yay!" Farni grabbed her hand and pulled her away.

They started with a step and a bow. Bobby laughed at Farni's serious expression as they stepped around each other with a small clap. Farni's "human" appearance was that of a slim twelve-year-old boy. His demeanor was one of fearless bright energy. He had taught her this dance during her stay at Spoons Forge the previous summer. He grinned and cocked his head to one side as they moved slowly around each other again.

"So?" Bobby asked gesturing to where they had left Maug and Katrin. "What do you think of Maug?"

"The dragon?"

"Yes," Bobby said, "the dragon."

"He's all right. The others are scarier. Maug is different, though. Even Ezra says so. It's because Charles Tampton is his foster father, you know."

"That's what Katrin said," Bobby replied, trying to observe Maug while he wasn't paying attention to her. "Then it's true, he spends a lot of time in the Geotic?"

"I guess."

"Does he have a girlfriend?"

The unicorn looked puzzled. "I don't know. Why?"

"Bobby!" A tall man who appeared close to Bobby's age stepped in front of Farni. His dark brown hair curled around his ears and he smiled. Eddie was one of the knights who served Spoons Forge and her grandfather. He was a Shadow, not quite a ghost, but not a living person either. "I've been looking for you."

Bobby was a little startled to see Eddie, she thought he had stayed behind at her grandfather's constabulary, but let him take her hand and lead her off the dance floor. Farni frowned, tagging along behind them.

"What are you doing here, Eddie?"

"It's the May festival," he said as if the reason were obvious. "And I am as much a part of Queen Titania's court as Ezra. We always celebrate the spring together. Ezra is in the White Rose Hall with the Queen already. I don't want you to miss the chance to meet her. Queen Titania said she was looking forward to it."

"Are you sure?" Her grandfather had made her promise to stay with Maug and Katrin.

"Of course."

She gazed at him, and he looked down at her with a solemn seriousness. Eddie never changed. He was tall, and appeared young, with no lines around his large brown eyes.

The side of his lip lifted as he tugged at her arm to pull her away. When she was little, Bobby had thought he was the most beautiful person ever. He was kind and always watching out for her. As she grew older, she noticed his unchanging appearance and had asked her grandfather about it.

What she learned broke her heart. Eddie was actually Sir Edwin McGaffy, knight of the realm, guardian of the gate, keeping those who shouldn't cross between the Geotic and Thaumaturgic Realms from doing so. And he was of one of Queen Titania's shadow knights—men who died, but whose souls were given the chance to live again if they served in the fairy's court. He would never grow old, never have children, and would stay as he was forever. It seemed so unfair. Bobby cared about him. He'd always been a sort of older brother to her, and her grandfather trusted him.

"All right," she agreed. "But we can't be long."

"Only as long as you like," Eddie agreed. Farni made to follow, but Eddie put a hand on the unicorn's chest. "You're not a member of Titania's court. You're not allowed."

"Neither's Bobby, but she's going!"

Eddie shrugged. "Go back to your room and try not to get eaten."

Farni stopped following them, and Bobby flushed with anger. She looked over her shoulder as they walked away. "That was mean."

He chuckled softly. "Farni is perfectly safe at the Keep. Come. Let's not keep the Queen waiting."

~ ~ ~

It was just as well the obnoxious unicorn had spirited Roberta Parks away. Maug needed to have a conversation with her friend that he was a hundred percent sure Roberta wouldn't understand. The small green dragon trembled while standing as stiff as she could, refusing to look in Maug's direction. While Roberta didn't seem to understand his exact nature, there was little doubt that the green dragon did. He crossed his arms as he stood behind her and spoke softly in the language of dragons. "When are you going to be in season, Katrin?"

She stiffened. "I'm sorry, I don't know Dragon that well. What… what does that word mean?"

Gods, was it possible she'd never had a season? "How old are you?"

"I'm twenty-two," she said, watching the dancers. "I only come to this realm in the summers, with Bobby. My… my parents are human."

"Not your real parents."

"No. My dam and sire were murdered when I was very young. Ezra took me in and found me a family."

"Gods," Maug muttered. Old Man Parks obviously didn't understand the peril he had put the young green in by bringing her here right now. She wasn't fully in season yet, but it wasn't going to be long judging by her scent. Three months? Maybe six? It was enough to turn every male dragon's head. Maug doubted he would have been able to put Turis off if she had fully scented as fertile. "You need to leave the Keep tomorrow. I'll give you my aunt's phone number. She lives in the Geotic Realm. I'll tell her you'll call."

Katrin finally looked up at him. She was a pretty thing, with bright green eyes, but too timid for Maug's taste. "I don't understand."

"Lord Turis has taken an interest in you," Maug said, changing the subject slightly. He had no intention of getting into a discussion about breeding and puberty with a female dragon about to go into her first season.

"He'll kill me," she whispered. Her breath caught, and she shook her head; he could smell her fear.

Maug frowned. "That is not his intention, I promise you. And to be honest, I have no right to interfere if I don't plan on keeping you for myself."

"What?" Katrin asked. "I-I don't understand."

"Just… stay close," Maug said, "And go back to the Geotic Realm tomorrow with Roberta. Call my aunt. She is far better at explaining these things than I ever—"

It was then the young unicorn came back, utterly dejected. His form was a human boy, around twelve or thirteen, and Maug didn't have any reason to doubt that wasn't his true age judging by his manner and behavior.

"Where's Lady Roberta?"

"Eddie's taking her to White Rose Hall. He told me to go back to my room, but I don't want to go. I wanted to dance with Bobby."

"Why would he take her there?" Maug glared in the direction of White Rose Hall where Queen Titania held court.

The unicorn shrugged. "He said Queen Titania wanted to meet her."

Maug frowned, feeling bright anger. While this courtier may have been well meaning, there was a reason for Ezra Parks entrusting Maug with his granddaughter for the evening. The old man would have to dance attendance on the Queen and, for whatever reason, he didn't want Roberta there. Maug smiled. "Let's go get her."

Katrin regarded him with a hint of trepidation. "Is that okay?"

Maug shrugged. "Lady Roberta is our companion for the evening. It would be unforgivably rude of me not to go after her. Besides, you want to see the skylights tonight, don't you? They are truly spectacular."

"Oh, yes!" The unicorn clapped his hands with delight. "I love the lights. It's my favorite part of the festival!"

"I've got a secluded spot for just the four of us," Maug assured him. "Now, let's find Roberta."

~ ~ ~

"Lord Turis." The black dragon heard his name near his elbow. The wolf woman materialized out of the crowd. Most of the revelers were keeping their distance from the dragons, but the hall had filled up as the evening progressed. Strains of music from the string quartet mingled with the hum of conversation.

Giet startled at her appearance and frowned in the wolf's direction. "Anywhere else and I'd pelt you for that, cur."

Laru arched a wry eyebrow at the dragon lord but turned her attention to Turis.

"What is it?" Turis asked.

"Lord Maug has decided to retrieve his companion from the White Rose Ballroom."

"The Queen's court?" Giet frowned. He looked around, trying to locate their red-haired lord brother. "He wouldn't be foolish enough to go alone, would he?"

"He could…" Turis inhaled sharply. "Is he going after the green?"

"No." Laru shook her head. "The other one. The human."

"Where is the green?" Turis's gaze swept the room. It was packed with revelers, but he spotted Maug's bright hair through the twirling dancers. Maug was nearly out of the door, pulling the green dragon behind him by the hand. "Curse his blood. He's taking her with him?"

Laru turned to look, leaning up on her toes to get a better view. "Apparently so, my Lord."

Turis bit back a hot, angry retort and pushed his way through the crowd to catch up with the idiot of a red dragon. The female was nearly in season and had no business being at court. But why would Maug wave her existence in front of the Fairy Queen?

"He can't go in there alone," Giet said as they moved through the throng; most stepped out of the way or were moved bodily aside. Even in their human guise, the dragons were large and formidable.

"I'll go," Turis ground out, understanding the urgency.

"We'll both go. If he starts something with that bitch of a Queen, we need to bear witness. We can either gut him for it or cheer him on."

"Gods." Turis frowned. "It's not time."

"Not yet," Giet agreed.

"Your pardon, Lord Maug," Turis called as they passed through the large double doors leading into the stone corridor of the castle proper. Maug turned and met them with hot irritation. The young green ducked behind Maug, keeping the red between her and the two blacks.

"What?" Maug snapped.

Ah yes. Turis smiled. Maug got that part of his temper from his mother, the Lady Jaylinn.

"I hear," Giet said pleasantly, stepping forward, "that you are going to pay your respects to the good Queen Titania. Now, brother, how could we not attend you when you do her such an honor?"

"Shove it, Giet," Maug said. "I'm going, and you can't stop me."

"We're not trying to," Turis put in, "But don't you think that, perhaps, the Lady Green may not be suitable company on such an adventure?"

Maug drew himself up and narrowed his eyes. He obviously suspected his motives, as he should. But he wasn't stupid enough to disagree. Then the young idiot proved that, yes, he really was that stupid.

"She stays with me. You even breathe on her, and you'll feel my claws." He turned on his heels, and the lady hurried after him, along with a young unicorn who watched the two dragon lords with a wary expression.

"C'mon, Farni," Maug called over his shoulder, "Don't loiter or Lord Giet will make a snack of you."

"I will not," Giet retorted as he fell into step, following behind them as they made their way to the White Rose Ballroom. "What a rude thing to say."

~ ~ ~

The White Rose Ballroom was similar in layout to the Crimson Ballroom, almost a mirror reflection of the other, but in white marble rather than red. The crowd was far more subdued, with the courtiers walking as if in a dream. Here, there were no dancers, and only a quiet murmur of voices as they passed the colorfully dressed revelers. Bobby wrinkled her nose, overwhelmed by the smell of roses; she sneezed twice.

They moved through a crowd that parted with a light drift. No one moved fast, but they didn't move slowly either. Eddie led her to the dais at the far end of the ballroom, upon which sat an ornate silver throne. Bobby blinked, recognizing her grandfather standing to the side of the

Queen. He was different. Younger. His hair nearly black, and not a line on his face. Her grandfather frowned upon seeing her and stepped forward.

"What's this?" Ezra Parks asked.

Eddie paused and looked to who could only be Queen Titania, immortal ruler of the kingdom.

"I asked Edwin to bring your granddaughter to us, Ezra," the Queen answered. She was thin and tall. Her long straight blond hair cascaded down her back past her waist; her dress was nearly sheer, with her nipples clearly visible. Bobby blushed brightly.

"This was not my wish, dear lady." Ezra Parks turned to the Queen. "We discussed this."

"And I found the discussion unsatisfactory." She ran a hand along Ezra's jaw in a gesture that was far too intimate for Bobby's comfort. She dropped her eyes, even more embarrassed. "Come, child. You should be mine, you know."

"What?" Bobby's mind mired in mud. She took a step toward the Queen's outstretched arms, then another. Something inside her told her to run as fast as she could. But she couldn't. All she could do was take step after step toward the Fairy Queen.

"Ah, Lady Roberta! There you are!" A bright, clear masculine voice cut through the fog. Bobby jerked her head around as Maug came striding into the hall, full of confidence and with a wide smile. A courtier moved to stop him, but Maug shoved him aside, and then the entire crowd seemed to turn on him. Maug had two large men at his shoulders, who stood ready to carry on the fight.

"Stop!" the Queen ordered. Her voice rang out, sharp with anger. "Lord Maug. Did my Lord Oberon let you off your leash? You are not welcome in my hall."

"Oh, my pardon good… Queen," Maug said the word as if it was distasteful. Bobby bit her lip, knowing this was bad—really bad. "But Lady Roberta Parks was entrusted into my care for the evening and stolen from my side through trickery and malice."

"That's not true." Eddie stepped around Bobby. "She came of her own free will."

"Did she now?" Maug questioned, dropping his voice only slightly. He moved forward, with his companions staying close to his side, watching for an ambush. Bobby saw Farni and Katrin lurking behind, sticking close together. "Then why does this hall stink of a coercion spell, eh?"

"Liar!" Eddie yelled back. Bobby blinked and put her fingers to her temples. Her grandfather moved to her side and put a hand on her shoulder. She felt a gentle wash of warmth as her mind cleared. The room's color changed from smoky rose to a white, near-blinding light. She winced against it.

Her grandfather gave her a little squeeze as he turned back to the Queen. "Please, my Lady, don't do this."

"I claim injury on behalf of good Queen Titania. This rogue sullies her name with his lies!" Eddie's voice rang through the hall. The crowd fell silent. Maug laughed.

"A challenge has been issued by my champion, Ezra," the Queen soothed as she turned to take her seat. "I cannot stop it now."

Eddie cupped his hands, summoning a blade in a bright flash of light. He approached Maug, ready to attack. The crowd twittered and pulled away. Maug said something to his companions at his side, and they nodded, stepping back. Maug stepped forward alone.

"Draw your weapon, dragon!"

"You think I need one?" Maug made a tsking sound. The contempt in his posture was clear. "Well, if you insist."

He held his arms high above his head, whispering something barely audible in a language Bobby didn't understand. Bright flames shot out of his hands, and a gleaming, golden broadsword appeared. Maug brought it forward with a flourish, moving into a defensive stance.

"Fuck," Bobby whispered. She turned to her grandfather, who made a reassuring motion with his hands. She bit her lip, crossing her arms in front of herself.

Eddie attacked with heat, but Maug deflected him with ease. He defended himself for only a few moments, then a wicked smile lit the dragon lord's features. He moved faster than Bobby had imagined possible, thrusting and attacking, beating Eddie back with his blows.

"Too much for you, Sir Knight?" Maug mocked. "Perhaps you should think twice before challenging a dragon lord. That is, if I decide to let you survive."

"Bastard," Eddie ground out and tried to beat the dragon back. But he was gaining no ground. Maug snorted with derision and launched a hard attack. A twist of his blade sent Eddie's sword clattering across the marble floor. He moved to get it, but Maug held his blade to the knight's neck.

"Yield," Maug ordered. "Sir Knight."

"I'll die first!" Eddie snarled back. A wistful smile flitted on Maug's lips.

"I can't kill what's already dead," he murmured. He raised his free hand, and it glowed with hot power.

"Stop!" A deep voice echoed through the silent chamber. Maug frowned and dropped his hand, but not his sword. A man, short in stature, wearing a rich black velvet tunic, strode in with a contingent of armed guards. He was a beautiful, youthful-looking man with black hair and a small circlet of gold on his head. His features were as smooth as a child's, but his face twisted in an unfriendly expression. He took in the situation, his lips twisting in contempt, and flicked his eyes at Maug. "Slumming?"

"I couldn't help myself, my Lord." Maug let out a breath. "My apologies."

"This is all your doing then, Titania?" The man moved forward, putting a foot on the dais of her throne. Maug's jaw tightened, and Bobby noticed his companions slipping out of the hall, taking Farni and Katrin with them. She wondered what sort of trouble Maug was in.

"I'm sorry!" Bobby bolted forward, wanting to make this right. "It's my fault!"

"Roberta!"

She ignored her grandfather and twisted away before he could grab her. She stumbled in front of the man, praying she didn't make the situation worse.

"I didn't know I wasn't supposed to come here," she said as she righted herself. "Maug was just coming after me,"

"Is that so?" The man focused on her and she felt an immediate chill. His eyes were dark and glittered like coal. They were cold, hateful. She shuddered under his gaze.

"Leave the child be, Oberon," Titania said in a bored voice. "She's a thousand years too young for you."

"If you can take a human lover, why can't I?"

Bobby was confused, not understanding the Fairy King's intention.

Maug stepped forward. "My pardon, sire, but may I take my kill?" he asked the Fairy King in a pleasant voice.

The fairy offered the dragon a long look, glancing at his pale, still wife, as if considering it.

Then.

"No," Oberon said. "Put your sword away."

Maug nodded, and the blade disappeared into wherever it had come from. Maug interposed himself between the King and Bobby, dropping to one knee with his hand on his chest.

"Then, my good Lord Oberon, might I ask a favor for denying me my rightful prey? He did, after all, challenge me first."

Oberon scowled. "Is that true?" he demanded of his wife.

"What of it?" she said with a dismissive shrug. "If you can't keep your dragon out of my court, what am I supposed to do?"

"Perhaps you shouldn't have your pet courtiers take on a standing Dragon Lord," Oberon mocked. "Very well, Maug. What do you want?"

"Lady Roberta's company, unmolested for the rest of the festivities."

"Granted. Take her and go."

"Oberon!" the Queen roared, rising to her feet. "You cannot give that poor child over to that beast."

Maug turned and held out his hand to Bobby. She lunged forward to take it.

"I just did." Oberon smirked. "Don't interfere. It could be true love, after all."

Maug pulled her from the hall so quickly Bobby didn't have a chance to hear any more.

~ ~ ~

"Come with us," the great black dragon ordered softly. Katrin had seen the Fairy King's entrance. The two dragons who had followed Lord Maug and stood at his side, willing to take on challengers with him, now seemed to be… running? She lifted her green eyes to meet his and shook her head. He took her by the upper arm and practically lifted her out of the hall. "Do not fight me, girl. This is for your own safety."

The other dragon moved Farni along. They darted through a few corridors before shoving her against a wall. The two dragons watched Katrin and Farni with a mixture of amusement and annoyance.

Farni bolted to her. He threw his arms around her waist and looked up at the dragons with hot belligerence. "Why did you leave Maug? He's in trouble!"

"Not likely." The dragon that spoke to her first stepped away. "He'll be along as soon as he dispatches Titania's shadow pet."

"But what about Bobby?" The unicorn glared at them. "You just left them. We could help!"

"And what could you do?" the second asked as he moved to grab hold of the unicorn. His hand came into contact with a shield, sparking at him. He winced and shook his hand, eyeing the boy with interest.

"Oh ho!" Lord Turis laughed. "The colt has a bite."

The other dragon snorted.

"Good," the other one said, "You'll need it, boy. But not against us."

"I don't trust you," Farni said.

"Good you don't," Lord Turis approved. Then he turned and pointed. "See? Here comes Lord Maug now."

Katrin stepped away from Farni and tiptoed to see. It was far enough from the unicorn's shield for the dragon to catch her arm and pull her close. He looked down at her from his height and closed his eyes, drawing in a deep breath. She shook in fear. He opened his glittering grey eyes, appraising her. He would kill her. Katrin was sure of it.

"You're close," he mumbled, "But not quite."

Katrin pulled herself free, not understanding what he meant.

Maug turned the corner and saw them, relief flooding his features. "You got them out. My thanks. I don't think Oberon saw them."

Katrin turned to Bobby with questioning confusion. Bobby shook her head and moved forward to take her hand.

Maug smiled. "So… the skylights? It's a bit away from the Keep, which is for the best at the moment. You up for a hike, good ladies?"

"Walk?" Giet made a face. "When we could fly?"

Maug frowned. "You're not invited."

Lord Turis laughed with good-nature. He clapped a hand on Maug's shoulder and leaned forward. "Giet will go back to Jaka, but you're not out of this yet. We travel in pairs until we leave the Keep. Especially now. Even Oberon's mages will be reluctant to take two of us on."

Maug ground his jaw and pushed his fingers through his hair.

Bobby touched Maug's arm and leaned up to brush a light kiss on his cheek. "Thank you," she whispered. "I don't know what…"

A bright blush flushed Lord Maug's cheeks.

Lord Turis made a rude noise and turned away. "You said something about a walk? Leaving the Keep?"

Maug nodded and motioned for them to follow him.

~ ~ ~

Because of his worry, they stayed out of Sebastian's Keep all night. They hiked to an expansive field about a mile beyond the fortress walls to watch the evening's entertainment. Fairy lights colored the sky with patterns, and playful songs echoed as they moved in a synchronized dance in the night sky. Maug had sent for some pixies who served his house, and they brought blankets and food. The young women curled up together, with Farni laying between them on the ground, warm and safe.

The girls, and especially the young unicorn, had delighted in the lights that lit the sky with fire, and after they ate their fill of the treats and pastries, fell deeply asleep under the bright stars of the Thaumaturgic Realm.

But the night did not lend itself for the dragons to sleep. They kept an uneasy watch, uncertain if Queen Titania would send forces to try and finish the job her shadow knight had started.

"Perhaps the king can keep his bitch in line," Turis whispered in Dragon.

Maug shook his head. "More than likely Titania is busy with Roberta's grandfather. May Day is one of the only nights Oberon will indulge her betrayal of his bed."

Turis turned his glittering grey eyes to Maug. "You mean to keep the green?"

Maug took a deep breath. He knew this question was coming. He could lie, but that would cause Turis to challenge him for her. In all the years he'd known the black dragon, he'd never seen him take such keen interest in a particular female. Sure he had bed-warmers, but they came and went. Most were eager for Turis's heat. Katrin and her sweet scent attracted the older black in a way Maug hadn't seen before. Maybe part of it was the chase, with Katrin's lack of interest enticing the older dragon. Maug did not doubt Turis's intent to have her. He was a dragon meaning to possess a female. And as Maug had told her earlier, by dragon law, he had no right to stand in his way.

"No," Maug said, "But I don't think you should pursue her either."

"Is that so?" Turis asked with humor, relaxing.

Turis had been ready to challenge him, Maug was sure of it, but probably didn't want to fight over a female any more than he did.

"Look, she's was raised in the Geotic Realm. You're confusing her. She doesn't understand."

"What's to understand? I'm a dragon, and she is a delightful smelling female," Turis said, clearly not getting the implication. "And what are you going to do, fledgling? Chase after the human?"

Maug's attention drifted to where Roberta was sleeping. A soft smile crossed his lips. She was sweet, smart, and brave. She was also a mage, with no little talent. Roberta was still training, but from what Charles had said, Parks was planning on making her heir to the Advocacy of Spoons Forge. If that were true, she would be one of the most powerful mages in the kingdom when she came fully into her power.

Besides, he liked her—a lot.

"What if I am?"

"She's human. She can't give you hatchlings."

"What makes you say that? Charles and Maggie—"

Maug stopped himself, wondering if he'd said too much. Turis eyed him but didn't speak again. They watched the sun rise; the two dragon lords keeping their own counsel and quiet brooding.

They woke the girls in the morning and made their way back to the Keep; the revelers from the night slowing as they came in from their merriment. Maug and Turis received sly grins, as many assumed they had enjoyed the soft pleasures of the flesh. Maug walked them to their door. Farni and Katrin went inside, leaving him alone with Roberta. She moved forward impulsively and threw her arms around him.

"Thank you." She lifted herself onto her tiptoes to whisper in his ear. "I'll never forget this night."

She brushed a kiss on the side of his face. He cupped her chin in his hand, leaned down, and tasted her lips. Maug felt like he was on fire as she opened her mouth and teased his tongue. He kissed her long and gently. They parted, and he bounced on his toes with a grin. "Thank you."

He glanced over his shoulder. He knew Turis lurked nearby, waiting to walk him back to the rooms he was sharing with Charles. "Hey. Would it be okay if I called you?"

"On the phone?" Bobby asked.

Maug laughed. Yes, here, that was a very strange thing to ask. "Yeah," he said. "On the phone. Give me your number, if it's okay?"

"I'd… like that." She whispered her phone number into his ear. He smiled and touched her lips again, pulling himself away.

"Be well, Roberta."

"You can call me Bobby," she whispered.

Maug shook his head once. "That's a boy's name," he chided softly. "No, sweet. You are my Lady Roberta. I'll call soon. I promise."

GIRLS WANNA HAVE FUN

It was 'Open Mic' night at the local pizzeria. It was a medium sized place, but worn around the edges with broken tiles on the floor and peeling paint. The tables had been pushed out of the way to make room for a small stage, which was little more than a box with a microphone in front of it. But the food was good, and it wasn't as expensive as some of the chain places around town.

Roberta had talked Maug into going since Farni had taken it into his head to be a stand-up comic. He wore a pressed white suit and was going over his 3 x 5 cards on the table. Nearly a month had passed since May Day, and Maug and Roberta were an "item" according to her brother. Bradley had made it very clear that if Maug didn't keep his hands to himself, he would be morally obligated to break them.

Bradley sat across the table from Maug, next to his sister. They were helping the unicorn pick out his jokes.

"I like this one," Bradley said. "'What is Mary short for?'"

"That's a terrible joke," Roberta said.

"'Because she had no legs!'" Bradley chortled with a deep laugh.

Maug's lips twisted slightly. Bradley would have made a good dragon in another life. He was fair-headed whereas Roberta was dark. Maug had met Roberta's parents and found that Bradley took more after them. Roberta's dark hair and light blue eyes came from her grandfather, Ezra Caleb Parks. Bradley had a little talent for magic but far preferred the mundane world.

"Did you tell Maug you were going to stay with Granddad for the summer?" Bradley asked.

"And if I didn't, he knows now."

"We've discussed it." Maug nodded, motioning to the waitress. She came over, and he ordered another round of drinks before asking when their food would arrive.

"Probably twenty minutes," the waitress said. "But I'll get the round discounted for ya since the kitchen is so backed up."

She offered Maug a wink and slipped him a piece of paper. He glanced at it as she walked away. Bradley looked at him with curiosity. Maug snorted and tossed it on the table. It had the woman's phone number on it.

"You dog!" Bradley laughed. "That's like the third one!"

"Jesus." Roberta frowned. She called out after the waitress. "I'm right here, you know." Then she paused, puckering her lips. "Maybe I should talk to her!"

"It's not your worry," Maug said as he reached over the table and tapped her nose. Roberta swatted at his finger with a laugh.

"Still"—she feigned a hurt face—"the hussy!"

"Hey." Katrin hurried up and slid into the seat next to Bradley. She gave him a quick peck on the cheek and smiled. "Did I miss Farni?"

"Not yet," Roberta said.

Maug frowned and lifted his drink. He had not been amused when he'd learned the green was dating Roberta's brother. "Where've you been?"

"Seeing Aunt Maggie." Katrin dimpled a smile. Maug did approve of that. His aunt had taken the little green under her wing, letting everyone know how vexed she was with old man Parks for not contacting her with the girl being so fresh out of the shell. Maggie loved children, whether they were human, dragon or otherwise. Katrin smiled at Maug. "She said Charles wants to see you."

"Yes," Maug said. He knew what Charles wanted and didn't care to have that conversation.

"Tomorrow," Katrin added.

"I am aware," Maug answered.

Roberta smiled brightly and kicked him under the table. "You're not going?"

"No."

"Well, I told you." Katrin smiled and reached down to take Bradley's hand. "I want to go dancing tonight!"

Farni looked up from his cards. "I wanna go dancing too!"

"You're too young," Katrin said. "Bad enough we can't go to over twenty-one bars for another month because of Bobby."

"I can be older," the unicorn said. Maug snorted. It didn't matter what guise the youngling took; he'd have that perennial innocence forever. That was just part of what a unicorn was. The lad raised his head and offered a wide smile. "Oh. Hullo, Eddie."

Maug's head snapped around with a low growl. Here? The knight was getting beyond annoying. He should have defied Oberon and turned the shadow to dust. It would have been worth whatever punishment the Fairy King dished out.

Eddie walked up to the table, throwing a hot look of hate in Maug's direction before staring at the unicorn. "It's time to go, Farni."

"But I haven't had my turn yet."

"Now."

"C'mon Eddie," Roberta said. "It's not that late."

"Are you his keeper?" the knight snapped.

Maug stood up and shoved the knight. "Watch your mouth, cur. Who do you think you're speaking to?"

Eddie glowered at Maug. It was clear he hated the dragon as much as Maug hated him, maybe more. Maug had what he so very clearly wanted.

"Roberta Parks," Sir Edwin said softly. "Granddaughter of Ezra Caleb Parks, Advocate of Spoons Forge."

The knight's gaze drifted to Roberta, and the dragon clenched his fist at his side and felt hot power stirring.

"Maug!" Roberta grabbed his arm and pulled him back a little. Maug turned to her, and his anger melted away. How could he blame the knight for his infatuation when Maug was losing his heart to her? "Please don't fight here."

Maug paused. He leaned forward to brush his lips on her forehead, incensing the knight further.

"Now, Farni!" the shadow ordered.

The unicorn wilted and Maug felt a pang of pity, but he took it for the gift it was. "Well," he said to the others as their food arrived. "I see no reason to stay here after we eat."

~ ~ ~

Turis, Dragon Lord of the North, walked up the simple cement path to the door and then knocked. Even a dragon lord had to offer the proper amount of respect to the home of a Thaumaturgic advocate. He felt the wards around the dwelling bristling at his presence. As much as he would have loved to take Maglin by the throat and demand answers from her, he knew that would be an act of war. And it wasn't just the advocate, powerful as he was, which made Turis pause, but her hotheaded blood nephew. Turis didn't care to fight the little bastard in a full fit of temper.

The door opened, and Maglin, the orange female of the House of the West, pinned him in place with a sharp glare.

"Hello, Maglin," he said politely. "I'm not very happy with you."

"That makes two of us." She put a hand on her hip. Her light orange colored eyes flashed with heat. "How did you find this place?"

"The green," he said simply. He'd set spies on the girl after her return to the Geotic Realm. They reported the girl was a regular visitor to another dragon. It didn't take a lot of deduction for Turis to figure out who that would be. "May I come in? We need to speak."

"Charles isn't here."

"Best that way," Turis said. "On my word Maglin, I have no interest in starting a war with Maug."

She weighed his words and moved aside so he could pass through the threshold. He felt a flash of heat and knew that had she not invited him in; he could never have breached the door.

"Follow me," she ordered. "I'm making tea. Care for a cup?"

"No," he said. Friend or not, he had no intention of eating or drinking anything that came from this human's house.

"Well, you can watch me then."

She led him through a long hall to a large, wide kitchen in the back of the house. It was decorated in bright yellows and greens. She pointed to the table, near the window overlooking the walled-in garden.

"Sit."

Turis hid a smile as he moved to a chair. He regarded her while she poured boiling water from the kettle into the cup. Turis was old and wise enough to wait before he spoke. Maglin had a tongue that could keep even a dragon lord in line. He eyed her figure with appreciation and a small smile. She had always been a beautiful female, with long brown hair and snapping orange eyes. Turis had considered keeping her for himself at one time, she being near his age. He had sent her to Ridges Hollow to be Maug's nurse when he'd learned the red was being raised by a human. He'd meant to take her back as a bed-warmer after Maug claimed the title of Lord of the West, but Charles Tampton asked for her. That was a debt he hadn't collected on yet. Since that was the man's debt, what he had to discuss with the orange had nothing to do with it.

"Katrin is little more than a hatchling. You should find some other prey." Maglin moved to sit in a chair across from him. "Maug told me you're pursuing her. Come now, my Lord, can't you find a more willing lady?"

Turis had no intention of discussing the green. She was young, true, but her scent told him she would be fertile soon. It teased his senses in a way no female had in close to fifty years. The only other to capture his interest was Maug's dam, Maglin's sister, the Lady Jaylinn. He still smarted over her loss to the black, Mugan.

"What are you doing filling the boy's head with the idea he can breed with a human?"

Maglin startled. "I've told him no such thing."

Turis frowned. "Are you aware he's courting a human?" He leaned forward and lowered his voice. "Damn it, Maglin, he's the youngest we have. We need the hatchlings he could—"

The back door flew open and a young voice called out, "Hey, Mom."

Turis jerked his head around as a young man ambled in. He was a tall lad, with brown hair like… his mother's?

"Sorry I'm late. The library closed and they… Oh."

"Daniel, this is… a friend of Maug's."

"Yeah? Hi!"

Turis leaned back and examined the human. Young, perhaps sixteen? Seventeen? And human, but he had the scent… just a breath, but enough for Turis to catch. Dragon blood, no question. The boy grabbed an apple on his way through the kitchen and then shuffled up the stairs. Turis fixed his pale grey eyes on Maglin. Her face had drained of color. She clenched her hands and rose from her seat.

"Leave!"

A faint smile flitted on Turis's lips. "So it is possible. Perhaps your red idiot isn't as stupid as I suspected."

"Now, Lord Turis. I want you out of my house, now!"

"Very well, Maglin," he agreed. "I got the answer I was seeking."

~ ~ ~

Maug's phone chimed as they walked to the next club. He frowned and pulled it out of his pocket, keeping one arm wrapped firmly around Bobby's waist. She leaned into him with a smile. Brad and Katrin were a bit behind them. Maug flipped the phone open and put it to his ear.

"Hey, Aunt Maggie," he said. Bobby felt him stiffen and slow his walk. "Did you call Charles? Why the fuck not?"

Maug pulled away from Bobby to push his fingers through his hair. "All right. It's all right. I'll take care of it." His voice sounded strained. "Fine."

He snapped the phone shut and scanned the tree-lined street. His eyes narrowed with a flash of temper. Bobby turned and saw the dragon lord she had met on May Day stepping out of the shadows. Turick? Turis, maybe?

"What is it?" Bobby asked, touching his arm.

He offered her a slight nod. Turis put himself in the middle of the street, blocking the way.

Maug brushed her face with a light kiss, never taking his eyes off the other man. "It's all right," he said softly, then raised his voice, straightening with a sharp gaze that never faltered. "Bradley, why don't you take the ladies to that bar over there?"

"You sure, man?" Brad asked. "You gonna be alright?"

"I'll be there shortly," Maug assured him.

Bobby followed her brother to the bar a short distance behind them. Maug remained where he was.

"Who is that guy?" Brad asked when they had gotten around the corner.

Katrin's eyes were wide with fear. "Lord Turis."

"Another dragon, right?" Brad asked.

"Yeah," Bobby said. "But I thought he was a friend."

"It's… not that simple," Katrin hedged. "Aunt Maggie explained it, but I don't really understand. The Dragon Lords stand together, but really, they're rivals. Maggie's just told Maug that Turis came to see her."

"You could hear that?" Bobby asked.

Katrin nodded. "My dragon hearing has to be good for something. Maggie sounded very upset. I don't think Lord Maug is too happy about it either."

~ ~ ~

Maug felt hot anger when he faced Lord Turis on the quiet side street. His lip curled. How dare the black go near one of the females of his house? He pulled on the natural energy of the streets and soil with his whispered call of power. The wind picked up as energy curled around his fingers. He wasn't going to kill Turis, but he'd make damn sure he hurt.

"I'm not here to fight you." Turis stepped forward. His hands lowered but Maug didn't trust him. The old black could fight seven ways backward. He'd already learned not to let his guard down with this dragon.

"I told you to stay away from Maggie." Maug's voice was low and tight, with a guttural growl. The older black paused and cocked his head to one side, readying a defense. The stench of ozone and hot power was unmistakable. Steam rose from the ground in wisps of vapor.

"I meant her no harm, youngling." Turis moved beneath the bright streetlight. Maug continued to draw power to himself; he didn't need Turis going after Katrin at the moment either. Not with Roberta's brother so close to her. "So it's true then, she and Charles Tampton had hatchlings?"

"What of it?" Maug threw back with hot belligerence.

"Yet Charles Tampton is unquestionably human." Turis folded his arms. "Care to explain how this is possible?"

"How should I know?" he snapped. "Some sort of spell, I think. They got it from Laru-baba."

"Ah, I should have known she'd have a paw in it."

"We're not so different, Turis. Dragons and humans. Shit, any of the races. We all have a common origin."

"A fairy tale," Turis mocked in a low voice. "Spun from Oberon's lips."

"I should leave you to Charles." Maug threw a hot bolt of energy. It exploded around Turis with a flash of light and clap of thunder. "But I don't care to."

Turis had shielded and regarded him with a sideway smile. "Very nice, hatchling, but as I said, I'm not here to fight you. I'll leave Maglin to her mate. But you stay out of my way with the green."

"Turis—" Maug yelled, but he was alone on the street. The other dragon had gone, probably through a portal. Maug tipped his head back, returning the power to its natural state as he fought to release his anger.

Maug didn't doubt Turis would keep his word about Maggie. It wasn't that she was the mate of another, dragons had played games of mate stealing and seduction throughout history; but rather that she was a blood relative of a standing Dragon Lord, and Maug had warned him off. If Turis were to do it again, Maug would be obligated to try and kill him, but he doubted the Lord of the North would push it that far.

Still, this thing with the green, Katrin, remained unresolved. Turis was an uneasy ally, and Maug didn't want to create an enemy of such a powerful dragon. Katrin wasn't of his house, and Maug wasn't making a claim for her. In truth, she was fair prey for the black, no matter how much Maug hated the idea. He'd hoped Turis would forget about her once she came back to the Geotic Realm and was out of his reach. But the black dragon's appearance belied that hope.

"Fuck." Maug shook his head and moved towards the bar where the others had gone.

"Here." Bradley Parks put a glass in Maug's hand. The bar wasn't a planned stop for the evening, but it would do to grab a drink and have a couple of dances. It had a laid-back vibe to it, more classic rock than trance or techno. It had booths along the wall, with tables scattered around a wooden dance floor.

"Where are the ladies?" Maug asked, not liking them out of his line of sight. He didn't think Turis would make a move tonight, but he wouldn't put it past the old bastard.

"Taking a piss." Bradley jerked his head towards the restrooms. "Tell me, before they get back. Is this normal shit trouble or magic shit trouble?"

"Is there a difference?" A faint smile touched Maug's lips. He took a sip of the offered drink and raised an eyebrow as it burned his throat.

"Yah," Bradley said. "I made it a triple. Well, the difference is that I can help you with one, but with the other, you're shit out of luck."

Maug paused, considering how much to tell the young man. Bradley had no hope of standing against a dragon determined to get a female, but Maug liked Roberta's brother and didn't want to see him hurt.

"Lord Turis is the standing Dragon Lord of the North. He went to see my aunt this evening."

"And that's a bad thing? I mean, Kat seems really shaken up, but if he just stopped by to say hello, what's the big deal?"

"He's a dangerous dragon, Bradley." Maug drained the rest of the drink and indicated to the bartender that he wanted another. The woman nodded, grabbing his glass. "Thankfully, I am also a dangerous dragon."

"Mm." Bradley nodded. "Big shit talker. I can see how Bobby wraps you around her little finger. Nice try."

"Your sister is not a fair example." Maug grinned. He felt a wave of relief seeing Roberta and Katrin leave the restroom and head in his direction. If he could see them, he could protect them.

"Yeah, well." Bradley waved Maug off when he tried to pay for the next drink and threw a ten on the bar. "Good thing I like you, or I'd have to kick your ass. Just remember to keep your hands where I can see 'em, buddy."

~ ~ ~

"That's the girl." Elizabeth Cho pointed without looking. Thaddeus Stanley turned. The young women had come out of the restroom and were making their way back to their companions at the bar. She'd had a premonition that the girl would be in this place, at this time. They'd had a couple of drinks, and Elizabeth had been pleased when they had finally shown up. Thaddeus had missed seeing the girl before she went to the restroom with her friend.

"Which one?" Thaddeus's voice was low and deep. Elizabeth felt the hum of excitement and found it intoxicating.

"Not the dark one," she said. "The one with the short black hair."

"You're certain?"

Elizabeth nodded.

Thaddeus was a middle-aged man, but still in his prime. His figure cut as sharp as his haircut. His blond beard was cut short to his face, and he had blue eyes like steel. Elizabeth knew she appeared similar in age to him and had done that on purpose. She was a short, thin woman or, at least, a reasonable facsimile. Her hair reached her neck and she had streaked the natural deep brown with a mixture of blond and red. As bothersome as Thaddeus was, he held her heart.

"I'm sure," she said. "My portents want this girl sacrificed."

"Such a waste." Thaddeus frowned. "I want to check with my own sources. She could be worth more alive."

"Why do you always question me? I'm telling you, my lady wants that girl dead and has promised a good reward for it."

"Who is she with?" Thaddeus started a small spell. One of the men, the one with bright red hair, jerked his head up and swung it around.

"Stop," Elizabeth whispered. But it didn't stop Thaddeus.

The young man turned and looked straight at them. Elizabeth put her forehead in her hand and whispered. "He's some sort of wizard."

"He's not," Thaddeus said with confidence. "There's no one of power here, and the girl only has middling talent."

~ ~ ~

It smelled bad.

Maug frowned. Having felt the spark of a spell, his focus was drawn to a table in the far corner of the bar. Two were seated at it, human as far as he could tell. A man and woman. The man was the one who had cast the spell. Maug tightened a shield around his party, obscuring anything the man might otherwise sense. He didn't think the humans would be able to discern it; most magicians in the Geotic

Realm were woefully unprepared to deal with a full mage of the Thaumaturgic.

"We should head back soon." Maug gestured to the clock behind the bar. It was nearly eleven, and Roberta had to work the next day. She wasn't taking any classes this summer but only because she would be going to her grandfather's soon. That thought brought a frown to Maug's lips.

Would the advocate of Spoons be willing to entertain his company? If not, he'd figure out a way. Maybe the wolves would help. The idea of a forbidden midnight tryst sounded romantic and exciting.

Maug supposed he would need to talk to Charles soon. Not only about Turis's bad manners, he needed to make his intentions clear about Roberta. The dragon hoped he'd have her consent before that discussion, though, which was why he had been putting it off. It would do him little good if she weren't a willing party to his plan.

"We should probably call it a night," Maug said.

"Aww," Roberta complained.

"Sorry, my sweet"—he brushed a kiss on her forehead—"but I have an early morning board meeting and then I need to speak to Charles."

"I thought you weren't doing that." Roberta drained her drink. Bradley took Katrin's and finished it for her. He offered the green dragon a bright smile and a quick, but ardent kiss.

"Take me home and keep me forever?" he asked Katrin in an earnest voice. Maug startled. That was a terrible idea. Who knew what Turis would do to a human courting his target.

"Not tonight." Katrin pushed him off in a playfully flirtatious manner. "I have a headache."

"You lie to me," Bradley complained. "You lie to me every night."

"Get used to it, human," Maug drawled. "It's what females do."

"I have never lied to you," Roberta scoffed, giving him a light punch.

Maug smiled. "Not yet, but the day will come."

"Don't be an asshole," she said. "I'm not like that. You going to walk me home?"

"I've done better than that. I called a car."

Bradley made a face. "It's not that far."

Maug shrugged. He would feel better if he could keep them under his protection for the night, but he doubted he could talk Roberta and the others into going home with him. He didn't have a house in Geneva but in nearby Palatine. He would have to use a small portal to get them there, but it was easily doable.

"You sure you have to work tomorrow?" Maug asked. "We could go back to my place…"

"No," Bradley interrupted, offering Maug a dark look.

"Everyone is invited, Bradley." Maug smiled at her brother, silently approving of his protective nature.

"Naw," Bradley said. "You're right. It's late. We should head home."

Maug nodded and the four of them headed to the door.

~ ~ ~

The long black car pulled up in front of the apartment building where the green dragon dwelled. Turis stood on the roof, watching as Katrin got out of the car and walked to the building with one of the humans. He leaned over the parapet wall of the four-story building with a frown. Maug had gotten out and was scanning the area. Turis crossed his arms and smirked, certain his shields would hide him from detection.

He had expected the young red to be furious with him over his visit to Maglin. What he hadn't expected was the ferocity and raw power of his response. Truly, the youngling was going to be unstoppable when he came to full power. Maug was bred true to his lineage. His mother had been powerful enough to be a Dragon Lord in her own right, had she not been female. And Mugan? Gods, no dragon could have stood against him. Mugan's death had been achieved through betrayal and poison.

Turis hadn't lied when he said he wanted no fight with Maug. In the days that were coming, Turis was counting on him being an ally. The others weren't so sure, they worried that Oberon had the fledgling enthralled. The Dragon Lord of the North smirked. As if that could happen. The red was far too hard-headed and stubborn to fall into a spell so easily. Turis had been watching their youngest carefully. Maug had already made his judgment of the Fairy King and found it lacking. It was only Oberon's hubris that he couldn't see the contempt the young dragon held him in. Or it was possible the Fairy King didn't care, seeing Maug as an amusement in his tepid immortal life.

The human returned to the car and got in, but not before Maug swept the area again. Turis stilled as the youngster narrowed on where he was standing. He watched the red dragon for a long moment, wondered if he had actually seen him. He held off calling power in defense, that would give his location away.

One heartbeat, then two. Maug turned his head and ducked back into the car. Turis let out a breath.

The fledgling was good; he had to give him that. Turis couldn't be sure if he'd been detected, or if Maug had decided against the fight.

He went back across the roof and opened the hatch to the building, climbing down the ladder inside. He came through the maintenance door and paused, spotting the green at her door, unlocking it. He moved behind her and pulled her into her apartment, closing the door behind him. She made a small noise as he pinned her body between him and the door.

"Don't," she whimpered. He smiled and breathed in her scent, running his nose along her neck. She shuddered beneath his touch.

She was young and wild. Her fear enticed the predator in him. He couldn't have given up the chase if he wanted to. Her scent was too sweet. Her spirit had a fragile quality, though, and Turis had no desire to break it. His ancestors had played this dance for thousands of years. The breeding imperative of a dragon was raw, natural and untamed. If Turis wanted civilized, he could try and breed with the yellow court-bred bitch of Tsui's. It took nearly all his self-control not to grab and ravage the lovely green dragon. He longed to savage her flesh against his and growled with real physical need.

Turis's gut twisted. If he did that, she would never willingly mate with him and would probably destroy their eggs as soon as she laid them. He knew what females were capable of. He was clearly the more powerful, but she held a different kind of power. That too was the way it had always been, and it was right.

He would have to proceed with care and cunning to get what they both needed.

He pulled back and met her leaf-green eyes, but didn't release her. "I'm not going to hurt you."

"You'll kill me," she whispered in a voice layered in fear. Terror marred her face. "I know you will."

Turis frowned, wondering what idiocy Maglin had filled the girl's head with.

"Why would I do that?" he asked with a snort.

"Because I don't want you."

He laughed low in his throat. She said she didn't want him, but every response and smell told him she did. How could she help herself? She was struggling against a dragon's very nature, and she was nearly in season, only a few months out. At that point, her body would move on its own and make her his. He just had to find the willpower and patience to wait, and keep the other males from seizing his conquest.

"I can wait until you do," he said. He leaned forward and kissed her softly, and then moved his lips to her ear. She nearly went limp in his arms. He could probably take her tonight, but a very small, rational part of Turis's mind told him to wait until she was ready—until she would accept him.

His fingers trailed along her neck and down her sides. She was soft and firm in all the correct places. Turis pressed against her, fiercely fighting his aching need.

"I will wait," he whispered hotly in her ear. A soft moan escaped her lips. "But remember, you are mine."

~ ~ ~

"Ten minutes," Brad said as he closed the car door, leaving Bobby and Maug in the back seat. "Then I'm going to haul your ass out."

Bobby held up her middle finger, and her brother made a kissy face at her.

"Tsk." Maug took hold of her hand and brought the finger to his lips. "Manners."

"Brothers," Bobby started as she moved to straddle him in the back seat, "don't get good manners."

Maug leaned back. He tipped his head as she moved forward to kiss his lips, and then moved to his bare neck. Maug groaned and shifted beneath her. He leaned in to return her kiss and then moved lower to her neck, slipping the shoulder of her loose top away so he could kiss the skin beneath it. His hands settled on her hips, drawing her closer. Bobby smiled, feeling the response in his crotch and leaned in to nibble his ear.

"Gods, Roberta," he gasped and pushed her away. Heat smoldered in his dark eyes. "We can't go too far."

"Why not?" She grinned, and then kissed his strong jaw and neck. He moaned and shifted his weight. Her fingers started to unbutton his shirt. "C'mon Maug. I know you like me…"

"Like?" He stopped, grabbing her hands, looking at her intently. Bobby bit her lip, wondering if she had said the wrong thing. "Roberta, I more than like you. That's why…"

"Why what?" She smiled, she pulled a hand away and toyed at the buttons on his shirt again, opening the first few. She slipped her hand inside the material and ran it up to his shoulder. "I bet we could get a lot done in ten minutes."

His smile broadened, and he leaned forward to part her lips and taste her tongue. He moved aggressively, and Bobby gave as good as she got. He paused, pressing his forehead against hers.

"We could," he agreed softly. "However, I want to make you mine with an entire night of pleasure. Not a stolen taste in the back seat of a car."

"When?" Bobby asked. She was ready now. It wasn't like she hadn't thought about it. About him. He paused, searching her face. She reached out and ran her fingers through his bright red hair and leaned forward to kiss him on the cheek, moving her lips to his ear. "When?"

He pulled her away and closed his eyes.

"Not long." He let out a small, short laugh. "I can't stand to wait much longer."

"Me either," she said. "I… I hope you don't think I'm some sort of…"

"What?" His eyes snapped open. "Truly, Roberta, I think you're wonderful. I just… we just need to make this… right, for it to work out."

There was a sharp knock on the window and Bobby threw herself against him and held him tight.

"I trust you," she said. Bobby paused and then spoke softly into his ear, "I… think I love you."

Maug reached out and cupped her face. He smiled, touching her nose to his. "You don't know how happy that makes me. Now go, before I decide to take you home and deal with your brother tomorrow."

~ ~ ~

"Let me help you with that," Maug called out to his aunt. Maggie Tampton was at the end of her driveway, unloading the groceries from the car. Maug had tried to talk her into using servants, but she wouldn't hear of it. He could tell he'd startled her and felt a pang of regret.

She was likely on edge from Turis's visit. Maug was still in his brown business suit, although he had loosened his tie. He'd had meetings with two of his brokers that morning. They had delighted him with record profits. Again. Maug was anticipating a good quarter over the summer.

He had earned his money the old-fashioned way—inheriting it. His father had his claws deep in the financial markets of the Geotic Realm for over five hundred years. After Mugan's death, Charles made sure that it went to Maug. The young dragon spent most of his life straddling the realms. He'd been educated in the best schools the Geotic had to offer and had nearly tripled the assets he had been born into. Maug was a very wealthy dragon.

He moved quickly to help his aunt and took three of the plastic bags in one hand, two in the other and smiled. Maggie eyed him with suspicion. Then she pointed towards the house with a shake of her head.

"Charles isn't here," she told him in a short tone. That elicited a good-natured laugh. Maug was well aware his foster father wasn't going to be home until after 5:00 pm. He had timed his visit to miss him. Charles was going to have some very pointed words for him. Maug could wait to have that talk.

"Can't I stop in and see my favorite aunt?"

"Mm." Maggie Tampton pressed her lips together. Maug found his way to the kitchen of the three-story brick house, immediately feeling comfortable. Over half his childhood had been spent in this house. Mostly with just Charles and Laru-baba. Maggie came later. He started to unload the items from the bags and set the boxes on the counter. He made a face upon seeing some of the pre-packaged foods. Maug paused, reading the ingredients.

"You know this stuff will kill you," he said as he held up a box in an offhand way.

"I'm certain you're not here to discuss our eating habits," Maggie quipped as she yanked the box out of his hand. He grinned, and she scowled. "Do you want some tea?"

"Sounds lovely." Maug leaned against the counter and crossed his arms, watching her fill the kettle at the sink. He helped her put the groceries away, and then they sat at the table with the steaming cups in front of them. Maug fiddled with a paper napkin.

Maggie Tampton sighed. "All right, you little shit. What have you done?"

"Aunt Maggie!" The young dragon smirked. "Language."

"You show up unannounced when you know Charles isn't going to be home, and you've got Lord Turis shadowing your steps. You do something illegal?"

"Not today, no." He picked up the cup and blew on the hot liquid. He took a few moments to compose his thoughts. "Tell me, how difficult was it for you and Charles to have children?"

Maggie set her cup down sharply. "So, it's true? You're courting a human?"

Maug closed his mouth and tightened his jaw. He'd find a way to get the black back for this. Maug hadn't wanted to tip his hand to Maggie so quickly. Charles had probably heard rumors, although it was entirely likely that old man Parks had complained about his dating Roberta.

"Laru-baba won't tell me how it's done," Maug said, deciding to avoid the question. Maug had learned many types of magic from the old wolf shaman. Most of the time she was eager to teach him; however, when he had raised this question a few weeks ago she had become evasive. Charles and Maggie had children, so Maug knew it was possible. Maug disliked the idea that Turis knew as well, but that was milk already spoiled.

"Gods." Maggie Tampton rubbed her temple. "Maug, don't tell me you're fertile."

"Not at the moment." He sighed and looked out the window, examining the garden at the back of the house.

His cycles were on a predictable five-year pattern since attaining his maturity. One unfortunate frustration of being a dragon was finding a partner that shared the same cycle. In days of old, when there were more dragons, it was far easier to find a mate. These days, with the dragons ever-dwindling numbers and long reproductive cycles, it was unheard of for anyone to be nesting. It had made Maug despaired to think he'd never find a mate.

That was until he met Roberta Parks. Having spent time with her, he knew she was what he wanted. What he needed. Just thinking about her made his lips upturn in a wistful smile. He hadn't expected to be so smitten with a human but then, when did things ever go as expected?

"Why are you asking about this now?" Maggie Tampton said, getting up to get more hot water. He considered for a long moment before answering.

Maggie Tampton was one of the few that Maug could trust to discuss this with. She was the wife of his foster father. Charles had raised the orphaned Maug from a near hatchling. That was, in fact, how the human advocate had met Maglin in the first place. Luck would have it that Maglin and Charles ended up falling in love and marrying.

Maug had spoken to Charles about starting a family. It was something that Charles encouraged, even though Maug found female dragons to be annoying at best. Charles blamed himself, saying he should have made more of an effort to see that Maug spent time with his own kind. Most of the dragons Maug knew were older and had their own agenda; which brought him back to what he wanted to discuss with his Aunt Maggie—the possibility of a human mate.

"There is a girl," he said finally.

"Of course there's a girl," Maggie stated flatly. "Human?"

He nodded imperceptibly.

"Maug." Maggie sat back down and pulled one of his hands into hers. "You'll kill a human mate. A human isn't going to be able—"

"But that's the thing," he said with a hint of excitement. "I think she could. I'd say she's going to be a pretty powerful mage when she's older."

"Older?" Maggie pulled her hand away and glared at Maug with suspicion. "How old is this girl?"

"Old enough."

"Maug!"

The young dragon grinned wickedly. He couldn't explain it to her. Hell, he couldn't understand it himself. Maug couldn't be certain when he'd decided that Roberta would be the one he'd take for a mate. But it had become a clear certainty for him. After she had confessed her feelings the night before, Maug was positive she was the one.

"You need to talk to Charles."

"Gods, no! He'd exile me to the Thaumaturgic Realm if he had any idea I was courting a human."

"He already knows something's up." Maggie frowned. "Why do you think he's been wanting to meet?"

"Don't tell him," Maug said, grabbing her hand with a light squeeze. Maggie eyed him for a moment and then sighed a little wearily. "I just… I want to be able to tell him when I'm ready. Please?"

There were a small number of people the Dragon Lord of the West would beg. Charles was one, Aunt Maggie the other. And now, he decided to add Roberta to that very short list.

"No, love, I won't tell him."

He grinned and grabbed her hand, pressing it to his lips. "Now be a good girl and teach me the spell?"

"For hatchlings?" Her lips pressed into a firm line. "It's not something I can teach. It takes a different kind of magic."

"What kind?"

"It's a sympathetic spell."

Maug nodded slowly, only now realizing why Laru-baba had put him off. That would make it more complicated. Those sort of spells required… active participation.

"Ugh, gods," Maug said. There was little use trying to get the spell out of his aunt now. She'd flat refuse him for many of the same reasons the wolf shaman had. He ran his fingers through his hair. Well, he'd just have to work it out, somehow, but at the moment he wasn't sure how.

~ ~ ~

Maug said he would pick her up after work. Bobby hoped he wouldn't show up in a limo this time. She didn't want her manager to get the idea she was dating a rich guy. She waited in front of the office supply store where she worked in a strip mall when he pulled up on a motorcycle. The large Yamaha was decked out in orange and yellow. He stopped and pulled off his full-face helmet with a playful grin.

"Ready?" he asked.

Bobby eyed the large machine with trepidation. "You sure you know how to drive that?"

Maug laughed and offered her his helmet.

"What are you going to wear?"

"Roberta, I am a dragon. I do not need a helmet."

She considered that for a moment and then pulled the helmet over her head. Maug helped her fasten the straps. She slung her purse across her body, swung a leg over the bike and moved closer to Maug. She felt a thrill of heat as she wrapped her arms around his waist.

He's nothing but muscle.

"Do you work out?" she asked.

Maug craned his head around and arched an eyebrow. "I suppose—if you call leading Oberon's war parties 'working out.'"

"That sounds like a story," she teased.

He shrugged and gunned the motorcycle into traffic.

Bobby had never ridden on a motorcycle before. She had to admit she felt a thrill as they zipped through traffic at high speed. She supposed she should be afraid, but somehow she knew, that with Maug, she was perfectly safe. Bobby doubted there was much in the world that could hurt her with a dragon standing by her side.

They pulled up to the Cajun restaurant decorated in bright yellows and reds, and he held the bike while she hopped off. She pulled the helmet off and smiled. "That was fun!"

He grinned. "Better than the limo?"

"Definitely."

Maug threw a leg over and grabbed her wrist, pulling her to him. She smiled at him.

"I'll keep that in mind," he said softly. "Although I like the privacy the car affords."

Bobby smiled and leaned on her toes to touch his lips.

Maug stilled, turning his head sideways as if listening for something. They were in the middle of the suburb and there was little in the way of grass and trees. A troubled expression crossed his features and Bobby looked at him questioningly.

"What is it?"

"Something," he said. He wrapped an arm around her waist and walked her into the restaurant.

"That other dragon again?" Bobby scanned the parking lot, trying to catch sight of whatever Maug had sensed.

"No. This stinks of something else. Let's go inside."

~ ~ ~

It had only been a moment, but Maug knew that scent. The acrid smell of rotting flesh in sewage, sharp enough for him to taste metal in his mouth. He wasn't alarmed. He'd faced down any number of these demons before. Enough so they made a point of staying clear of his path in the Thaumaturgic Realm.

A sardonic smile twisted his face.

Was it possible the idiot creature was hunting him?

Maug's immediate concern was that Roberta be put out of harm's way, but she would be safer with him. Maug didn't know how much training her grandfather had given her, so was uncertain if she could defend herself. Even a simple shield could be a high draw spell if you didn't know how to work the natural magics to borrow the power.

"How many tonight?" the hostess asked as they walked in the door hand in hand. Roberta held up two fingers with a smile. Maug was happy to let her take the lead in this. The establishment was a little garish for his taste, with bright primary colors assaulting them from every direction. Even the tiled floor was patterned in green and orange. Maug was wary, trying to get a sense of where the demon was lurking.

"Great," the hostess said. "Right, this way then."

Roberta followed and Maug trailed behind, making a small gesture with his hands. The floor glowed, but only he could see the magical trail. He noticed a discoloration and traced it to a table where two people sat.

Them?

He frowned and moved to take a seat across from Roberta.

"Your server will be with you in a few moments." The woman smiled, handing Maug and Roberta a menu each.

Maug recognized the couple from the sensory spell he'd blocked at the bar the other night. He'd thought it was some middling hedge wizard that was curious. However, seeing them twice in his proximity made him believe this wasn't as random as he first thought.

"Hello! Welcome to Billy Joe's." The waitress moved to the table with a pad and pen ready in her hand. "Have you been a guest before?"

"I have," Roberta said.

"I have not," Maug said. He smiled at the server. "Tell me what's good, and then bring it."

"The BBQ ribs are on special," the woman said. "Half rack for $16.95, it comes with two sides. May I get you something to drink?"

"It's unfortunate to ruin perfectly good meat with fire," he said, a smile playing on his lips. "Roberta?"

"I happened to like my food cooked," Roberta said. "Ice tea, please."

"Sir?" the woman asked.

"Water."

"I'll be back to take your order in a bit." She moved away from the table.

"Do you really eat raw meat?" Roberta leaned over to whisper. Maug arched an eyebrow and offered a short laugh.

"I do," he said. "But I prefer to have hunted it myself. Nothing like a fresh kill."

"Ugh," Roberta made a face. At least Maggie hadn't had this issue with Charles. He already knew what dragons preferred, having raised Maug.

"Not to worry my sweet. I can eat cooked meat; it's just not the way I prefer it."

"Mm…" Roberta looked at the menu while Maug took a moment to feel out the natural magical currents beneath the tiled floor. A concrete barrier hindered his attempt to pull power from the earth. For a lesser mage, it may have caused a problem, but Maug had a store of power. He could offer a full fight without touching the environment if he had to. He doubted the demon would have the same ability. He flicked his eyes in the direction of the offending couple. Only to have the man nod at him with a smile.

So arrogant.

Maug knew a good deal about arrogance. Too bad the other wouldn't have much to back him up once Maug got his claws in him. The woman startled and paled. Interesting, she could sense his killing intent. Good. He liked his prey afraid. It enticed the hunter in him.

"Do you know what you're going to have?" Roberta asked, glancing over the top of the menu.

Maug grinned. "Yes."

"Well, I think I want the pulled pork. What about you?"

"I'll have the steak." That would be his starter anyway. He'd get the other two later.

"What about sides?" Roberta said. "I can't decide between the soup or a salad."

"I'll just have the meat."

Roberta paused and glanced over her menu. "You know"—Bobby closed her menu—"Katrin eats vegetables. Vegetables are good for you."

"Being a green, she would." Maug smirked. "No, sweet, I am a true carnivore. Bad enough it's going to be burnt."

"Are you ready to order?" Their waitress came back with their drinks and they put in their order. Maug leaned back to watch the couple watching them. He wondered if he could put a spy on them while he took Roberta home.

Damn pixies, never around when you need one, he thought to himself.

~ ~ ~

It was a not a coincidence, truly.

"What luck," Thaddeus said.

Elizabeth shook her head and took a sip of her drink. "No, I knew."

"If you say so, my dear." He took on a patronizing tone. She couldn't decide to be irritated with him or happy that he said 'my dear.' She sighed, and as with many things, let it go. Her infatuation with the human wizard made her let a lot of things pass.

That's when she felt a sharp chill. She jerked her head and met the eyes of the redhead. They were dark, unfeeling, those of a killer. She sank deeper into her chair.

He means to end my life, she thought. *Fortunate for me I don't have a life to end.*

"He knows we're here," she said in a soft voice.

Thaddeus shrugged. "What of it?"

There was little point in trying to gainsay him. Thaddeus had his own mind on … well, everything. He was arrogant, rude, and condescending. But still, something about him enchanted her. His heat in the throes of passion was like nothing else in the world.

She glanced back at the girl and the young man. The redhead was ignoring them for a moment, so she took the opportunity to get a better read on him. She frowned, not feeling the power that she was usually able to call. It was slow, as if mired in ice. She frowned and noted the red-haired man smirking at her.

Was he affecting the magical currents around them? What sort of control did he have? He lifted his chin with an arrogant flash of a smile and turned his attention back to his dinner companion, dismissing her with contempt.

He could rival Thaddeus in arrogance, she kept the thought to herself.

This didn't bode well.

Elizabeth had summoned a demon spirit to guard them while they ate. The portents had warned that the young couple would be here. She could sense the creature lurking nearby. It was interested in the couple as well; she felt its hunger as if it were her own. It focused on the man, longing to devour his power. Just as well. The man meant them harm, no doubt. His intent to kill was a palpable thing to her.

Still, should the creature feast on the girl, she would be unavailable as a sacrifice to her Lady. She offered an exchange for underlings like the one lurking, and other gifts of power for doing the Lady's bidding in this realm. It was what she had to do to keep "living." Her well-being tied to what her powerful patron would provide.

Even Thaddeus didn't know the whole truth. Elizabeth was the true power in their partnership. She kept him around because he enchanted her, and she loved him.

She considered and decided.

"Take the man," she said in a quiet voice. "But I want the girl."

The creature rebelled silently, and Thaddeus laughed low. "This should be amusing," he said. "When?"

"Later," Elizabeth said. "After they leave the restaurant. We will get them on their drive home."

~ ~ ~

"I'll be leaving for Granddad's next week," Bobby told Maug. He frowned a little, crossing his arms. "What? You know I have to go."

"Yes, but I don't have to like it."

"You can come see me," she said brightly.

Maug rolled his eyes. "Oh, the advocate will love that."

"I don't understand why not." Bobby spooned desert into her mouth. "You're my boyfriend. At least I… well…"

"Oh, I'm more than that, my sweet." Maug smiled, leaning forward and reaching for her hand. "But your grandfather is a member of Queen Titania's court, and I am a member of her husband's. They are bitter rivals and have little use for each other. That spills over to the members, like your grandfather. I am not his favorite because of it."

"Aren't they married?" she asked. "The Fairy King and Queen?"

Maug shrugged in an offhand way. "Neither keep their vows."

"Oh?"

Maug shook his head. "I don't indulge in the court gossip."

Bobby frowned. It was more than that. He didn't want to talk about it at all.

"I shall ask if the advocate will receive me. We may not be able to see each other for a month. Maybe more if Oberon sends me on a campaign."

"A campaign?"

"We've got trouble in the west," Maug explained. "The north too. It falls to Turis and me to deal with it. We've got hordes massing at our borders. They are going to try and have another go at us."

"Hordes of what?"

"Minor demons mostly, but there are all sorts of undead creatures. They look to the lands of the kingdom to feed their hunger. They are a blight, but we can usually keep them out. They make a push every few years, and we push back."

"We?" Her grandfather never talked about such things. Instead, he worked with Bobby to develop her power, training her to hold the land, and its wild magics; how to bond with it and bend it to her will. The advocates kept the power of the land from running amok, at least, that's what her granddad said.

"The Dragon Lords," Maug said. "We control a good portion of Oberon's army. If too many of the dark forces get in, the advocates may not be able to hold off disaster. Our world hangs in this balance of power. It's a real mess, to be honest."

"How come?" Bobby asked, making a note to take some of this up with her grandfather. At least Maug was willing to talk about it.

"The Thaumaturgic and Geotic hang in balance with each other. What happens in one, is often mirrored in the other. The Thaumaturgic is affected by climate change, pollution, deforestation; all of that is happening in the Geotic. Because of these things, equal parts of the Thaumaturgic are becoming uninhabitable. That feeds these dark creatures power."

"How can it be stopped?"

Maug frowned and shook his head. "I don't think it can, my sweet. I think eventually, the two worlds will merge back into one."

"Back?" Bobby finished her small sundae and pushed the dish away. "What do you mean?"

Maug toyed with the spoon and then tossed it aside. "I don't know how much of it is true. A lot of pre-history is shadowed in legend and outright lies. You should ask your grandfather about it."

Bobby watched his face and then nodded. "Yeah, I think I will."

~ ~ ~

Dinner was a passable fare, but Roberta seemed to like it. Maug couldn't decide if he was irritated or amused with the couple watching them. He would have preferred more privacy with Roberta. They were waiting for them to leave, he was sure. Maug thought to call a car to take Roberta home while he dealt with them, but decided against it; their time together was limited and he rather selfishly didn't want to give it up.

He paid the bill with an American Express Card and Roberta laughed. "You have a credit card?"

"No, it's a charge card. I pay the balance every month. Or one of my accountants does."

"You have accountants?" She took his hand as they walked out of the restaurant. Dusk was setting, and the sky had turned a burnt orange.

"Many." He smirked. "What, did you think I stole my money?"

"I thought it was magic," she said bluntly. Maug laughed. He glanced around the parking lot warily. It would be fully dark soon.

"This is so woefully mundane. I'm sure I've disappointed you."

"Don't be silly." Roberta held the helmet and frowned. "Maybe it's better. I can see the IRS trying to investigate tax fraud. I'm not sure they would take 'magic' as a way of making money."

"No fear of that." Maug leaned down and gave her a quick kiss. "I pay taxes. A lot actually."

She pulled the helmet over her head with a bright smile and then he started the motorcycle. She hopped on and pressed her body against him. He closed his eyes briefly, relishing the feeling of her body against his.

"Thank you," she said over his shoulder. "I had fun tonight."

"Perhaps the night isn't over." He glanced back. "How about a little ride? See the city lights from the hills?"

"Sure."

Maug smiled. If he could keep her out and in his company for as long as possible, he would be a very happy dragon.

He pulled the bike off the main road, and they started up the long winding road above the city. There was only the hum of the bike under them, with the single headlamp lighting the darkness. There was no other traffic, and he twisted the throttle to give the motorcycle some more gas as it hugged the twist and turns of the road.

The bike hit an invisible wall, stopping it instantly, throwing them violently off. Maug cursed himself for not sensing the attack and threw out a soft magical barrier to catch Roberta. Maug didn't fare so well; having tumbled head over tail, tearing his pants on the gravel road as he landed in a crouch. He sank his fingers deep into the dirt with a snarl.

That was the demon's mistake. It should have taken him near concrete and steel, which block the natural eddies of power. But it would have had trouble pulling power for itself there. It probably, wrongfully, believed this spot would leave Maug more vulnerable, away from any potential allies. Here, just outside of the city, Maug was able to sue the full resources of his surroundings.

The demon soared out of the sky and landed in front of him with a hard thud. It stood a good five meters tall and let out a mighty roar as it took a swipe at Maug. The dragon grinned. Why it was such a little thing. And so bold to show itself. Maug decided to end this quickly. Roberta could be injured the longer this went on.

"No!" Roberta screamed from behind him. Maug waved his hand and threw up a shield to protect her. Her voice muffled as she shouted his name. He wished he could reassure her. It was a small matter, really, one he didn't need his true form to take on.

"Oh, you're a bold one aren't you?" Maug's face lit with grim delight. He threw a hard bolt of energy and the creature screamed in pain as it tore into its flesh, making it stagger backward. Maug laughed and summoned his broadsword with a burst of flame, holding it high above his head. "All right then," he said. "I'll make this quick."

He moved forward as the demon threw fire at him. Maug stepped through the flames with practiced ease. Using fire? The idiot creature had no idea what it had taken on. It tried to swipe him with foul claws that reeked of death. Maug dodged the blows easily, then leaped in the air, and with a thrust of his sword, cleaved the monster's head from its body.

Maug watched without emotion as he dropped lightly to his feet. The demon's body staggered and then toppled to the ground with a *thud*. Maug held out his hand; it glowed with a bright red color. He sought the tendrils of power connected to his attacker, knowing it would lead to the woman. Her stench was all over the creature. He sent a sharp bite along the demon's link, and although it wouldn't kill its mistress, it would wound her. He'd finish it later, after getting Roberta to safety.

"Maug!" Roberta ran to him. As soon as he knew the creature was dead, he'd released the shield holding her back. She threw her arms around him and cried. "Are you okay? Oh my God! You're bleeding!"

He put his fingers to his head and inspected the blood with a shrug. He'd likely banged it in the tumble off the bike, but his bones were stronger than those of a human's. It was little more than a scrape, but Roberta didn't understand that and was near hysterical.

"It's fine." He tried to sooth her, grabbing her hands. "Are you hurt?"

"No!" She pulled off the helmet and her pale blue eyes welled with tears. "Hold still!"

He smiled and put his hands on her shoulders, offering her a light squeeze. "Listen, love, it's fine."

"No." She shook her head and held her hands forward, they were glowing white, hot with power. Fascinated, Maug watched her power rolling over him. It was bright and warm, and he moaned under her touch.

"Roberta, stop!" She was draining her own resources to heal him. He frowned. Hadn't she learned to take power from the environment? She was starting to flicker, and he shook her, trying to break her hold. She collapsed in his arms, unconscious. The minimal pain disappeared, and his head had stopped bleeding. He lifted her into his arms, summoned a small portal and stepped through. It took him to the walled-off garden at his house in Palatine, where he was currently staying in the Geotic realm.

A healer? He nodded in thought as he carried her through the back door and up the stairs to his room. *A powerful one too.* She just lacked experience and judgment. Her raw talent was easy enough to see. He could taste her power, and it was sweet and pure. He could feel what her heart had poured out to him without realizing what she'd done.

He laid her gently on his bed and caressed the side of her face with the backs of his fingers, leaning down to touch his lips on her forehead before he straightened.

This girl. She was… everything he wanted. Everything he needed. He didn't care what he had to do to make her his.

Roberta Parks would be his mate. And he didn't care who he had to go through to make it so.

MIDSUMMER'S DREAM

It had taken cunning to elude the hunter. She had let it catch her trail because she had worried it would go after Thaddeus if it lost her. It had nearly gotten Elizabeth Cho twice. If she hadn't been a shade, it would have succeeded.

She had never seen a creature like it. Long, huge, with massive wings. It was the size of a semi-tractor trailer. She'd only glimpsed the shadow of its form as it crept through the alleys, but that was enough. The backlash she'd gotten during the demon child's death throes would have killed a mortal creature. Even as a Shadow, it had hurt, bad, and it hadn't given up until near dawn.

But it wasn't giving up, not completely. She could feel its pleasure in the chase. Its enjoyment of the game it was playing. Elizabeth knew she would have to leave the area. Even then, she wasn't sure that it wouldn't be able to find her elsewhere. All she could hope was that it would find other prey.

But what was the monster doing with that human girl? It had managed to hide its true nature from Elizabeth during their first few encounters. She couldn't even be certain what it was. Some backward bastard cousin of a high demon, that was for sure.

Her mobile phone vibrated in her pocket. She opened it and put it to her ear.

"Where are you?" Thaddeus asked sleepily. "It's nearly dawn, and you didn't come home."

"The girl has a protector." Elizabeth decided to share only a small portion of the truth. Thaddeus would think he could bargain with the monster and would likely be eaten for the trouble. It was implacable and would kill them both.

"Oh?" His voice was rough, having just woken up. "Did you get the redhead out of the way then?"

"He's the problem, Thaddeus."

"He wasn't much," Thaddeus said with a yawn. "You know, I'm really disappointed in your minion, Elizabeth. When are you coming home?"

"Not for a bit," she said, glancing over her shoulder. She thought she would stay away for a few days, just in case the predator had a way of tracking her. But she had to think of something to get Thaddeus out of the way. A light smile crossed her lips. "Perhaps you should broker us a stronger ally? They respond better to you."

"That's true," Thaddeus said. "But I'll have to go to the northern caves."

"I'll hold things here," she said. Thank god for the man's hubris. In this case, it could save his life. "I'm going to check the mirror. Perhaps my Lady will offer me aid."

"All right," he agreed. "I'll see you in a few days then."

"Indeed."

~ ~ ~

Maug woke to a wet wolf tongue licking his face. He batted the nose away and sat up on the couch. He'd been trying to find that sorceress bitch all night, but without much luck. There was something strange about her scent, though, every time he was sure he had her it seemed to disappear. With dawn coming, he'd abandoned the hunt. He didn't want Roberta to wake on her own, with no idea of how she got there.

"Gods, Laru-baba." He made a face of disgust. "There are better ways to wake me."

The wolf sat on her haunches, regarding him with a scowl. "Perhaps the Lord Maug would care to explain what a human female is doing in his bed?"

"Since when do you care who I have in my bed?"

"Since this human female is the granddaughter of the advocate of Spoons Forge." Laru-baba's tone was full of reproach. "Are you looking to start a war, my Lord?"

He stood and pushed his fingers through his hair. He could use a full day's sleep, but doubted he would have the opportunity; if Laru was here, he didn't doubt who his next visitor would be.

"You can tell Charles I'm not keeping her. At least, not at the moment."

"I do not approve."

"Like I care. Go on. Get out."

Laru-baba offered a withering glare before shimmering away. Maug knew it wouldn't be long before Charles showed up. Couldn't the mongrel keep her nose in her own den? He left his study and went up the stairs, quietly opening his bedroom door. He stepped into the expansive oak paneled room, he'd always enjoyed the comfort older, larger homes bought him.

He smiled. Roberta was still sleeping soundly. He perched on the edge of the bed and leaned down to kiss her lips.

"Mm." She stirred and made a noise and then startled when she opened her eyes. "Where…?"

"Shh." He smiled. "We're at my house."

Roberta glanced around, sitting up on her elbows. "How'd I get here?" Then her eyes went round. "Oh my God! That monster! It hurt you!"

"It's okay." Maug smiled, taking her hand. "You healed me."

"Did I?" She dropped back down on the pillows. "I've… I've never done anything like that before."

"You were very good at it, but you need training. You drained your internal resources and exhausted yourself. There are better ways to go about it."

"I didn't think I could draw from the earth in the Geotic Realm."

"Well, it's harder, but not impossible." He paused and brushed her hair away from her face. "Roberta…" he stopped himself and then snorted. He felt like a raw hatchling fresh from its shell. "I need to discuss something very serious with you."

"What?" She sat up and put a hand on his cheek. He leaned into it, drawing deep on her scent. Gods, she smelled good.

"I desire you very much," he said, his gaze meeting hers. A slight smile lit her face.

"Well," she said in a low, teasing tone. "You aren't the only one feeling that way."

He laughed quietly. No, he supposed not.

"But I desire more than to just sleep with you," he said, holding her pale blue eyes with his. "I mean to wed you."

"Wed? You mean like get married?"

"Yes, silly one." He leaned his forehead against hers. "Marry. That is if you want to."

"I…" Roberta bit her lip, offering a slow nod. "But can we get married? I mean, you're a dragon."

"I am."

"Is that allowed?"

"If you agree." He leaned forward and ran his nose along her cheek. "I will make it so. I swear it."

"Yes," she answered impulsively. He pulled back, cocking his head to one side. Roberta nodded, her eyes never wavering. "Yes. I love you, and this feels right. I will marry you. When?"

Maug laughed. He kissed her hard on the lips and eased her back on his bed, his hands wandering down the soft curves of her body.

"It'll take a little time. These things are a formal affair. We have to post the banns and get permission from your guardians, but as long as you're in agreement, we can start the process."

Her arms came around his neck. "I'd like that. I'd like that a lot. I want to get married as soon as we can. You make me happy."

"Gods," he breathed. "You don't know what joy you bring me."

He kissed her, feeling his blood heat. She started to undo his shirt and pushed it from his shoulders. She nibbled along his jaw, and Maug rolled her under him. He ran his tongue along her neck and jaw, knowing he had gone too far to stop now. He pulled at her shirt and slid it away, cast her pink bra aside, and circled her nipple with his tongue, teasing it with his teeth. He moved his lips to her neck, nipping along the back of it. She gasped, tightening her fingers on his bare shoulders. He pressed his body against hers, pinning her to the mattress.

"There's one more thing," he said, his voice low and hoarse. For him to truly mate with her, he had to do this. "Please. It will seal our promise."

"I want to do this," Roberta said, moving her lips to his jaw. "I want to make love to you."

He growled softly and buried his head in her neck, losing himself to his nature as he moved more aggressively. Roberta clawed at him with the same heat. He pulled her slightly forward; Maug examined the smooth pale skin of her neck and moved his nose along its curve, drawing a deep breath. First, he lightly kissed it and ran his tongue along her neck. Then the dragon growled under his breath and pulled her tightly to him. There—that would be the place.

Maug sank his teeth deep into the young woman's shoulder. Roberta screamed, clutching his shoulders before falling unconscious. Maug closed his eyes and shuddered, feeling his venom enter the wound. If he hadn't yearned to mate with her, he could easily have devoured her at that moment. Instead, he licked her neck tenderly, lapping up the blood. Maug would never forget the taste. It seared into his soul like a hot brand.

He lifted his head away to see the wound closing. As his poison spread, a familiar light grey diamond pattern appeared across the top of her shoulder and down the back of her neck. He leaned forward and whispered a small spell, drawing power to add to hers as her body worked to heal itself.

The dragon smiled with smug satisfaction as the pattern darkened. The wound faded, leaving only his mark on her pale skin. Roberta was a strong mage to be able to fend off his poison and heal herself. He'd known he would have to aid her some, but her power was true, bright, powerful and amazing. Most humans would have been cold and dead in his arms from the mating bite of a dragon. Roberta was a mage of the highest potential. Power drew to power, and Maug knew this mating was right and true.

Every dragon's poison created a different pattern; a mark that was personal to each dragon. By biting her, he had marked her as his. Now it would be impossible for even Oberon to interfere.

And by marking her, he had bound Roberta to him until one of them died. This wasn't a simple act. There was a price to be paid. Roberta was tied to his soul, as he was to hers. He felt her love shining inside him, making him more complete than he'd ever been. And she would feel his dragon nature; it would become part of her as well.

But she could also be used as a tool to harm him, should she fall into the hands of his enemies. Her grandfather could use her to revenge himself on the dragon, but it would cause Roberta horrific pain if he did. In truth, the man couldn't harm Maug through Roberta unless he was willing to shatter her soul. Maug swore to himself, and a whisper to her, that no harm, not ever, would come to her. He was strong enough to protect a mate and defend a nest. And he knew it was possible to have hatchlings. The red dragon understood what he had undertaken, and now that Roberta had felt his bite, she would know too.

Roberta stirred in his arms with a soft moan. The mark was light grey against her white skin. As she healed, it would go black. Once they fully consummated the making, it would turn a brilliant red to match his colorful hide.

Maug kissed her lips, fully intending to finish the mating.

"Mm," she moaned, opening her blue eyes to slits.

Maug cupped her face and kissed her urgently.

"Oh God," she gasped. Her arms came around his neck, and her fingers trailed along his shoulders; their bond was igniting her desire for him. She uttered a soft moan of pain and Maug lifted his head, looking at her with concern.

"What is it?" he asked tenderly, running a thumb along her bottom lip.

"My neck hurts," Roberta whimpered.

"It'll be tender for a few days." Maug smiled with a kiss. "I made you mine."

"I… understand," she whispered, even as she pressed her lips against his. Her breath quickened, and Maug felt her heartbeat against him. She drew a deep breath, leaning back against the bed. "Oh, God. I…understand… I understand everything."

"No regrets?" he teased, moving his lips to her neck. Her fingers clung to his head.

"Never," she breathed, returning his kisses hotly.

"Lord Maug!" Laru-baba slammed the door against the wall as she burst into the room in human form. Her yellow eyes flashed with hot anger. "What do you think you are doing?"

"I think," Maug growled, pulling his head away from Roberta, "that I am going to pelt a wolf."

"You will stop this instant!" Laru-baba ordered shrilly. "And you will take that girl back to her family!"

Maug leaned on his elbows with Roberta still under him. He clenched a fist, curling power in it to vaporize the wolf where she stood. How dare she interfere with his mating?

Roberta reached for his hand. "Don't," she begged quietly. "It's… it's okay. She's right. My folks will be worried."

Maug leaned his head against hers. She was right. He needed to speak to her family, to her father. He had to do this right, or they could make it harder for them.

He kissed her softly. "It doesn't matter," he whispered in her ear. "We're mated now. I can be patient."

"I don't want to be patient too long." Roberta buried her head into his chest while Maug threw a hot glare at Larubaba. The wolf, for her part, crossed her arms and regarded him icily.

"Lord Maug is foolish and rash," the wolf bit out. "We will be discussing this with Charles."

Maug moved to get out of bed, shielding Roberta from the wolf's view. He stepped close and glared down at the wolf menacingly.

"Watch yourself, bitch," he said in a low voice. "I am your lord. You serve me. I'm warning you now; you interfere with this, and I will banish you from the House of the West forever."

~ ~ ~

They rode back to Bobby's house in Maug's limousine. The journey from his house in Palatine to hers in Geneva was close to an hour. Bobby fell asleep against his chest with his arms wrapped around her waist. She couldn't explain the contentment she felt in his arms. It was like she had waited for this moment forever; she had never felt more right.

Maug insisted they eat before he took her home, and had his servants serve hotcakes and bacon for her, and a platter of raw meat, with a cup of black coffee, for him. She thought she would be squeamish about it, but it didn't seem to bother her.

She called her folks to let them know she was okay and would be home later. They were relieved to hear from her, but she expected they were mad at her too. She'd stayed out all night before, but only with girlfriends. This was the first time she'd spent the night with a guy. And while they hadn't finished what they'd started, Bobby knew it would happen soon. *Not soon enough,* a whisper in her mind said. She wasn't sure when she should tell her parents she had got engaged, but was smart enough to know this morning would not be it.

Maug woke her as they arrived in town, and leaned down to brush a kiss on her lips.

"They'll think we slept together," she said in a soft voice.

Maug smiled. "They can think what they want."

"I wish we had," she whispered. He lifted her chin with two fingers and parted her lips, teasing her tongue. Bobby moaned softly, feeling a deep ache. He smiled and touched his lips to her ear.

"In time, my sweet, and I promise to make the wait worth it. Now, I need to speak to your father and make things right. I don't want to make an enemy out of him."

Bobby felt herself shiver. She wanted him—badly. The ferocity of her desire surprised her, and she knew it must have something to do with the bite. They were tied together somehow, but it didn't scare her. She was going to marry a dragon. She loved him. This bond was just an unexpected part of that.

They pulled up to her house and the driver got out and opened the door. They emerged from the car hand in hand. Bobby's mom sat on the porch swing while her dad paced up and down. Her father was a slim man, dark-haired like her grandfather, while her mother was fair.

Maug straightened his shoulders and escorted her to the house with his hand on the small of her back. James Parks offered Maug a hard look, and Bobby reached for the dragon's hand.

"Go in the house with your mother, Bobby," her father ordered, his voice calm and measured. Oh yeah, he was pissed, and there was no arguing with him when he was like that. Bobby's mother took her arm to lead her inside. Bobby mouthed the words "sorry" over her shoulder as she went inside.

"Care to tell me what happened?" Tabitha Parks was in her mid-forties but appeared ten years younger. Her honey-colored hair was pulled back from her face in a ponytail. She looked rigid, and pale, like she hadn't slept. Bobby felt a pang of guilt. She had put that worry there.

"I'm really sorry, Mom. There was an accident…"

"What sort of accident?" Brad was sitting on the stairs, leaning back on his elbows. He was half watching their father and Maug out the long window.

"One involving magic," said Eddie as he stepped out of the kitchen. "I went looking for you. I found the motorcycle and the smell of a freshly burnt corpse."

"Some sort of monster attacked us," Bobby admitted. She bit her lip and turned to her mother. "But it wasn't Maug's fault, Mom. He got hurt fighting whatever it was. I healed him and passed out."

"The Dragon Lord has enemies." Eddie crossed his arms. He let out a long breath. "You aren't safe in his company."

"No! I was safe because of him."

Eddie shook his head with a snort. "Ezra wants you in Spoons. Pack your things."

"What? No!" Bobby looked at her mother in horror. *Leave Maug? Now?*

Tabitha Parks nodded. "Just until we figure out what's going on. I'm sorry, sweetie, this isn't a punishment. Your father and I have spoken to Ezra about this. It's for the best."

"Don't worry," Brad said. "I'll tell Maug what's going on. Maybe it'll give him time to figure out who was after him. If I know him, he'll like the idea of you being somewhere safe."

"Well, I don't. It's not fair!" Bobby fumed, crossing her arms. "We didn't do anything wrong!"

Bobby's father entered and closed the door behind him. "Maug explained what happened. I told him your grandfather wants you to go to Spoons Forge and he agrees it's a good idea."

"Told you," Brad said, moving to his feet. "He might be a dragon, but he's a stand-up guy."

Bobby threw a hot look of anger at all of them and then bolted out the door. She hopped down the steps and ran to the car, catching Maug's arm before he got in. "I won't go!" She felt real panic at the idea of leaving him. "They can't make me!"

"Ah." He set a hand on her neck and pulled her forward, wrapping her in a hug. He leaned down to speak softly in her ear. "Go to your grandfather's. You'll be safer there. I'll find who's behind this and put an end to it."

"I don't want to leave you. Not now. Not before we—"

"Come to Sebastian's Keep for Midsummer's Night. We'll finish this."

Maug kissed her softly on the forehead and got into the car. Bobby bit her lip as she stepped back and watched the car pull away, feeling as if the world had just turned very dark.

~ ~ ~

The portents were being difficult.

Elizabeth frowned and pushed her brown hair out of her eyes. Thaddeus would be back soon. She clasped the silver hand mirror and whispered the words again. This was the fourth try, and so far, her plea had been ignored.

"Queen of the delight, your most devoted daughter calls to you," Elizabeth said. "Again."

"Such petulance does not become you, my child." A light, musical, feminine voice laughed from the mirror. "What favor would you ask of me?"

"A little thing." Elizabeth disliked pushing her luck. Her Lady could be indulgent, or fickle and cruel. The shade never knew which she would get. "There is one hunting this child. I need to know how to defeat it."

"Mm?" There was a lilt of curiosity in the tone. The mirror danced with pastel lights, and flashes of gold and silver. "I am curious. What could harm one such as you?"

Elizabeth closed her eyes and held out her hands. She'd captured a hint of its power the night before. The energy crackling in her hand raged bright red. She contained it for only a brief moment. It flashed with a snap and disappeared, leaving blood-red smoke as it vanished. She hissed in pain and shook her hand. Whatever the monster was, it was stronger than anything she'd encountered before.

"Oh dear," the soft voice said. It sounded… worried? That startled Elizabeth more than anything else.

"High powers of all, what is this thing?"

"Did you make this one your enemy?"

"I did," Elizabeth admitted, not liking the hint of rebuke in her Lady's tone. Her face flushed. "Tell me, Mother of All, how can I defeat it?"

"You cannot," her Lady's voice returned. "It would have been best if the beast had not noticed you, child. This is a fearsome monster, the worst of all the magical creatures. It has no heart and lives a remorseless, murderous existence."

"It's hunting me." Elizabeth closed her eyes. "But it can't hurt me—can it? Not when I don't truly live. You've said so yourself."

"What cannot be killed can be destroyed," the White Queen of Elizabeth's heaven said. "Perhaps it is time for you to leave that realm and come home to me. I have a place ready for you at my side."

"May Thaddeus come?"

"No. He is not welcome in my court."

Elizabeth bit her lip and felt tears start in her eyes. If she couldn't be with Thaddeus, she didn't care if she would survive. Better to stay here and protect him from his own folly.

"Tell me, my Lady, what is the name of this monster, so I may better protect myself?"

"A dragon." The Lady's voice faded as the entity released the connection, and the object returned to being a simple hand mirror.

~ ~ ~

The red dragon straightened his shoulders before knocking on the double wooden doors to Charles's study. He heard the assent and opened the door. The room smelled of books and old leather. Charles sat at his desk, writing longhand on a piece of parchment. Maug took the chair opposite him and leaned back, seeming far more relaxed than he felt.

Charles was nearly seventy years old, but his sandy hair was only flecked with white. In truth, he appeared to be barely forty. Maug wondered if it was his bond with the land in the Thaumaturgic Realm that held the secret of his youth, or that he had mated and bonded to a dragon. Aunt Maggie was over three hundred years old herself. Which in dragon terms wasn't even middle-aged. Maug could see Maggie lending her life force to keep her mate at her side longer. Maug had already decided to do the same with Roberta.

Thinking of her, he sighed and sank back in the chair.

"So?" Charles didn't look up. His glasses perched on his nose as he continued to write. "Why do you appear now, Maug?"

"I may have done something," Maug said, his voice low and deep.

Charles glanced up with the ghost of a smile. "Oh?"

Maug felt his face color; making Charles Tampton smile wider. How could this man still make him feel like he was ten-years-old, caught killing the neighbor's chickens for the third time?

"Damn it, Charles!" Maug jumped out of the chair and moved around it to lean on his hands. "I've chosen a mate."

"Have you now?" He put his pen down and watched Maug with a hint of amusement. "You know, mating a human is a terrible idea."

"Like you're one to talk!" Maug exploded. "Gods, Charles! Have you heard of the pot?"

Charles grinned and got up from his chair. He moved over to where he kept a small stash of spirits and poured two glasses. "Maggie is vexed. Honestly, boy, why do you have to keep my mate stirred up?"

"Mind your own nest," Maug snapped. Charles handed Maug a drink, and he downed the glass, nearly choking on the potent liquor. Charles arched an eyebrow and drained his glass without making a face.

"You are the son of my heart. I've raised you as my own, so I do have some say in your stupidity."

Maug drew in a deep breath and let it out slowly. "I need your help."

"Ezra has expressed some concern," Charles said. Maug looked at him with surprise. "What? Did you think I didn't know what you've been up to? Tell me, why do you want this girl? Surely there's another female that would be more suitable."

"What?" Maug said, stricken. "No! Roberta is the one."

"Her grandfather may not agree," Charles said, returning to his desk to open a drawer.

"It doesn't matter," Maug said. He lifted his chin belligerently. "I marked her."

"My, my." Charles chuckled. "You are moving fast."

"Shut up." Maug threw himself back into the leather chair. "I intend to marry her."

"If Ezra is so inclined," Charles corrected.

Maug glared at his foster father. "He can't stop me. I've claimed her. She's mine."

"Biting her doesn't make her yours."

"Does too!" Maug's sat up, his eyes flashed with temper.

"I've been doing some checking," Charles said. "You're the talk of both courts. While Titania doesn't approve, Oberon has chosen not to involve himself."

"I don't want him involved!" Maug felt a small panic. If there were anyone who could make trouble for him, it would be Oberon. As a member of his court, Maug had sworn loyalty to the King. He knew it bothered the other dragon lords, but he saw it as a way to a political goal. But that didn't mean he trusted Oberon. The Fairy King was fickle and cruel. He toyed with others for sport. Maug didn't want his mate drawn into a power struggle between the two monarchs, but he was aware that it was a very real possibility.

"He'd likely side with you just to irritate Ezra." Charles picked up a pen and toyed with it. Maug watched him for a long moment and then raked his fingers through his bright red hair.

"I don't know what to do," he admitted softly. "I need your help to make this right."

"Admit you acted rashly by not coming to me first." Charles took off his glasses and set them on the wooden desk. Maug felt himself wilt under Charles's steady gaze.

"I may have acted rashly," Maug admitted. But he'd learned long ago that asking for forgiveness was far easier than asking for permission. "But Charles, she's the one. I know it. I can feel it. Can't you understand?"

"I can see something has stirred you," Charles said gently. He reached into the drawer and handed Maug a small scroll of parchment. "And if you were stupid enough to mark and bond her, then I assume you are serious in your intention. Look that over. It's a copy of the marriage contract I sent to Ezra on your behalf."

Maug glared at him with irritation. "When? Gods! You made me grovel for help when you already—"

"Groveling is good for you." Charles got up and walked around the desk, setting a hand on Maug's shoulder with a light squeeze, "and entertaining for me. Read the contract. I expect Ezra will have some changes."

"You're an asshole," Maug muttered as he started to leaf through the marriage proposal document.

~ ~ ~

Bobby sighed as she made her way through the long marble halls of Spoons Forge. She'd been there nearly a week. Usually, she looked forward to the magic and strangeness of the place, but this time, she longed to be elsewhere.

With Maug.

Just thinking about him made her nearly weep from the need to be with him. Without Maug, the sun didn't shine as bright. She knew she was turning into a greeting card cliché, but she didn't care.

"Bobby! Bobby!" Farni ran towards her at a good gait, his bright hooves chiming across the marble. She smiled as he slid to a stop beside her. She loved the bright white unicorn. He was a sweet boy and an even better friend. "Ezra sent me to get you!"

"Oh?"

"There's a visitor!" Farni said. "Goodness. She is so cool. I've heard amazing stories about her, but I've never actually met—"

"Who?"

Farni turned and clip-clopped next to her. "Laru-baba," he said in a hushed voice. "She is like, the most powerful shaman in the whole of the Thaumaturgic Realm."

"Laru..." Bobby mused thoughtfully. Then her face flushed, remembering. "Oh. Her."

"You don't understand. She is a legend!"

"Doesn't she serve Maug?"

The unicorn paused and cocked his head. "I don't think she serves anyone. Except maybe Queen Titania. I think they're close."

Bobby frowned. Maug had clearly told the Laru woman that she served him. Bobby followed Farni through the halls to her grandfather's office. Farni shimmered into his human form and knocked on the door. His hair was as white as when he was in his true form. He offered Bobby a saucy wink as they went inside.

"Ah, Roberta." Her grandfather stood up as they came in. Bobby nodded and looked him over with a start. He was younger than before. His hair, which had been grey that morning, was now stark black. And his face didn't have a single line.

"Is everything okay, Granddad?"

"Sorry, child," he said as if realizing her discomfort. "The closer I get to Midsummer—"

"Ezra?" a voice interrupted. Bobby turned and saw a grey dog sitting on its haunches, watching Bobby with sharp yellow eyes.

"Yes." Her grandfather went to stand next to the dog. "Roberta, this is Laru-baba. She is the shaman of the great wolf pack out of Ridges Hollow."

"We have met before," the dog—no, wolf—said, and shifted to become a tall, slender woman. Bobby blanched, remembering her rebuke at the woman's hands in Maug's bedroom. The memory made her flush three shades of red. "Remember?"

Bobby dropped her gaze. "Yeah."

"My Lord Maug requires the girl to be trained in her art," the wolf woman told Bobby's grandfather. "As such, he has made this my task."

"Yes, yes," Bobby's grandfather dismissed with impatience. "I know about the dragon's interest in my granddaughter."

"This goes beyond his interest." Laru-baba sniffed. "If it were just that, I would have refused."

"Would you?" Bobby's grandfather asked archly. The woman turned a cold expression on him, and Bobby shifted uncomfortably. "Don't toy with me, wolf, but enough of this. I will allow it, Laru-baba, if only because I know she could ask for no better tutor. However, I need to speak to Roberta first. Alone."

The woman offered a small smile, shifted to her canine form and trotted out of the office with her tail held high.

"You too, Farni," Ezra Parks said. Farni frowned and gave Bobby's hand a quick squeeze.

"Come see me later," he said in a low tone, and then shifted to his colt form before bolting from the room.

Her grandfather closed the door. "Sit," he said. "We need to talk about this."

"What do you mean?" Bobby went to a low couch, and her grandfather sat down next to her.

He took her hand and looked at her earnestly. "Tell me the truth, Roberta, do you even like this dragon?"

"What? Maug?" Bobby asked. This was not the direction she had expected the talk to go. Her grandfather nodded. Ezra Caleb Parks had always been an easy confidant. As a child, she told him things she had never told her parents. But this was different. This wasn't a childhood thing. But as she met his eyes, she knew she had to tell him the truth. "I love him, Granddad."

"Why?" His voice strained as he drew in a long breath.

She didn't expect that question either. Bobby rolled it over in her mind. Sure, they had buckets of sexual attraction. But there was something else; something undefinable. Maug was… "He's right."

Her grandfather offered a look of askance and started to speak, but she interrupted.

"We're different," Bobby admitted. "And it's not just because he's a dragon. He's strong, powerful. He's a warrior. I get that."

"His values fall outside of my Lady's court." His tone was severe, almost cold.

"But not King Oberon's," Bobby said impulsively. Her grandfather crossed his arms impatiently. "I've been reading in the library. It's the King's forces who hold evil at bay, keeping the kingdom safe. That's true, isn't it?"

"There is some truth to that, yes. But King Oberon's methods are harsh and cruel. As are the members of his court."

"Maug wouldn't hurt anyone that didn't have it coming. He protects the kingdom."

"That's naive. You're not thinking clearly," her grandfather told her. "However, Maug's advocate is a very old friend of mine; a good friend. Charles raised Maug from a near hatchling. If that weren't the case, I wouldn't be entertaining this at all. Maug wants to marry you. Did you know this?"

"Well, yeah." Bobby laughed. "He asked me, and I said yes. Do you think he'd try and marry me without talking to me first?"

"He is a dragon, Roberta. Do you understand what that means?"

"Probably more than you do." Bobby bit her lip.

"Dragons are violent killers without remorse; predators incapable of love. And Maug isn't just any dragon, he's one of the seven standing Dragon Lords. He murdered the previous Lord of the West for that title. And he'll only hold it until another dragon kills him for it. He's soaked in a good deal of blood already. This is not a good match for you!"

Bobby's jaw tightened. She hated that she couldn't deny everything he'd said, but she understood Maug's nature in a way her grandfather never could. When he bit her, his soul had opened to her. Yes, he could kill without remorse; but there was always a reason. And saying he was incapable of love was a lie. His love for her burned brightly, and she could feel it, even when they were apart. She hadn't told her grandfather about the mark, and now she was glad she didn't. It burned hot on her skin and made her long for Maug. She wanted him, needed him. "I'm going to marry him."

"Not if I don't approve!" Ezra Parks shook his head and stood up. "Things are different in the Thaumaturgic Realm, Roberta. I have a copy of the proposed marriage contract from Lord Maug's advocate. You will not marry until I've settled the terms and approved it."

Bobby tightened her jaw. "I'm sorry, Granddad, but I am twenty-one. I can marry whoever I want—whether you like it or not—and I don't have to do it in the Thaumaturgic Realm!"

~ ~ ~

Lord Maug's sure step echoed as his boots hit the stone floors of Sebastian's Keep. He wore his colors in the form of a brilliant red tunic and a cape that fell from his shoulders to just above his knees. He wasn't sure Roberta's grandfather would allow her to come to the Keep for the Midsummer's revelry but he hoped so, and if what he was able to gather was true, Ezra Parks would be in Queen Titania's company for most of the festivities.

Midsummer was the one night of the year that Titania and Oberon were forced to exercise their wedded rights. If tradition followed, it would also be the night that the other would seek the bed of one of their favorites to wash out the foul taste of their spouse. Parks had been Titania's lover for years. It was madness in Maug's mind.

The only touch Maug longed to feel was Roberta's. He prayed that old man Parks would bring her to the Keep for the night, but he couldn't be sure. If he didn't, he would cross into Spoons territory tonight, act of war or not. The young dragon was tired of waiting. Tonight he would taste the flesh of his mate.

He stepped into the Blood Hall, sure that if he were to find her, it would be here. A smirk crossed his face. Had Roberta been taken to the White Rose Hall, he would follow her there again. Queen Titania might cry insult, but Roberta wore his mark now. Given that, he could legally follow her anywhere.

"Oh?" a soft feminine voice said. "So it is you, Lord Maug?"

Maug turned his attention to the owner and snarled inwardly, even while putting on a pleasant face.

"Lady Trin." He offered a slight incline of his head. Maug was glad he'd never attracted the yellow dragon's attention. Trin was the daughter of Tsui, Lord of the Southwest, one of Oberon's weak picks for their ranks and the oldest standing Dragon Lord. He was over a thousand if he was a day. He only survived this long due to the Fairy King's backing. A younger challenger should have rightfully taken his title years ago. The yellow female lifted her haughty eyes to him and stepped forward. Maug eyed her with contempt.

"I am seeking Lord Turis."

Maug's lips twisted. *Yes, I'm sure you are.*

"Do you know where he would be?"

"No," Maug said. Turis had been a nagging worry to him. So far, he hadn't seen him, and hoped he would stay away from the festivities at the keep. Maug frowned, hoping that he wasn't stalking Katrin, but knew that hope was faint. "Why would I?"

"You are his subordinate, are you not?"

Maug scowled. "Has the lady perhaps forgotten that I am the Dragon Lord of the West?"

"Oh." She laughed in a conspiratorial tone and put a hand on his arm, which he jerked away. "That is only in name, surely. A boy of your age couldn't possibly—"

"Quiet!" Maug snapped, pushing only a hint of power at her. She very nearly stumbled backward, her bright yellow eyes going wide.

"What our young dragon means," a smooth voice came from behind as a hard hand rested on his shoulder, "is that he is clearly too impudent to be anyone's minion."

"Lord Giet," the yellow bit out. Maug cut his eyes in the direction of the black Dragon Lord of the South, shaking off his hand with irritation. It earned him a smile he longed to claw from Giet's face. Trin paused for a moment, looking at Giet, and then turned and fled. Giet kept a pleasant face until she was out of sight and then scowled, giving Maug's shoulder a rough shove.

"Mind your manners, youngling. This is Court after all."

"What are you doing here?" Maug threw an equally unpleasant glare in his dragon lord brother's direction.

Giet shrugged. "If you dumb bastards keep coming to Court, what else can I do?"

Maug drew in a deep breath and let it out slowly. "Turis is here then?"

Giet made a small nod. "Tauc and Lein too. They are all hunting that green."

"She's here?" Maug jerked his head to look into the filling hall.

"Can't you smell her?" Giet chided. Maug didn't answer him. The only scent that teased him was own mate's, the way it should be. But this didn't sound good for Katrin. There would be challenges for her. Maug disliked the sound of that on principle.

"You know, Turis has pretty much claimed her," Maug told Giet.

The black regarded him and nodded once. "I have different prey."

Maug's heart froze. He leveled his gaze on Giet with sharp intent. "Oh?"

"Oh?" Giet repeated softly, and a faint smile crossed his lips. "Does our young brother have a female he's chosen for himself this night?"

There was no point dancing around it. They would learn of it soon enough. The faster Maug staked his claim and warned them off, the better.

"I've marked a female," Maug said in their own language. His words low and quiet. "Go near her, and I'll feed her your beating heart."

Giet let out a breath. "Good. That means you won't be in the way of the female I've chosen, youngling."

He stepped around Maug without another word. Maug eyed him as he passed and shook his head.

The music swelled from the four-piece band playing in the corner as Maug made his way into the ballroom. It was an old time tune, likely from the early 17th century. Not for the first time, the young dragon wondered why they didn't have more modern music. Even something from the Big Band era would be better than this.

And the fashion? Oh, ye gods.

His dark eyes swept the room, and it only took a moment to locate Roberta. A wide smile touched his lips as he went towards her. Relief washed over him. Her grandfather had allowed her to come after all. Her back was to him as he approached, but she turned and offered a smile over her shoulder, sensing he was near. Maug's heart melted. She looked as beautiful as he remembered her in the high-necked gown of bright blue. Her shoulders and arms covered, which was just as well. If his black mark were visible, she would be pursued by every dragon seeking a conquest.

Once he turned it red; only a dragon lord would be so bold.

Thinking on that, he turned around to see if he could spot Turis. But he couldn't see the Dragon Lord of the North anywhere in the ballroom.

"Lady Roberta." Maug came around and offered a small bow. She threw herself into his arms and hugged him tightly around his neck. He smiled softly and indulged her, even as some of the matrons twittered in disapproval. He moved his lips to her ear. "I've missed you."

Then she pulled away and gave him a light shove. "Why did you send that wolf to tutor me?"

"Laru-baba isn't treating you well?" he asked with surprise.

Bobby rolled her eyes even as she took his arm and pulled him away. They walked to one of the patio doors leading to the expansive rose gardens.

"She's okay," Bobby said. "But I don't think she likes me."

"She doesn't like anybody." Maug smirked. "Don't take it personally."

It was nearing the end of the day, and the air was warm rather than sweltering. Other revelers walked along the stone paths lined with colorful roses from all over the realm. With Roberta on his arm, Maug was so happy, he couldn't keep the grin off his face. And then he spotted the red Tauc eyeing him from across the courtyard.

"Did Katrin come with you, my sweet?" he asked before the red got too close. Bobby nodded as the Dragon Lord of the East came to stand in front of them. Because he was a red, he also sported bright red hair. Tauc was the next youngest dragon lord, after Maug. But he was still over a hundred and had a good inch on Maug, his body also had more depth due to his maturity.

"Lord Maug," Tauc drawled, clearly more interested in Roberta than the younger dragon. Maug stepped in front of Tauc with a tight smile.

"Lord Tauc," Maug acknowledged. "What brings you here on this Midsummer's night?"

"A wild, wicked scent," Tauc said, leaning up to look at Roberta from over the top of Maug's head. He frowned. "But she is not in your company?"

Maug offered a faint smile. "Perhaps you should inquire of Lord Turis?"

A wry smile crossed the other red's face, and he offered a small shake of his head. "I don't care to challenge Lord Turis," Tauc said. "At least, not today." The older red dragon craned his head around to take another look at Roberta. "Who do you have with you?"

"Your death," Maug replied pleasantly. Roberta jerked on the back of his cape, which only made Maug smile wider.

"Don't keep him, sweetling," Tauc offered as he walked away. "The hatchling has a terrible personality."

"Maug?"

"He's not your worry," he said, before returning his attention to her. "So where is Katrin?"

"She didn't want to stay," Roberta said. "I felt bad that I didn't go back to Spoons with her, but I really wanted to see you."

"Ah." Maug relaxed. "Then she returned to the Constabulary?"

"Yeah," Roberta said. "She said this wasn't a good place for her to be."

"She's right, it's not," Maug said. "I'm relieved she went back to Spoons. Maybe you could talk her into returning to the Geotic Realm?"

"What's going on?"

Maug paused, holding out his hand with a brilliant smile. "That's for later my love. Dance with me? I've really missed you."

~ ~ ~

The green didn't stay at the Keep long. While that was bothersome on one level, Turis had to give her credit for common sense. She'd drawn the attention of more than one dragon, and even his brother Dragon Lords were taking an interest. Giet of the South, Lein of the Northeast, and Tauc of the East were all in attendance for the Midsummer festivities. Oh, and the red idiot of the West too. But he was more concerned with the human bitch.

While Maug's pursuit of the human troubled Turis, he was content to leave the hatchling to his own devices for the moment. It meant one less challenger for him when it came down to it. In truth, Turis felt confident that he could hold against the others if they wanted to fight him for the female. Maug? That one was an unknown quantity. The youngling was cagey and didn't show his true power often. Turis had gotten a small bite of it when the fledgling went after him over Maglin. Even then, Turis knew Maug was holding back.

Out of all the Dragon Lords, Maug was the one that Turis didn't care to fight. He didn't know how it would go. The only other dragon lord that eyed Maug with caution was Giet. The Lord of the South had already fought with the young Lord of the West. Turis took his unwillingness to re-engage as a sign that there was far more to the red fledgling than most gave him credit for.

Turis made his way to his rooms and changed into his travel leathers. If the green wasn't here, there was no reason to stay. But unlike his brothers, he knew where she had gone and was more than willing to pursue her.

Entering the Constabulary of Spoons Forge uninvited could be considered an act of war. But the advocate wouldn't be there. He was at court, enthralled in the Fairy Queen's bed. Turis was willing to take the risk; he'd had enough waiting.

If necessary, Turis was certain he could beat the old human in a fight. Especially, if he tried to bar a dragon lord from a potential mate.

Turis left Sebastian's Keep the mundane way. Oberon had forbidden their dragon form within the grounds generations ago. But once outside its magical boundary, Turis leaped into the air, beating his powerful black wings against the wind. This was what it was to be free.

It only took a small portal to arrive at the edge of Spoons Forge. If he didn't use magic inside the constabulary, he would be able to avoid detection by the advocate. He'd rather focus on the pursuit of the green, than a battle to get to her side.

His wings beat across the sky, and cool air washed over him. As he came closer, he slowed his speed, moved to the ground, and shimmered into his human form.

He pulled his hood over his head and walked the rest of the way.

As he got closer, her scent teased him. He closed his eyes, drawing it in, allowing it to lead his steps. Turis knew it was foolish to follow the green back to Spoons Forge, but he was old enough not to care.

With the advocate away, there were few guarding the constabulary proper. Turis moved with practiced ease around them, slipping into the palatial building along the shadows. The green's smell was drawing him deeper into the marbled halls. He knew that he shouldn't be here; the lure of the soft pleasure overcame his common sense. The hunter in him thrilled with the chase.

Turis found her door and slipped inside. He scanned the dimly lit room. Her scent nearly overwhelmed him as he crept to where she was splayed on the large four-poster bed on top of the soft blue bedding. The curtains on the patio doors billowed softly in the breeze. She wore a small pair of white shorts and a matching camisole, a sharp contrast to her nearly golden brown skin. He could tell by her deep, even breathing that she was fast asleep.

Turis sized up the open patio door as his route out of the room should he need to make a quick exit. He moved forward, pulling off his shirt and slipping off his boots as he crept onto the bed.

He paused for a moment, his ice-colored eyes looking over her delicate form. Then he moved deliberately, pinning her to the soft mattress. She moaned as he ran his tongue along her ear.

Her bright green eyes flew open, and she opened her mouth to scream. He clamped his hand over her mouth and shook his head. "Quiet," he ordered. "Let's not alert the watch, mn?"

She bit his hand, and he shook it with a soft curse. She pulled away, pressing her body against the headboard.

"You can't be here," she hissed.

Turis raised his eyebrows and offered a low laugh as he crawled towards her. "Don't be so foolish, girl. Did you honestly believe I would give up so easily?"

"I can't," she whispered. He reached out and held his hand to her. She shook her head. "I won't."

"You're a female who is delightfully close to being in season. You want this as much as I do. Stop your foolishness and come to me."

She stared at him for a long moment; her large eyes were frightened and unblinking. He stilled, waiting for her to make her choice.

Greens tended to be more timid and fearful than most dragons. In true form, they were the smallest of the dragons, whereas the blacks were the largest; the nature of a green more fearful because of it. Common sense told her that Turis was dangerous, and she wasn't wrong. If he wanted her to accept his overtures, he had to coax her. Hesitantly, she reached out and took his hand, her face holding a solemn expression. Turis smiled and clasped it, gently pulling her towards him. He leaned forward and met her lips, his kiss full of heat and possession. Her arms came around his neck and he rolled her under him.

Her body arched against his and she closed her eyes. "Yes." She shuddered; tears started down her face. "God, I need—that."

"And I will give you what you need," Turis promised. He reached under her top and divested her of her small shorts.

She hotly returned his kisses as he pulled her against him. It wasn't long before he was nude against her body. He closed his eyes, feeling his shaft half-slip to its true form before he speared her under him. She wet against him, and he stilled, feeling the throbbing pulse of his member, as if it had a life of its own.

He opened his eyes and met hers. Tightening his jaw, he ground against her. She moaned quietly, clinging to his shoulders.

"That's right," he murmured, relishing her touch and breath against him. "Give yourself over to me, my silly one."

She nodded, meeting his lips even as he moved to dominate her.

~ ~ ~

They didn't stay at the dance long. Bobby wasn't surprised. Maug had watched her with glittering eyes; there was no question of his intent. Many were pairing off and disappearing. Some moved off in clusters of three or four. Maug threw her a wicked smile and took her hand, leading her into the dark stone corridors. He spoke quietly, "Everyone has their own pleasure to chase on Midsummer's Night."

"I can't see," she complained softly. He squeezed her hand as he led the way. She didn't want to trip and break her nose.

"I can," he whispered back.

They walked a long while before he quietly opened a door and then whispered a command. The room lit with a low glow.

"Magic?" she asked as she leaned against the door watching him.

"A small indulgence," he admitted. "But I have to be careful. Oberon dislikes us to use much. He believes that lighting a room would lead to a conspiracy against him."

Maug threw off his cape and moved to catch Roberta in his arms. "Are you ready?"

"Ready?" Bobby asked, giving him a teasing smile.

He moved his lips to her ear and neck, undoing the fastenings at the back of her dress.

"Oh. Um. I guess."

He paused and pulled her fingers to his lips while he studied her face. "I guess? Didn't I promise you this night?"

"Yeah." Bobby nodded as she wrapped her arms around his neck. "You did."

He growled softly and pulled her into the next room. He unbuttoned his shirt, pulled it off, and then helped Bobby to remove her dress. She slipped out of it and stood in her bra and panties. Maug lifted her with ease and set her on the wide, tall bed. He yanked his pants off and crawled up to join her.

"Jeez." She laughed. "I guess you are ready."

"You have no idea," he breathed settling on the bed and moving over her. "This is all I've been able to think about for weeks."

She leaned back as he pressed his body against hers; he pulled her underwear away, and they were nude against the other. She drew up a knee as he moved between her legs. Bobby felt him hard against her abdomen.

"Is this going to hurt?" she asked. He froze and then pulled back to meet her eyes.

"You've never done this before?"

Bobby bit her lip and shook her head. He twined his fingers in her hair, pressing his forehead against hers. "Thank you for telling me. I didn't realize. It might, but only for a moment. I'll be careful."

She closed her eyes while he lifted his hips and eased himself into her. She felt a hot bolt of pain and cried out, gripping his shoulders. He kissed her ear tenderly and leaned in, going deeper. He jerked hard, and she felt a stab of heat and pain. He stilled, kissing her neck. Bobby panted against the pillows.

"I know. Here." He rolled over, putting her on top, with him still buried deep inside. "Brace your knees, and move yourself."

Bobby wasn't sure what he meant until he started making short thrusts. She felt a wild heat of desire and nearly went limp against him.

"Come on, love," he coaxed with a soft laugh. "You can do this."

She pushed herself until she was nearly upright, her hands against his chest. She ground against him, and he moved with her. It didn't take long before she was riding her body; feeling the well of passion inside. She shuddered and felt a wave of heat wash over her, leaving her boneless against him.

"All right," he murmured. He rolled her around, pulling himself out.

She whimpered. "No. Don't stop!" Bobby begged.

"It's all right." He moved up on one knee and drove himself deep inside her. Bobby yelped, and he covered her mouth with his, his lips and tongue dominating her. The dragon moved faster, slamming his body into hers. It hurt a little, but she wanted more. His mark burned on her neck, and he ran his tongue along the pattern; it seemed to glow white-hot. He gripped her against him with strong arms as he pushed on.

She lost herself in his touch, with his breath against her. Sweat beaded and rolled off them both, even as he continued his campaign with her body.

"Shit," she gasped as she felt her wetness. He moaned and redoubled his efforts. Moving smoothly, beating himself against her. He stiffened and shuddered, driving deeper inside her, then dropped on top, panting. Roberta kissed his ears and his cheek. He moved to take her lips and delved into them deeply. She managed to gasp out "I love you," with her head tipped back against the pillow.

He lifted his head, his red hair dripping, his dark eyes glowing with heat. "Gods help me, Roberta. You truly are the reason I live."

LOVE, SEX, AND ROCK & ROLL

Terra Su Mudan was the oldest of the dragon holdings in the Thaumaturgic Realm. Lord Turis was lucky that it sat in the middle of a glacial field on his lands in the far north. He walked through the winding stone corridors, feeling the magic of his ancestors humming in the walls. Truly, its defenses were so impenetrable that you had to be a dragon, and looking for it, to find it at all. The wards were ancient but bristled with bright power. The Dragon Lords of Legend had poured their blood into fortifying its defense. And for good reason; it held a vast library of not only their history, but spells and curses of all types, not only the dragonic.

If a dragon could do it, it was documented here.

Turis hadn't found this place on his own. He'd learned of it nearly half a century ago. Maug's sire, the black dragon mage Mugan, had told Turis of it. Mugan, and his clutch mates, had been raised here by their sire, the great dragon Sarzan. They had been orphaned by their mother shortly after their hatching nearly six-hundred and fifty years ago and the holding had been ancient then. Mugan had known more kinds of magics and had more power at his call than any dragon Turis had ever heard of. He was also a rotten lying bastard who would often cheat and held more arrogance in one claw than any dragon lord, even though he did not stand in their number.

Mugan had been the first of their number to sound the alarm to Oberon plotting something vile. He had the evidence he needed but not the allies. He held nothing but contempt for the Dragon Lords because they had aligned themselves with the Fairy King, unknowingly courting their doom. For whatever reason, Mugan had chosen Turis to confide in and sent him to Terra Su Mudan with the then newly named Lord Jaka, to do their research on Oberon's treachery. Turis's life hadn't gotten easier that day, but he had found a renewed purpose for living. The gift of Terra Su Mudan was probably the greatest that Mugan had given to their people.

If he stood quiet, on the high cliffs, Turis could swear he heard the whispers of their ancestors speaking in their ancient tongue.

Turis and a few of the other dragon lords had started to fortify this holding; moving in supplies, dragons, and servants. They were acting quietly, not alerting anyone to what they were doing. The time was coming when this place would be their refuge.

When the time came to stand against Oberon.

Turis shook his head and brought his mind back to his task. He was in the great library, a vast cavern with high shelves with baskets full of books and scrolls. There were ladders along the walls. It smelled of old parchment and ink.

He was searching for a spell. He'd seen it before but hadn't paid much attention at the time. However, with his sweet little green Katrin coming into season, Turis had to find a way to force his fertility. He wouldn't go into season naturally for another year. Turis was certain Katrin could bear him a clutch of eggs when it was time. He was high on a ladder, picking through a basket of parchment papers. A faint smile touched his lips as he held an ancient yellowed piece of script. Ah, there it is. He studied it and frowned. It wasn't complete. He shook his head with frustration and looked around the long tall shelves, it had to be here, somewhere.

"Lord Turis?" Lord Jaka entered the great library, and Turis grinned at the younger dragon. He was pleasant enough, and while not powerful magically, his mind was brilliant. If there was a dragon who could figure this out, it would be Jaka.

"Jaka," Turis acknowledged. "Come up here and take a look at something for me?"

Jaka nodded and moved to climb the wide ladder.

"Giet is asking for you," Jaka said as he climbed. "Oberon is on the move. He's ordered the Dragon Lords to war."

"He's just hoping we're stupid enough to get ourselves killed," Turis said without humor. "Is Giet in the council chamber?"

Jaka nodded.

Turis handed the parchment to Jaka. "See if you can find the corresponding chain. I need all four parts of the spell to make this work."

"Fertility?" Jaka asked with some interest. "Do you think this can help? No one has nested in years. My theory is that no male's cycle matches to a female. If we can force a male's fertility when a female is in season…"

"It's worth checking," Turis said. He wasn't of a mind to tell Jaka this was for his own benefit. Should the others learn of Katrin coming into season, he would fight at least Lein for her, if not Tauc, and maybe Giet as well. He moved to the ladder and walked out of the library; through the stone caverns, passing through the indoor grotto with a hot spring and climbed back up three levels.

"Ah, Lord Turis," Giet said as he came into the council chamber. Lien and Tauc were also present. They each offered him a slight nod. They were looking over a map of the Thaumaturgic Realm, laid out on a large stone table. It had small pieces on it that represented various armies. "Did Jaka tell you?"

"That Oberon is trying to kill us again? Yes."

"He has called all of us to service this time." Lein, black Dragon Lord of the Northeast, said. Lein was a tall, serious dragon, a little older than Giet. His black hair was short on his head and his eyes a bright blue. Lein was one of the most formidable in their number. "Usually, he is content with just you and that idiot hatchling."

"Odd," Turis said.

"There is a lot of activity from that bitch demon, the Southern Queen," Giet said. Turis nodded. The female ruler to Giet's southern border had long been a problem for the Lord of the South. "She's launched an invasion into my lands."

"And we've got the demon riders pushing Maug's borders here and"—Tauc pointed—"here."

"At the same time?" Turis frowned. He turned to Giet. "Are they working together?"

"Usually, I'd say no." Giet crossed his arms in thought. "But I can't see this as a coincidence."

"This could make building up here more difficult," Turis said.

"I disagree," Lord Tauc said. "Oberon will be busy with this war. We'll keep moving dragons and supplies. We can use the campaign as cover while we do it; no one will think much of it if we request more supplies. We can divert a portion here."

"When do you plan to bring Lord Maug into this?" Turis asked, glancing up from the map. They had already decided they wouldn't advise Lord Tsui of their plans. The ancient yellow was firmly under Oberon's influence. But Maug's loyalty was still in question. Giet looked troubled and nodded to Lein.

"We can't trust him." Lein leaned forward, folding his arms in front of him with a troubled expression. "He's a member of Oberon's court. There is no reason to believe he won't be loyal to the King."

"You don't give him enough credit." Turis set a hand on his hip. "He is his father's son. And trust me, that's not an endearment."

"He claims to have marked a female," Giet said in a speculative manner. "On Midsummer's. If that's true, he'll be marked for death by Oberon. Do you know anything about that?"

Turis frowned sharply. Would that impossible brat do such a thing? The only female the fledgling had an interest in was that human girl. Did he have any idea what he was opening himself up to by marking and bonding with her? Turis felt his stomach turn and shook his head. Turis had a bond-mate once. Even brushing that memory brought pain. It had taken him a long time to recover, and in some ways, he never had, not truly.

Hatchlings with humans are possible, he told himself with irritation. *Still, I hope it's a pretty blue and the human is a bad attempt at diversion.*

"We'll need Maug when it's time," Turis said, turning the subject away from Maug's stupidity. "All seven of us will be required."

"Ah yes, the spell," Giet said, pausing before continuing. "Is Jeremiah Kincaid even alive?"

"Oberon would have made a show of it had he been able to get him," Turis said speaking of their erstwhile human ally. Jerimiah Kincaid had thrown his lot in with the dragons years ago, searching for a spell that would break Oberon's immortality. Turis hadn't spoken to him in over twenty years. "My sources say he's somewhere in the Geotic Realm, far from Oberon's reach."

Giet looked thoughtful. "Charles Tampton and Kincaid have always stood with us in the past." He raised his dark blue eyes to meet Turis's. "We need to know where Tampton is going to stand in this conflict. Maug will likely follow the advocate's lead. Go to Ridges Hollow and speak to him. It's possible that he knows where Kincaid is as well. After that, we can make a judgment on whether to bring Lord Maug in or not."

Turis agreed with Giet, but he'd rather chew glass. Maug had warned him away from the orange Maglin. Turis didn't doubt Maug would be equally furious for him going to speak to his foster father.

"Very well," he said. "I'll leave at first light."

He smiled to himself as he left the chamber. He already had plans for the night. Charles Tampton could wait until morning.

While Turis longed to stretch his wings in flight, he knew that he didn't have much time. It was full night, and he weighed losing the hours flying and made an easy decision.

Summoning a portal, he stepped through just outside the territory of Spoons Forge. He'd made this trek nearly every night for the past three weeks, ever since Midsummer's Night. Turis was tall and muscular, even in his human form, but he could be whisper quiet when necessary. He walked for approximately half an hour before making his way through the marbled halls of the constabulary proper.

Katrin, for all her earlier resistance and games, never locked her room to him. Not that a dragon couldn't get through one simple lock, but the point that she didn't try to keep him out wasn't missed on Turis.

He slipped into her room quietly, wondering if he would wake her. On more than one occasion, the green dragon had been asleep by the time he came to join her. The Lord of the North would content himself by curling around her until near morning and softly kiss her before he escaped into the dark.

Tonight she sat up in bed when he entered. Turis moved quietly, pulling off his shirt and unsheathing his blade, laying it within reach on the floor near the side of her bed. She crawled forward and met him at the edge. He set a knee on the bed and pulled her close, her lips going along his jaw and neck. The black dragon smiled and tangled his fingers into the green's dark brown curls, feeling a tight heat of anticipation and greed. He longed to fully possess her and keep her; guard and protect her from all others.

"Lord Turis," she breathed, begging into his ear. "Please…"

The black dragon knew a good portion of this was due to her breeding heat. He couldn't gauge exactly when she would be in full season. But her scent told him it wasn't far off now. He silently hoped that Oberon's war wouldn't cost him this window of opportunity.

"I'm here," he assured her, leaning her back on the soft bed. He had been ready to take her since he'd stepped into the constabulary. Katrin's soft fingers found the tie at his waist and pulled at his trousers. A quiet growl of need escaped her, and he licked her ear, returning the sound.

Katrin delighted him in ways no female had in more years than Turis cared to remember. He was going to have her for himself. He was willing to give her time to come to terms with that. If her ardent behavior in bed were an indication, it wouldn't be long until he could offer her a place in his nest at Terra Su Mudan.

Turis delved into her flesh, relishing her breath against his skin with a soft smile before he met her lips.

"I'm here." He braced himself on his elbows, thrusting deep with smooth motion, arching to press his head against hers with a groan of pleasure.

~ ~ ~

It had been a really long day. All morning, Bobby had done drill after drill with Laru-baba. She was happy that it was easier to use magic in the Thaumaturgic Realm, and the wolf shaman was teaching her how to bond with the reservoir of magic deep under Spoons Forge. The wolf was a stern teacher, but Bobby appreciated everything she was learning from her. Her grandfather had done an okay job but had only taught her how to do things. He'd never taken the time to explain how magic worked.

Magic in its natural state was destructive and wild. It was the Advocates of the Thaumaturgic Realm that kept it in check. It simmered under the surface of the earth, teeming with life.

"But where does it come from?" Bobby had asked. "And can it be used up?"

"Energy can be neither created nor destroyed, but can change form," the wolf told her.

Bobby frowned. "That's science, not magic."

"Magic is science you don't understand," Laru-baba said rolling over on her back. "The state of the magic changes with its use. Magic is like water. It has oceans, rivers, pools, and deep underground reservoirs that can be called upon. All life energy feeds it."

"So why can't everyone do it?" Bobby asked as she made a small light dance on her hand. She could push it one way or the other, make it change color. It was showy and didn't really do anything, but it was more than any of her other friends in the Geotic Realm could do. It was more than most could do in the Thaumaturgic. She was learning that even "magical" creatures didn't always have 'magic.'

"There are certain kinds of power, magic, that are passed down in blood lines." The wolf laid her head down and watched Roberta with sharp yellow eyes. "Lines of power that are ancient. Ezra Caleb Parks is not the first in his family to hold the power of an advocacy. And he won't be the last."

"Okay, so why does magic work better here? In the Thaumaturgic Realm, I mean. It barely works at home. I have to use what I have stored rather than pull it from around me."

"Because it's used more here," Laru-baba said. "The Geotic's magic is touched so seldom that it's nearly frozen in place. You have to use your inner reserves to prime it, but there are stores of magic available to use."

It was then that the wolf decided that it was too hot to continue, and they should go swimming. Bobby didn't blame her. The wolf shaman preferred to be in wolf form and had to be miserable. They headed to a warm spring-fed waterfall and pond for the rest of the day. Katrin and Farni came along too.

It didn't end well. The goodwill she had earned with the wolf woman vaporized once Farni made an unwelcome observation.

"Farni wanted to know what my 'tattoo' was," Bobby told Maug as they lounged together on her bed. She was on her back, and he was leaning over her on one elbow. He had surprised her after dinner, slipping into her room without anyone in the constabulary being any the wiser. He'd pulled her into his arms and growled softly against her neck, leading her back to her bed. Now they were naked under the sheets, enjoying the warm afterglow as Bobby told him about her day.

He smiled at her, ran a finger along her jaw and leaned down to kiss her.

"It's not a tattoo," he murmured.

"I know that. But then Kat asked when it turned red. Laru-baba woke up and demanded to know what I thought I was doing. Didn't she already know? I mean, she was kind of there when it happened."

"No," Maug said with a playful grin. "I didn't let her see it. She would've scorched my ears if she had. Ah, well, so much for my peace."

"She told me it was dangerous for you," Bobby said. *And stupid,* she added silently. Only the words the wolf had used were 'foolish' and 'rash.' "Is that true?"

He shrugged. "It could be," he admitted. His fingers played with her hair as he watched her. "But I won't let that happen. The wolf worries too much."

"What could happen?" Bobby asked. It wasn't that she was afraid for herself because she wasn't. But it would kill her if Maug got hurt because of her.

"Because we're bonded." He leaned down and started to kiss along her neck, and then moved lower, between her breasts. Bobby felt a hot jolt from her ears to her crotch. Her fingers tangled in his bright red hair. He spoke in a whisper against her skin. "You could be used to get past my magical defenses. I wouldn't be able to fend off that kind of attack."

"She was really pissed," Bobby said. She gasped as he teased her left nipple with his tongue. He laughed in a low tone, pulling away.

"I'm sure," he said. Maug sat up, and Bobby leaned on her elbows. He reached over to the table next to the bed for a small box. "I have something for you."

"Oh?" Bobby pulled the sheet around her chest as she sat all the way up. She was pretty sure he planned to stay the night again. She was looking forward to going home next week and spending the night with him, without worrying about someone trying to kill him if he got caught. The long broadsword lying next to the bed reminded her of that danger. "What is it?"

He grinned and opened the box. She blinked in shock.

"A ring?"

Maug nodded and held out his hand for hers. She gave him her left hand, and he slid it onto her ring finger. It was a large diamond solitaire ring. She uttered a small squeal of delight. "An engagement ring?"

"I'm late, I know," he said with a small amount of contrition. He pushed it on her finger with a small frown. "But I wanted to pick it out myself, and shit's been crazy in the west."

Bobby felt a light tingle of magic. He moved the ring with a nod. Bobby laughed, realizing he'd re-sized it on her finger.

"You should be a jeweler," she teased.

He arched an eyebrow with a smirk. He ran his hand along her jaw and kissed her softly.

"It's beautiful. Thank you."

"Not as beautiful as you."

Bobby dropped her eyes and then raised them to meet his. "You know, Granddad doesn't like you much."

"He's a member of Titania's court, my heart. He'll hate anything that is remotely tied to Oberon."

"I am going to marry you anyway," Bobby said firmly. "I don't care what he says."

Maug said thoughtfully, "Roberta, I am a dragon."

She broke into a full smile and leaned over to kiss him. "That has been established." She laughed. Maug kissed her back and then held her shoulders and looked at her seriously.

"Dragons don't marry," he told her. Bobby frowned drawing her eyebrows together. "No, not marry. I mean, they don't marry each other. Dragons don't have a tradition of 'marriage.'"

"I don't understand. You gave me a ring, buddy, and I'm holding you to it."

Maug offered a wicked lopsided grin and leaned her back down on the bed, kissing under her chin.

"You're human," he assured her. "And yes, I'm going to marry you. But if you were a dragon, I wouldn't have to. We're mated, Roberta. Marriage will make things right with your family. But in terms of dragons? We're mated. My mark is our bond. That's what dragons do."

"Then we don't have to get married?" she asked leaning her face away when he tried to kiss her.

"Try and stop me." He kissed her ear. Bobby closed her eyes as he started to make love to her with hot intent. "No, my love, we'll be both mated and married. We'll follow the traditions of both dragons and humans. That will satisfy your family and mine."

"Isn't that sort of silly?"

He jerked his head up, looking at her with mock horror. "Are you making fun of me?"

"Yes."

He laughed and placed his hand between her thighs and kissed her.

"Shame on you," he murmured. "Just for that, I may not let you sleep tonight."

"Promise?" Her head tipped back as he pushed into her urgently.

~ ~ ~

Maug quietly left the Constabulary of Spoons Forge just before the sun came up, bare-chested and carrying his boots. He'd managed to slip into Roberta's bedroom for the night on four different occasions. The old man was getting his revenge on the young dragon by dragging out the marriage negotiations. When Maug complained, Charles had snapped at him.

"Perhaps if you weren't sleeping with his granddaughter in his own house, this would go a little faster?"

The red dragon grinned. It was worth it.

He stopped short, turning a corner and pressed his body against the wall. He put his hand on the hilt of his sword. It was that ridiculous knight with a small knot of watchmen. They looked like they were on the alert, searching for something. Maug played with the idea of turning the shadow knight to dust and then shook his head. He would be found out for sure, and then he'd be barred from Spoons entirely. While the old man didn't like him here, Maug hadn't given him cause to have him banned from his constabulary. Parks knew Roberta was wearing his mark and what that meant. He would only interfere if the dragon gave him just cause.

They moved off in different directions, and Maug smirked, going the opposite way. One more corner and he would be nearly out of the constabulary proper.

Maug paused, seeing a shadow slip around the corner ahead of him. He glanced over his shoulder. Did Parks have any kind of security here? Shit, maybe it wasn't Maug the knight had been tracking. Worrying this might be a real threat, he grabbed the man's shoulder, spinning him around.

Turis blinked at him. A sly smile crossed the black dragon's face. "I should have known," Turis's voice was low, barely a whisper. Maug tightened his jaw. If Turis got him caught, he'd flay him alive. "It's true then; you bedded that human girl?"

"Let's just go," Maug said quietly, and they slipped out of the constabulary together.

They walked in silence for nearly ten minutes, until the sun had risen above the horizon.

"I hope you're not forcing the green," Maug said. He wouldn't put it past Turis. It was the dragon thing to do. Shitty, but not outside of what draconic culture considered customary.

"I could say the same of the human," Turis said. "But I wouldn't care if you were. And neither should you."

"Katrin wasn't raised with dragons, Turis."

Turis turned on him. He shoved him hard against the garden wall and held his forearm under Maug's throat. The red dragon didn't even have a moment to react. Turis was strong and powerful. But that didn't mean Maug was weak. He eyed Turis while he clenched a fist, pulling from his reserves, not caring to disturb the magical eddies in Spoons.

"Don't you even say her name," Turis hissed into his face.

Oh, the black had it bad. And he was behaving irrationally, the way any male dragon claiming a mate would.

"Let go," Maug ordered. He didn't want to go head-on in a fight with Turis here. That was another thing that would get him banned.

Turis met his gaze and dropped his arm, but he didn't step back. "The green is mine," Turis said. His grey eyes flashed with temper. "Don't interfere."

Maug nodded, hoping he wouldn't have to. But if Roberta's brother ended up in the mix, Maug would have to stand between his future brother-in-law and the Dragon Lord of the North.

"There is something else," Turis said. "I'll be speaking to Charles Tampton this morning."

"What? Why?" Maug demanded.

"Not your concern." Turis stepped back and caught Maug's fist as he threw a punch. He held it while it crackled with power. Turis had more brute strength than Maug, and slowly lowered his hand. Turis quenched the energy as if was nothing, his eyes never leaving Maug's face. This was truly a dragon Maug did not want to fight. "This isn't an act of war, fledging. It concerns matters that date before your birth."

Maug yanked his hand away, shoving Turis before stalking away. "If any harm comes to him, Turis," Maug snarled in warning; he may not want to fight him, but if Turis even breathed wrong on his foster father, he would. "I will tear out your heart."

~ ~ ~

"Lord Turis." Charles Tampton inclined his head as he allowed Turis into his office at the Constabulary of Ridges Hollow. The stark difference between this and the one in Spoons Forge was profound. Where Spoons had marbled floors and were more like a palace, Ridges was made of natural wood and stone. Ridges Hollow was warm and welcoming, Spoons cold and sterile. Turis knew that by coming here, to the seat of the advocate's power, that Charles Tampton was less likely to feel threatened. "What brings you to my side of the realm?"

"Jeremiah Kincaid," Turis said. He moved to the offered chair and sat down. It creaked slightly under his weight. "Is he still alive?"

"Now, how would I know that?"

Turis frowned and crossed his arms. "Let's not dance around this, Advocate. Was Jeremiah not your previous heir? Before you decided to lay this burden on that impetuous juvenile?"

"He was." Tampton smiled, splaying his hands on his desk. He looked over his glasses at Turis.

"So in truth, Jeremiah is still tied to the magic reservoir of Ridges Hollow," Turis said. "So I ask again. Is Jeremiah Kincaid alive?"

Charles Tampton frowned and took off his glasses, rubbing the bridge of his nose. He sighed and leaned back to regard the dragon. "He is, but I don't honestly know where he is."

"I'm not concerned with that," Turis said. He leaned forward and dropped his voice. "When the time comes, as long as he is alive, he'll give us what we need."

Another reason to come to Ridges Hollow was that not a spy could be found there, not ever. Laru's great wolf clan kept security for the constabulary. Turis himself had tried to plant spies, to no avail. There was no chance that Oberon would have any luck. Turis felt confident this conversation would never leave the room.

Tampton pressed his lips into a thin line. "I don't want Maug involved in your civil war, Turis. He's settling down. Found himself a mate. Hopefully, once he's wed; he and Roberta Parks will have a nest full of hatchlings."

"Mate? With a human?" Turis frowned. There were no words for how much the Lord of the North disliked this notion. He knew the young red was satisfying his adolescent needs with the female, but Turis hoped he had enough sense not to keep her. Giet had told him Maug claimed to have marked a mate at Midsummer's; Turis held fast to the hope that it was a lie to warn others off. The red's sire, Mugan, was the master of deception, after all.

"Don't sneer. It's insulting." Charles grinned and cocked his head to one side. "Maggie told me you came to see her."

"What of it?" Turis felt a flash of temper. Advocate or not, this was still a human speaking to a dragon lord.

The man's eyes glinted in the light. "Don't do it again."

"I'm not here for a fight," Turis said as much to remind himself as to reassure the human. It was difficult to do when the human's posture was offering a challenge. Turis had to fight against his instinct to lash out at him.

"Good," Charles Tampton said, regarding Turis with a cool expression.

"I want to know if you are going to stand with Oberon, or with us."

"Ah." Charles Tampton smiled and moved to stand next to his chair. "I'll side with whoever Maug sides with."

"He'll follow your lead."

"He won't." Charles shook his head with a snort. "So the good Dragon Lords haven't figured him out yet? It's not that hard, Lord Turis. He is Jaylinn's temper and Mugan's arrogance. Maug will do what he's going to do. Anything I say isn't going to sway him."

Turis had already guessed Maug would stand with them, but he needed to hear it from Tampton's lips. Turis had known the young dragon's parents better than the other dragon lords. Both the Lady Jaylinn and Mugan were Turis's friends. The others had admired the lovely Jaylinn as a prize they could never win; Mugan had rebuffed any overture of friendship for hundreds of years. Turis had only been close to the old black because of childhood stupidity. He'd been of a mind to challenge Mugan to make a name for himself when he had been just a little older than Maug was now. The older black dragon had beat him bloody, took him in, healed his wounds, and got him drunk. Turis didn't know why Mugan hadn't killed him outright that day, but to hazard a guess, it was because he amused the older dragon in some way.

"That's not useful," Turis said. He'd already made the case to the others. What they wanted to know was where Charles Tampton would align himself when the time came.

"Oh, but it is Lord Dragon." The man had the audacity to laugh. "Seriously. Mugan was my good friend, and Ridges Hollow was his home and hunting ground. I know you were close to both him and the Lady Jaylinn. Where did they stand when it came to the Fairy King? Their son isn't going to be any different. And that worries me above all else."

"Worry?" Turis questioned. "I'd say that's where he needs to be."

"Yes." Charles Tampton was clearly troubled. He moved to look out of his high window for a long moment, and then turned back to face Turis. "But that's not going to be the safest choice. My concern is for the safety of my son. You bastards can go fuck yourselves."

A smile spread on Turis's face.

Ah, now *there* was the man a female dragon had given her heart to. Too often Charles Tampton danced behind the guise of being friendly, affable, and helpless. Turis knew there had to be a dangerous edge to him. He had to be a powerful mage to hold his Advocacy too. Tampton would never have been able to control a young male dragon or woo and win the heart of a female otherwise. Charles Tampton may not like it, but he would stand with them.

He stood and readied himself to leave, having got the answer that he needed. Turis offered a polite smile. "Good day Advocate."

~ ~ ~

"Excuse me." Elizabeth looked up with a start. A tall young man with dark brown curly hair stood in front of the information desk in the library. "Are you Elizabeth Cho?"

She paused, eyeing the man for a moment. There was something off about him, but she couldn't say what. She chided herself, and forced a pleasant smile. Having been continually hunted for the last few weeks, she was feeling more than a little on edge.

"Yes."

"My name is Eddie McGaffy." He said, reaching out with his hand. It glowed and faded, then became real again. Elizabeth blinked. She stared at him with a hint of wonder.

Like me?

"How did you find me?" Elizabeth gathered up the papers on her desk. Her eyes darted around. *Shit, if this kid could find her, know what she was, that damned dragon wouldn't be that far behind.*

"I'm alone," the man said. "Actually, I am here to help you. I hear you have a problem."

"What if I do?" She grabbed her paper cup of lukewarm coffee and started off the library floor. He followed closely behind. Elizabeth's eyes flicked back and forth, worried this was a trap.

"You and I may have the same problem," he said reasonably. He kept his pace next to her with an easy stride. "I am here at the behest of Queen Titania."

"Who?" Elizabeth asked, not stopping.

He cocked his head to one side and smiled. He moved in front of her, blocking her way. Elizabeth frowned at him.

"I know more than you do." He took the books from her arms and smiled. He was handsome and seemed sincere. "And I'm here to help. Really."

He didn't act like he was going away either, and he had half her books. Elizabeth made a motion for him to follow her. She led him past the "Employees Only" sign and down one of the half-lit corridors. She turned, and they went down another set of stairs.

"This goes to the fallout shelter," she said over her shoulder. "I've been staying here. Hiding, really."

His dark brown eyes watched the shadows. They were teeming with dark creatures that would help protect her and do her bidding. His stiff posture and frown indicated that he didn't approve, but who was he to judge? She was running for her life.

They entered a long narrow room. There was a conference table in the middle. A cot was made up in the corner, where she had been sleeping. She hadn't yet gone back to the apartment she shared with Thaddeus. She worried she would lead the beast there. The ground was littered with take-out cartons and empty drink bottles. She motioned to the table. "Put my things there, and tell me who you really are."

"I am Eddie McGaffy. He made a motion, and his clothing changed from twenty-something grunge to a medieval tunic with a long sword at his side. "Actually, Sir Edwin McGaffy. I am a full knight in Queen Titania's court. She is sympathetic to your plight, but she can't help you with this creature. It is one of her husband's pets."

"Oberon?" Elizabeth asked, keeping the table between herself and the knight. Her memories were sketchy about the other place; most of the time she didn't even trust them to be real. She remembered her Lady, though, bright and beautiful. She also remembered being miserable in that place. Which was why her Lady allowed her to come back home, to this… realm? Yes, that was it.

He nodded.

"Queen Titania again offers you safe passage to Sebastian's Keep." He held out his hand. "She is who sent me."

Elizabeth's brows furrowed, something was dancing away from her memories.

"But Thaddeus can't come," she whispered.

"The man?" Sir Edwin asked. Elizabeth nodded. "No, he can't. He isn't a Shadow, and he is not welcome. Due to his ties to Oberon, Queen Titania does not approve of your liaison with him at all."

"I love him."

He drew a deep breath and let it out slowly. "I know about love. I've died for it before, and it doesn't look good for me this time either."

"I can't leave Thaddeus. I-I just can't."

He watched her for a long moment. "I could help you with the dragon."

"Why?"

"There's a girl," he said simply. "If you truly love the man, you know why."

Elizabeth felt her face flush, and she turned away with a nod.

"The dragon is involved with the girl I love. I want to take her away. She isn't safe with him. If he doesn't kill her himself, someone else will. From what our Queen says, she and her husband don't agree with the match either."

"Then why do they allow it? Aren't they gods?"

"The dragon has allies, and he serves a purpose. Better if the girl just disappeared. If you help me get the girl and keep her away from the dragon, I'll do my best to make sure he's got enough on his mind that he'll forget you exist."

"You think it that simple?"

He shrugged in an offhand manner. "He's a dragon. All they think of is murder and sex. This really isn't going to be as hard as you think."

~ ~ ~

Sitting in a shitty bar with Bradley Parks was not Maug's idea of a good time. But Bradley had called him, and Maug liked the younger man. They both had drinks in front of them. Bradley sat on a stool facing the bar, and Maug turned around, watching the door.

"You seen Bobby?" Bradley asked. His forehead crinkled. "I keep thinking one of these days, Granddad is just going to keep her there."

Maug nodded. That was probably the advocate's original intention. Maug knew what he wanted—to marry Roberta—but he wasn't sure that would change old man Parks's plans. Roberta had been listed as a favorite to inherit the Advocacy of Spoons after Parks died, but Ezra Parks had never made it official. Charles had made no secret of Maug being his heir, and he was even conditionally approved by the Senate. Spoons and Ridges shared a long border to the northwest, and Ridges Hollow was only a small part of the western territory that Maug held. When it became time, they could combine the two constabularies, but that could stretch their ability to hold the magical energies of the land too thinly. He'd prefer it if Roberta were passed over for another candidate. There was a good chance Ezra Parks would feel the same way now she was bonded to a dragon.

"I've seen her," Maug answered. "On Midsummer's, and I've slipped into the constabulary for the night a few times."

Bradley chuckled. "If Granddad catches you, he'll pin your hide to his wall." He leaned close. "Hey, you're not banging my sister, are you?"

Maug paused and then nodded. There was no point in lying. Anyone could see the bright red mark glowing on her skin. Bradley frowned.

"I mean to marry her," Maug put in. "If that makes a difference."

"Damn." Bradley sighed. "Naw, it's cool man. It's not like you can get her pregnant, right?"

"Not at the moment," Maug admitted. It would be three years before his next season. By then they would be married and could try for hatchlings with whatever spell he could find. Maug knew it wasn't a guaranteed proposition and hoped Laru-baba would have warmed enough to the idea by then to help.

"So." Bradley stared down at his drink. "Is Kat doing okay?"

"She hasn't called?" While it was true that communication was spotty between the realms, there was a telephone service in most of the constabularies. Some enterprising young elf had made a killing when she brought easy communication between the worlds.

Bradley shook his head. Maug felt a strong pang of pity. He didn't know what he'd do if he hadn't heard from Roberta.

Then he paused, yes he did.

He took a long drink, narrowing his dark eyes. He'd fly to wherever she was and kill his rival. Unfortunately, that was not an option for Bradley.

Maug knew more about that situation than he cared to share. Turis had been in Katrin's bed; there was no question about that. Maug didn't know if Katrin was a willing participant, but in the end, it didn't matter. Lord Turis had claimed her. Whether the black dragon planned to keep her, the younger red dragon didn't know. And while he knew Bradley and Katrin dated, he didn't believe they were intimate. Something for which Maug was eternally grateful. If they had been and Turis learned of it, he would kill Bradley Parks without a second thought. And if it came down to that; Maug would have to stand between them.

"They'll be home tomorrow," Maug said. "Then we can all get back to normal."

And maybe once the green was back in the Geotic Realm, Turis would move on to the next female.

Maybe.

"What about that thing that attacked you? Did you take care of it?"

Maug made a face.

It wasn't like he hadn't tried. The female had to be a shadow by the way she moved and could disappear. But what was she doing outside the fairy court? Shadows were a favorite of both Oberon and Titania. Maug guessed it was because they were like the fairies and never truly died. But they didn't live either. The Shadow Knight that served Roberta's grandfather was a good example of that.

"The woman responsible has stayed out of my way," Maug said. Irritation crept into his voice, and he drained his glass. "Perhaps she was warned off."

"Is that what you think?"

Maug nodded to the bartender to refill their glasses. The female sorceress was better than he had first given her credit. A sardonic smirk crossed his face; fear was an astounding motivator.

"I think she was after your sister, not me," Maug said honestly. "Roberta's light shines brightly. I use barriers, so mine doesn't. The woman didn't know what she was taking on until I destroyed her demon."

"So what are you going to do?" Brad asked. Maug frowned and shook the ice in his glass, and set it down.

"Protect your sister," Maug said. It was all he could do at this point. He didn't mention that he was having border issues in the Thaumaturgic Realm as well. He had demon riders pillaging the mountain villages that fell under his protection. He could see the signs and was surprised he hadn't received notice from Oberon yet. War was blowing in fast. "It could be she's given up. That would be the more intelligent thing to do."

Bradley nodded and downed the last of his beer. "Maybe I can help you?"

"I'm counting on it," Maug said. "I may have to go away for a bit. There's trouble in the Thaumaturgic Realm. I'll be depending on you to keep her safe."

"She's my sister," Bradley said, giving him a faint smile. "Taking care of her is my job."

"Surely not after we're married," Maug laughed. Bradley was a good man and an even better brother. But Maug was not only a dragon—he was a dragon lord. He could protect his own mate.

"Dude." Bradley smirked, nodding to the bartender when she brought their drinks over. "Even after you're married. Anything happens to her, I am so kicking your ass. You have any sisters?"

"Actually, I do. Charles and Maggie have a daughter, Victoria. She's fifteen and pure trouble. So yeah, I get it."

"Good. So, now that we got that taken care of, when do you plan on getting married?"

~ ~ ~

At last, it was time to go home. Bobby was heartily ready. Between Eddie's near-constant sniping about Maug and Laru-baba's drills, the only thing that had made the summer bearable was Maug's occasional visits at night.

And that wasn't nearly often enough. Bobby bit her lip as she shouldered her bag and headed down to the courtyard where her grandfather was waiting to take her home. Katrin came out of her room with a downcast expression.

"Why so sad?" Bobby asked cheerfully.

"It's nothing." Katrin had her hair pulled away from her face in a tail that curled halfway down her back. Bobby wished her hair was as thick and curly. Her hair was black and straight and did nothing. She toyed with the idea of cutting it off and wondered if Maug would like it, and then chided herself. He'd like it if she did.

"All right then, Roberta." Her grandfather offered her a smile. "You ready then."

"Yes, Granddad," she said. "Thank you for having us."

"Always a pleasure," he said. But Bobby knew that this time, that wasn't true. She and her grandfather had been at odds over Maug, and the situation wasn't close to being resolved. He'd been even more unhappy after she started wearing her ring. And her mark? Oh, God.

Laru-baba indicated there was a deeper political reason than Maug being a dragon. Maug had told her the same thing. Her granddad seemed to think he could stop her from getting married. She planned on telling Maug they needed to go to the courthouse next week. She smiled to herself, and her grandfather interrupted her train of thought.

"We just have to wait for—ah, there you are, good lady."

Laru-baba walked out in human form; her long silver hair was braided into a single tail that hung below her waist. She was impossibly thin, and while Bobby had the feeling she was very old, there were no lines on her skin. It was hard not to mistake Laru-baba for an unworldly creature, even when she presented herself as human.

"I am ready," the wolf shaman said.

"Ready?" Bobby asked.

"Laru believes you need more tutoring," Bobby's grandfather said bitingly. The wolf lady offered a wan smile. Granddad wasn't completely happy with Laru-baba teaching her, but that went back to Maug too. Laru-baba was acting on Maug's order, and while Ezra Parks knew there was no better teacher, he hated it all the same. "Seems I haven't done a suitable job."

"You've done your best, Advocate," Laru-baba sniffed. Bobby hid a smile. The wolf was probably the only one in the world that got away with speaking to the Spoons Forge advocate in such a manner. "However, you are only human, and Roberta has only limited time in the Thaumaturgic Realm. Besides, since we're going back to the Geotic, there is work we can do to sharpen her skills there."

"Work?" Bobby asked bleakly. Katrin stifled a laugh, and Bobby offered her a wink. Kat hadn't been herself at all lately. Bobby wondered if she was missing Brad. Maug came when he could, but Katrin hadn't seen Brad in nearly six weeks.

Maybe next summer, if Bobby decided to go back, she could talk Brad into coming. Then she remembered, as her grandfather called the gate and a wall of nausea washed over her, why Brad disliked traveling to this realm. He preferred using one of the crossings. Gates made him throw up.

As they reappeared in the backyard of Bobby's childhood home, she didn't blame him. She felt ill from the jump.

"Hey! Good to see you!" Brad had been sitting in a lawn chair, clearly waiting but not waiting for them. He gave Bobby a quick hug and then moved to Katrin. Bobby grinned. Brad had probably missed Kat more than Kat had missed him. Now maybe she'd cheer up a little. "Really good to see you, Babe. How was the trip?"

Katrin paled but wrapped her arms around him and leaned into his shoulder. "I've missed you, Brad," she said quietly. "So much."

~ ~ ~

"I am so mad at you!" Roberta walked into the small club and practically yelled across the bar at Maug. He lifted his drink and raised his eyebrows as his mate stalked across the floor and gave him a sound kiss. He returned it, wrapping an arm around her waist with his eyes going to Bradley. Her brother shrugged, answering the unasked question; Katrin followed, holding his hand.

Maug wanted to be at Roberta's house when they arrived but thought better of it. Ezra Parks was still stalling on the contract, and he didn't want to put the old man off any further than he had already. Maybe, if he gave him a little space, he'd get around to giving in to Charles latest demands.

Nothing so far had been utterly outrageous. Most having to do with lands and titles. What Roberta would get to keep, should their union break.

Maug snorted softly. He was a dragon. They mated for life. The human was trying to put conditions in the document that didn't apply to their situation.

But other things, like the provisions for children, which were typical in human contracts, had made Maug furious. Parks wanted to limit the number of hatchlings to two, which was clearly unacceptable. How were they supposed to know how many they would have until the eggs were laid? A typical first clutch was five to eight eggs. Did the old man think they would only have one? And what were they supposed to do with the "extra" eggs?

Charles said Parks was certain they wouldn't be able to have children, so these provisions were moot. Maug told Charles that anything to do with hatchlings couldn't be included. If Charles wanted to lead old man Parks on that they couldn't have children, then fine. But Maug knew better and was not going to have any reason for Roberta's family to call foul later down the line.

"Why are you mad at me, my sweet?" he asked pleasantly, pulling out a chair for her.

"Laru-baba? You do know that she's moved into my house?"

"I do." He'd ordered it himself. Since he had been unable to ferret out the shadow sorceress, he told the wolf to keep Roberta shielded and protected. Laru-baba had agreed, but she had that calculating look in her yellow eyes. Maug knew the wolf would revenge herself on him later, but if it kept Roberta safe, he was content with whatever torment the wolf chose to visit on him.

What he was not content about was Katrin hanging onto Bradley's arm. The fair-headed young man was happier than Maug had seen him in weeks. Katrin beamed with a smile, and that set the young dragon on edge. He cast out a light spell and set a few magical trips that would warn him of another dragon's approach. But would Turis appear here? Maug couldn't be certain. He didn't know if the old bastard's interest in Katrin was more than fleeting. He had little experience with male dragons and their females. Too often, though, females set the males up for a fight, if only so they could mate with the strongest.

His dark eyes narrowed on Katrin, wondering how much of her behavior was instinctual and how much she was aware of doing. Her scent was obvious; the green was getting closer to her season. Had he not been bonded with Roberta, Maug may have been tempted to see if she would entertain him. But at least he would know what he was stepping into. Bradley? He didn't have a chance in hell against the standing Dragon Lord of the North.

Maug finally got a chance to speak to Katrin when Roberta and Bradley went to the jukebox, arguing over what to play first. Maug had filled Roberta's hands with quarters and asked for some 80's hair band. Bradley threw him a look of sheer horror and tried to talk Roberta out of playing *Poison.*

Maug grinned. *"Talk Dirty to Me,"* sounded just fine to the dragon.

Katrin sat at their table, staring at her glass of beer. Maug leaned back and regarded her critically. "What are you playing at Katrin?"

She jerked her head up with wide, stricken eyes.

"I know Lord Turis has been coming to the constabulary. You are aware he'll gut Bradley if he catches you with him."

"He won't." She bit her lip. "I haven't seen him in over a week. He stopped coming."

"Oh?" Maug asked. "Does this upset you?"

"Yes," she snapped and then colored with a whisper. "No. I-I don't know."

"Don't you know your own mind?" Maug teased gently. She bit her lip and glanced at Bradley. He was on his knees, begging Roberta not to put any more quarters into the jukebox. She was cackling with glee. Maug laughed. Roberta was his joy.

"I do," Katrin said. Maug turned his attention back to her. She was a lovely dragon, with warm brown skin and dark hair that softly curled to her back. But truly, it was her bright green eyes that were her most beautiful feature. Being a green, she was too timid by nature for Maug's tastes. He liked bold and fearless. That was probably what attracted him to Roberta. But he understood why Lord Turis enamored with the young green dragon. Any male with a pulse would appreciate her. "I love Brad. I love him so much, but I want children. Don't you, Lord Maug? Don't you want hatchlings?"

"Of course I do," he retorted. Katrin gripped the side of the table, her knuckles turning white. He remembered going into season, the need to breed was almost a living thing for a dragon. It wasn't rutting for the sake of sex, no matter how delightful that was, the end goal was to find a mate that could give you children. Having hatchlings was a primal drive that no dragon could deny. "Why would you ask such a thing?"

"Bobby is human." She dropped her voice. "You can't—"

"That is not open for discussion." Maug's voice went cold. Gods, the last thing he needed was for her to think she could breed with Bradley. Maug didn't even know how he was going to do it yet, only that he would. His Aunt Maggie must not have told Katrin about her children with Charles, thank the gods.

"I am a green," she said, her voice whisper soft, her eyes full of pain. "I'm not a fit mate for a dragon lord, but he— God. I need him. I can't explain how I feel when he–"

"Ah," Maug said, understanding. So that was it. Then he had to wonder how much Maggie had told her about a dragon's fertility. "Just because you're fertile, it doesn't mean Lord Turis will be."

Katrin bit her lip and nodded, turning away.

"I won't do anything with Brad that could hurt him," she said with real heartbreak in her voice. "I love Brad. I don't know how I feel about… *him*. And I don't think he likes me, not really."

"Katrin," Maug scolded softly. "I don't think that's the case."

"It doesn't matter," she said. "I'm not going back to the Thaumaturgic until next summer. He won't come here. He's gotten what he wanted."

Maug wasn't entirely sure of her estimation. Turis was one of the most powerful dragons he knew and a standing Dragon Lord. The Lord of the North had claimed her; he'd warned Maug off, telling him the green was his. It was not in the black's character to let this go, but there was no sense in upsetting Katrin about it.

Perhaps she was right. Maug didn't fully understand the way male and female dragons interacted. But then, like Katrin, he hadn't been raised with dragons. He wasn't the best one to give advice. Maug was content to have mated with a human, something that was completely unthinkable to most dragons. But from what he did know, love rarely entered into the equation with dragons. Their breeding cycles were too erratic. If you found a mate whose cycle matched yours, you were damned lucky. An affection could grow from the mutual goal of sexual satisfaction and a nest full of hatchlings. Even the romantic story of his parents didn't start with love, but rather dominance, need, and trickery. But their story ended tragically, with one not being able to live without the other. If that wasn't love, Maug didn't know what was.

Roberta and Bradley returned to the table when the jukebox started spitting out *Poison*. Grinning, Maug got up and caught Roberta in his arms. The top of her head came to just below his chin. Maug smiled and cupped her face. "Talk dirty to me?" he asked in a low tone, playfully nipping her ear. She rewarded him with a shudder and a smile.

"Maybe, but you have to dance with me first."

~ ~ ~

For the first time in over a month Bobby finally felt free. Oh, her granddad was nice enough, but he had been practically sitting on her from the time she arrived in the Thaumaturgic Realm. Well, not exactly. It had started after Midsummer's night when he saw the pattern burning bright red on her neck.

"No need to explain what that means, Roberta." His voice had been low, reproachful. Bobby had been startled. He had never spoken to her in such a way. "You are of age. It's too late to urge caution, but I cannot believe you truly understand what you've done."

But Bobby did understand. Part of her soul was linked to Maug and she knew… everything. She knew how he felt about her in no uncertain terms. Bobby felt the same. She tried to tell her granddad that he was prejudiced because Maug was a dragon.

"You don't understand what that means either."

"I do know," she whispered as she rocked to the music against Maug's chest. His arms and body wrapped around her as they moved to the beat of the song. He made her feel warm inside. Her heart melted when he offered that wicked lopsided grin, or when his eyes danced with amusement. "And I want it."

"What do you want, my sweet?" Maug softly asked, his head resting on top of hers.

"I want to marry you," she said, pulling away. "I don't want to wait. Do you think we could do that? I mean, can you? Here? In the Geotic Realm?"

He smirked. "I've got a social security number and a birth certificate, so I don't really see much trouble in getting a marriage license. But we should marry in Thaumaturgic Realm first, love. Otherwise, it'll never be recognized by those that hold power there."

"Granddad is being a butt, isn't he?"

Maug drew in a deep breath and let it out slow with a nod.

"Charles promised to talk to him, but I think we can get married before next summer."

Bobby looked stricken. "I don't want to wait that long."

"We don't have to wait for anything," he whispered in her ear. "Spend the night with me, Roberta?"

Bobby bit her lip and glanced over to where Brad and Kat were dancing, speaking in low tones. She was relieved to see them together. Kat was sad most of the summer, and now she finally seemed happy. She turned back to Maug and bit her lip.

"My folks will worry if I don't call."

Bobby had talked to her mom and dad about marrying Maug earlier that day and showed them her engagement ring. Brad nodded his approval, but her folks were a reserved about it. They wanted to get to know Maug better, which was understandable. Her dad wasn't happy about his father negotiating a marriage contract; especially since this was the first he'd heard about it. Bobby told them that she loved Maug and was going to marry him. They had questions, but once they learned Maug spent half his time in the Geotic Realm, they seemed better about it. They were worried she would disappear into the "magic" land forever.

Bobby promised that would never happen.

They stopped dancing. Maug took her hand and brought it up to his lips with a serious expression. "Actually, I'd like it if you would move in with me. I have a beautiful home for us in Palatine."

"Before we get married?"

"We're mated, Roberta." A smile played on his lips. "Making us wait for our marriage vows won't change that."

Heat flooded through her body, her mark tingled while a lump grew in her throat.

Yes, that was true.

"I'm going to use the bathroom, and then I'll call Mom and Dad. And then-"

"Then?" The red-haired dragon smiled with bright indulgence.

"I'll be yours all night."

"No, Roberta," he said, quietly meeting her eyes. "You are mine forever."

Bobby smiled. She headed toward the restroom. A moment later, Katrin pulled away from Brad and chased after her. *I can pee by myself,* she thought with irritation.

She would rather Katrin and Brad got things ironed out. Katrin had been distant at her grandfather's. Bobby hoped it was because she was missing Brad the way that Bobby had missed Maug. But she wasn't sure. She'd tried to talk to her about it, but Katrin had steadfastly refused to tell her anything.

Bobby wasn't paying that much attention when she opened the door and nearly flattened a woman.

"Oh my God!" Bobby exclaimed. "I'm so sorry! Are you okay?"

"I'm fine." The shorter woman stepped back. Bobby cocked her head to one side. There was something familiar about her. But as she tried to recall where she might have seen her. A lilac scent layered the air, and her lids felt heavy.

"Do I know you?" Bobby asked. She took another look at her. Short, Asian… black hair… Something. Darkness fell around her as Katrin screamed her name from very, very far away.

~ ~ ~

"Bobby!"

Maug reached the restroom before Katrin's scream had died away. A snarl on his lips and his fingers glowing with hot power. He shoved his way into the bathroom. There were shouts from behind, but he heard Bradley blocking others from trying to follow him.

"It's okay," Bradley was saying. "He's my sister's boyfriend."

"What happened?" Maug demanded. Tears smeared Katrin's face.

She shook her head. "I don't know! I don't know!" Katrin put her fingers to her face and kept shaking her head.

Maug grabbed her shoulders. "Where is my mate, Katrin?" he growled, real panic welling in his chest.

"There was a woman…"

Maug shoved her away. Damn it! He closed his eyes and held his hand over the drain. A wisp of smoke materialized. It held the outline of a small sprite. He whispered his order to the creature in its language and the spirit took off.

"The sylph will track her," Maug said. Katrin nodded. He turned on his heel and stalked out of the bathroom.

"Hey! We don't need any trouble here," the bartender yelled at him.

"We're leaving," Maug told Bradley. Roberta's brother looked confused as Katrin hurried out of the bathroom to join them.

"Where the fuck is Bobby?" Bradley demanded.

"She's been taken," Maug said, striding with purpose towards the door. He had to get out of the bar and take his true form. That bitch was not going to get away with stealing his mate. "Don't worry, I'll find her."

He slammed the door nearly off its hinges, only to be blocked by that idiot knight who served Roberta's grandfather.

Maug growled deep in his throat. "Out of my way shadow. I don't have time for you."

"Too bad," the knight muttered. His eyes swept the area, and Maug tensed. He didn't trust the bastard to do something stupid.

Sure enough, the knight summoned his blade and swung it in Maug's direction. The dragon ducked with a growl. The knight missed his head by a hair but hit his shoulder, cutting deep into the dragon's flesh.

"Shit," Maug ground out in pain. He dropped to a crouch and threw a hot bolt of power at his attacker. Sir Edwin blocked it with his sword and launched forward with another attack.

"Brad!" Katrin yelled. "No!"

Bradley Parks threw himself in front of Maug, wielding a sword of his own.

"Out of the way, cur!" Edwin McGaffy ordered. His countenance was hard and full of anger. Bradley blocked a series of blows and returned a hard swing.

"Fuck you," Bradley snapped. "Where the hell did you take my sister?"

Rage boiled in Maug's veins as he realized why the knight was keeping them from the chase. The dragon shifted into his true form and let out an ear-shattering roar, his claws cracking the asphalt under his feet.

"Stop!" Katrin yelled as she ran towards the fighters. Maug summoned a portal and she ran through it before she could stop herself. Satisfied he had sent the female to a safe place, Maug turned back, whipping his head around.

"What did you do?" Bradly demanded over his shoulder. For his part, the young man didn't seem all that startled by a gigantic red dragon. "Where'd Kat go?"

"Females don't belong where there will be death," Maug answered. That was a dragon truism he'd lived with even as a hatchling. Maug stepped in front of Brad with one leg half hovering over him. He lowered his head to meet the eyes of the knight and drew back the skin around his mouth, showing his teeth. Maug's growl was like rolling thunder. Onlookers screamed and ran away, but his focus was on the Shadow Knight. Maug in his true form was nearly invincible. It would take over a hundred such knights to be even a small challenge. The knight threw a hateful glare and shimmered away as Maug unleashed a hot wall of fire that would have turned him to ash.

"Jesus," Brad muttered, turning his face from the heat.

"Damn him!" Maug bellowed with fury. He quickly shifted back to human form. His shoulder was bleeding profusely. He put a hand to it and used a small spell to slow the flow of blood. He didn't have time to attend to it properly. Maug had been wounded far worse than this on the battle line. He was furiously angry with himself for having taken the hit. He was clearly too complacent in this realm.

Bradley set his long sword across his shoulder and nodded. His blond hair ruffled and his face dripping with sweat. Maug eyed him with a frown. "Bradley."

"Yeah, I know." Bradley shrugged. "Let's just say Granddad didn't totally let me off the hook with this magic bullshit."

Maug heard sirens. He grimaced. Charles was going to have his ears for this. He was not to appear in his true form if he could help it. Hopefully, it would be reported as a hallucination of a few drunks, but he'd worry about that later.

His head jerked, hearing the sharp call of the tracking sylph. With a snarl on his lips, he created a portal and grabbed Bradley's arm, yanking him through it with him.

They stepped into an alley deep in the city, but arrived as the call died away. Maug felt a small bolt of panic as his eyes darted around the narrow, rat-infested alley. It stank of urine and garbage. Bradley made a face and shook his head.

"Damn, what is that smell? And where are we?" Bradley asked. Before Maug could speak, they were rushed by a small demon. Small being six meters tall. It thundered down the alley with a roar. Maug threw a ball of red lightning, vaporizing it to black ash. He tried to catch his mate's scent, but he was having little luck amongst the other stenches of the city.

He stopped and breathed deeply, trying to reach out through their bond. Maug worked to quiet his anger and touch the part of her that was in him with love.

"Come on, Roberta," he whispered, weaving the spell. "Tell me where you are, my sweet."

Maug?

He opened his eyes with a slow smile and motioned for Bradley to follow. Maug had an idea of the direction his mate was in, and she hadn't been harmed yet. As they got closer, he caught her scent. As he walked, he seethed with quiet anger.

First, he had to find Roberta and get her to safety.

Then the dragon was going hunting, and nothing would stop him from taking his kill.

~ ~ ~

"Wake up, girl!" A rough male voice ordered. Bobby struggled to open her eyes. She felt as if she was cocooned in a warm, soft gauze. She moaned softly, and her stomach turned.

"Oh, God." She rolled over and pulled herself to her knees before retching the entire contents of her stomach. She coughed a few times and tried to focus on the two figures standing around her. When she spoke, her voice didn't sound like her own. "Who are you?"

"Your better," the man said. He grabbed her arm and yanked her to her feet. She swayed for a moment before pulling away, feeling righteous indignation. She was in some sort of run down industrial space, a warehouse maybe? It was large and nearly empty, other than stacks of rusted barrels.

"Not on your best day," she ground out. Hot anger welled. She moved back, putting out her hands to ward them off. "Stay back!"

"And what are you going to do, child?" the woman asked in a cold voice. Bobby turned her attention to her. Maug's mark burned her neck like it was on fire.

"I will kill you."

What? Where did that come from? Bobby didn't have to worry because her threat didn't instill much fear. The man and woman laughed at her. *How dare they?* An inner voice hissed. Bobby felt her hands glow with hot power.

"What are you doing?" the woman asked sharply. "You can't possibly believe you can fight us."

"Lady Roberta?" A small sylph appeared, flickering in front of her. Bobby thought she saw a slight nod, followed by a high-pitched screech that nearly pierced her eardrums. Bobby dropped to her knees, covering her ears as her face contorted with pain.

"Stop that, you silly creature!" the man bellowed. There was a sharp blast and the screaming stopped. Bobby shook her head and put her palms to the ground.

I can do this. I can.

Laru-baba had been working on this one. The wolf said it would be harder here, and she wasn't kidding. Trying to draw power was like swimming through sand. She gritted her teeth. She needed words. Laru-baba told her she would eventually be able to do such things with no effort. But she wasn't there yet; and certainly not in the Geotic. "No one can harm me. No one can touch me. There is nothing strong enough to break my *shield*."

"What are you doing?" the woman asked.

Bobby opened her eyes and felt something click as if a door had swung open; bright white enveloped her.

"You… stop this!"

Sweat beaded Bobby's forehead from the effort. The man tried to move forward, but a spark snapped at him. Bobby met his blue eyes, and he started to smile. It was slick and evil, hungry. As if he knew something she didn't and planned to use it on her. He was older, close to her dad's age, but he was cut square with a tight beard. His short blond hair also clipped short.

"I think our kitten has claws," he said. "How delightful."

"Now is not the time to be impressed!" the woman snapped out. "Break that barrier."

And he did try. Bobby felt it falter and nearly threw up trying to hold the shield in place. She heard a small explosion and the sound of feet running. She didn't dare turn to see who it was.

A wolf snarled and a shadow leapt over her. The animal stood in front of her. Its grey fur stood up on its back, glowing with ethereal power.

"How dare you!" The wolf's voice was half a growl. Laru-baba! Bobby felt a wave of relief wash over her. "You will die for this trespass."

"You dare!" The man threw a bolt at the wolf, and she caught it as she shimmered into human form. Wearing leathers, her white hair trailing and her yellow eyes glowing with power.

"My, my," the wolf shaman spoke. "What a pretty little power you have, human."

The man snarled and threw another attack at her, but Bobby saw the other woman start a call of power. She was going to sneak an attack.

"Laru-baba!" Bobby cried, her voice broke from the effort of holding the shield. The wolf jerked her head and pinned the woman in her gaze, cocking her head to one side.

"A shadow?" Laru-baba asked. "Here?"

"Now, Thaddeus!" the woman yelled to the man. Bobby watched in horror as he tried to rush at Laru-baba. But she shouldn't have worried. The wolf made a motion with her hand, and the man was thrown off his feet. His female companion rushed to his side.

"Roberta!"

Bobby turned to see Maug and Brad running towards her. Bobby released her shield, and her brother caught her in his arms. Maug growled. His hands glowed with bright red power. Bobby's captors glanced at each other and then clasped their hands together before shimmering away.

"Damn it!" Maug exploded in rage. He shook his head and turned to Brad, who propped Bobby on her feet. Happy relief washed over her. Maug moved to her side and ran his hands along the side of her face.

"Going hunting, my Lord?" Laru-baba turned back to them and smiled, looking more wolfish than she did in canine form. Maug's face etched in anger. Bobby pulled away from her brother and lurched forward, nearly stumbling.

"Maug!" Bobby felt like she was going pass out again. Darkness swarmed around her, swallowing her. Maug lifted her into his arms and leaned his head against hers.

"Shh," he soothed. "It's all right. You're safe now. You did well, my love. Now leave the rest to me."

And her world went black.

~ ~ ~

Maug eyed Roberta with worry as he held her in his arms. He didn't sense anything wrong with her other than utter exhaustion. He'd caught her scent two blocks away. When they got closer, he sensed her drawing power. Half a smile touched his lips.

Oh, my love, he thought with bright affection, you are going to be a mage to watch when you come into full power.

But he'd already known this.

"Laru-baba?"

The wolf nodded and stepped forward. He placed his mate into the wolf shaman's arms. Laru-baba was inhumanly strong. She lifted Roberta easily, met his eyes, and then stepped through a portal she created. He didn't need to speak; she knew what to do. The wolf would take his mate to his house and guard her until he was able to join her. Maug felt a twinge of pain in his shoulder as he turned back to Bradley.

"Females aren't where there's death?" Bradley asked. He cocked his head to one side. "I'd be willing to bet that Laru-baba has seen a lot of death."

"She's a wolf," Maug said as if that answered the question, for him it had. "I'm sending you home. Tell your parents Roberta is safe and I'll bring her home in the morning. I need to speak to them as well. We have much to discuss."

"Yeah, you do," Bradley agreed. "What are you going to do?"

"I caught the human's scent," Maug replied. A predatory smile spread on the young dragon's face. "The woman must be a shadow; that's why I haven't been able to track her. But the man is human. I can find them now."

"And?"

Maug met his eyes with a small smile. He didn't need to answer that.

Bradley nodded. "Let me help you."

"No." Maug didn't even have to weigh the answer.

Bradley frowned.

"Tell me the truth, Bradley Parks. Have you ever killed?"

"Have you?"

"Oh yes," Maug answered with a tight feral smile. "I was fighting small border skirmishes for Charles at sixteen. At nineteen, I challenged the Lord of the West to combat and tore out his beating heart to claim his title as my own. I am a dragon, Bradley. We are killers by nature."

Bradley paled and dropped his gaze. He turned back to Maug after a moment. His blue eyes steady, so very like his sister's. "There's more to you than that or Bobby wouldn't love you. She might be a pain in the ass, but I trust her. And I want to help."

"You did help," Maug assured him. He waved a hand, creating a portal that would take Bradley home and away from the fight. "That sword of yours will draw blood someday, I'm sure. But today is not it. Go home."

Bradley clenched his hands to his side and stepped through the portal. Maug nodded. The Lord of the West didn't care to be responsible for Bradley's first blood.

And there was going to be blood.

He closed his eyes and let his rage burn brightly.

These two, the sorceress and the wizard, did not know what they had done by endangering Maug's mate. No dragon would tolerate such trespass, but a dragon lord? Their fate was sealed the moment they had touched her. If Maug could devise a way for them to die a hundred times over, he'd do it.

Maug walked out of the squalid warehouse and shifted to his true form in the alley outside. He used a glamor so he couldn't be seen by any without magical talent. He tipped his large red snout in the air and growled, showing his teeth as he pushed himself into the air.

The scent was faint, even though they hadn't left the city. They were in the direction of the lake. They would not escape him.

~ ~ ~

Elizabeth Cho and Thaddeus Stanley appeared near the waterfront in Grant Park. It was still dark, but the paths were brightly lit by ornate streetlights. The shadow sorceress bit her lip. Where was her ally? He said he'd help! He promised to keep the dragon distracted!

"Who was that?" Thaddeus demanded. "I've never seen anything with that sort of power!"

Elizabeth slowed her step. "A dragon," she said quietly. "And we need to get away from this place because it's going to come after us."

Thaddeus grabbed her arm and pulled her around to face him. "Dragon's aren't real."

"And demons are?" Elizabeth smiled and pressed her hand to his chest. She shivered, more from fear than from the light nip in the wind off the water. "It may have a human form, but that was a dragon, and it is very, very real. My

Lady says there is no creature more fearsome, and they are nearly impossible to kill."

"But why is it after us?" Thaddeus asked. He pulled off his jacket and wrapped it around her shoulders. She smiled and pulled it tighter, breathing in her lover's manly scent, tangled with his cologne.

"The girl," Elizabeth said. "The dragon is involved with her. My Lady doesn't approve. She wants the girl to die. The dragon may not have her."

"This doesn't make any sense. Elizabeth, who are you involved with? What haven't you told me?"

"Did you get that offer from that college in Kentucky?" Elizabeth asked, changing the subject. There was a lot she didn't care to share with her human lover.

"The University of Louisville, yes."

"Take it." She felt a change in the air pressure around her. How could the beast be tracking them so quickly? She caught another whiff of Thaddeus' coat, and her brown eyes widened. He could smell him. He could track Thaddeus. Damn it!

But she had his coat, and she had an idea.

"Listen," she said hurriedly. "You need to get away. Head for the main street and take a cab into the city. Get in a crowd of as many people as you can. Then go to Kentucky. We need to separate."

"Why?" Thaddeus stepped closer. "Please, Elizabeth, what aren't you telling me?"

"He'll find you if you don't run."

"Let it." Thaddeus leaned down to touch her lips. "We've got allies. And I think it's high time we used them."

"Not this time," she said. She created a portal and shoved him through it. He fought to reach her but then disappeared. Elizabeth nodded, satisfied. She tightened the coat around her body and started down the park path.

The dragon landed directly in front of her. The ground shook and she was nearly thrown off balance. It stretched its long wings and hissed at her, showing its teeth. She stood in front of it, clutching the coat tightly.

She was going to die.

Not the first time, she mused with dark humor. But rather than attack, it drew itself up, lifting its head high in the air. "Where's the wizard, bitch?" the beast demanded. It stepped forward, its sharp talons crunching the gravel. "You will both die for touching my mate."

"Far away from you!" Elizabeth spat. "And do your worst. I've died before!"

"There's no coming back from this," he said, in a low growl. She felt the rise of hot power and a burning wind whipped around her. The beast was weaving a fire spell.

"Stop this!"

Elizabeth jerked her head in horror. Thaddeus was standing next to her again. *How?*

He grabbed her hand and gave it a squeeze. "Trust me," he whispered.

Her heart sank.

They were both going to die.

The dragon bellowed, engulfing them with flames. Elizabeth felt a sharp bite of pain as she was jerked away, reappearing on a high-rise rooftop overlooking the park. She dropped to her knees, slapping her smoldering clothes. Thaddeus dropped beside her, smelling of smoke and burnt fabric.

"What…?" she choked out.

"A decoy." Thaddeus pulled her tight against him. "The beast will find bodies, but they're not ours."

"Whose?"

He shook his head. "It doesn't matter. It'll be satisfied we're dead and that's all that matters."

"No. It'll find us." Her body shook, and Thaddeus pulled her into a tight hug. She closed her eyes, pressing her head into his chest.

Thaddeus laughed, running his fingers through her hair. "It won't know to look. Listen, I'll take the position in Louisville, but you're coming with me. I'll find a way to destroy this dragon, but don't you ever do that again. We're stronger when we stand together."

He pressed his lips to her forehead. "Promise me."

"I love you," she murmured. He laughed low in his throat.

"That's not a promise."

Elizabeth closed her eyes. "It is for now," she assured him, feeling safe for this first time in what seemed like forever.

~ ~ ~

Bobby stirred and awoke with a start, trying to figure out where she was. She was sprawled out on a soft bed in a dimly lit room. She saw what she thought was a dog's head lift, but then realized it was a wolf.

"Laru-baba?" she said, her voice hoarse. The wolf had been curled up next to her with her head lying across one of Bobby's legs. "Where am I?"

"Lord Maug's," Laru's voice was soft and quiet. "He hasn't returned yet. You did amazingly well tonight, Lady Roberta. You made me very proud to be your teacher."

"Oh, jeez. Thanks." Bobby felt more than a little embarrassed by Laru-baba's warm, gentle words. She sat upright and winced, putting a hand to her head. It felt like it was going to split in half. "Shit. What happened? Where's Maug?"

"You were abducted," the wolf told her. "We found you, and I brought you back here. This is one of his houses in the Geotic Realm. It's not far from where you live. Don't fret, he'll be at your side soon, I'm sure."

"Who was it?" Bobby saw there was a tall glass of water on the nightstand and reached for it. She took a long drink. "My head is killing me."

"Little surprise," Laru-baba said. "You pulled a great deal of power and you're not accustomed to it. In time, it'll get easier."

"If you say so."

She heard a door slam from somewhere inside the house and startled.

"Roberta!"

"Maug!" She stood a little too fast and dropped back onto the edge of the bed. It didn't matter, it was only half a heartbeat before he was throwing open the door. He moved to her side and ran his hands along her face, kneeling in front of her.

"Are you all right?" He pulled her hand to his lips and kissed it urgently. "Were you hurt?"

"No," she said and pinched her lips together. "Maybe a little sick, but I'm okay."

"Gods." He stood, and pulled her into his arms. Bobby smiled and leaned against him. He glared at Laru-baba. "Get out."

"Maug! Don't be so rude."

"It's all right, Roberta," the wolf said as she hopped off the bed. "He did not have a civilized upbringing. I will check on you in the morning."

"Only because you helped raise me, you flea-bitten cur," he muttered. Bobby gave him a small shove, and he turned to smile at her.

Laru-baba padded out, Maug kicked the door closed behind her.

Bobby frowned up at Maug. "You should be nicer to her. She did save me."

He snorted and stood to pull off his leather jacket. Bobby's gasped when she saw his shoulder soaked in blood. "Oh my God. What happened?"

He glanced at it with a shrug. "It's nothing."

"Maug!" She got up and went to his side. "I can do this. I can heal you."

"Roberta," he chided, taking her hands and bringing them to his lips. "It's not necessary."

She closed her eyes and whispered, calling raw power to her. She would heal him. Bobby knew she could.

"Laru-baba teach you that?" He leaned forward and kissed her ear.

"You're distracting me."

"Oh, my sweet, I plan on doing far more than that."

Later, in the morning, Bobby felt the sunlight warming her face. She blinked and yawned against it. She stirred and turned. Strong arms wrapped around her waist and she felt utterly content. Maug smiled. He observed her through partially opened eyes, regarding her quietly. Bobby smiled and ran a hand along the side of his face, pausing before she pushed her fingers through his bright red hair.

"I love you."

He smiled and moved to nuzzle her ear with a soft kiss.

"Ugh. My mom and dad are going to kill me. I didn't get a chance to call them."

"It's all right," Maug assured her, sitting up on his elbows. "Bradley said he would tell them you were safe. Besides, it wasn't your fault. I took care of the problem last night."

Bobby pulled away from him. "What does that mean?"

"What do you think it means?" Maug frowned. "I am a dragon. I can't allow an attack on my mate to go unanswered."

Bobby felt a little queasy. "Maug…"

He shook his head and got out of bed, jerking on a pair of jeans. "It's fine," he assured her in a short, clipped tone.

There was a light rap on the bedroom door. Maug moved to answer it, blocking Roberta from view. It was probably Laru-baba again.

"What? Now? Gods. All right. Tell them to wait." His normally calm voice sounded strained. Bobby watched as he stiffened, satisfied that his shoulder wasn't bruised and was healed from any mark. He shook his head. "I'll be back in a moment."

Curiosity got the best of her. Bobby got up, grabbed one of his shirts, and pulled it on. She went out to the hall, trailing behind him.

The house was beautiful; the second-floor landing was large and wide with a carved ornate wood trim running along the floorboards and around the doors. If Bobby had to guess, the house was one of the older ones in Palatine. There was another flight of stairs up, and one down. On the walls, beautiful pieces of art were displayed. The house was decorated better than any place she had seen outside of a museum. Maug had told her that he had money, and having seen his house, he hadn't been joking.

Bobby grabbed the banister. Maug stood at the bottom of the stairs, two fairies in full court regalia before him. He took the parchment they offered him and glanced at it. They bowed their heads and walked to the front door. Maug crumpled the paper in one hand as they left.

Roberta went quietly down the stairs. She wrapped her arms around his waist and pressed herself against his back. "What is it?"

"Oberon." Maug drew in a deep breath and turned. "There is war in the west. The king has called me to service."

"What does that mean? For how long?" Maug was going to leave her? He was going to war? She bit her lip and looked at him with stricken eyes. He sighed and tipped her head up, leaning down to meet her lips.

"Not long, surely," Maug answered quietly. "Oberon has demanded all the Dragon Lords stand with his armies this time."

"We were going to move in together."

"And we will," he promised, pulling her fingers to his lips. "This isn't the first time I've been called to fight in the King's war, love. It'll just be for a bit. Yule at worst."

"Yule?" she choked out. "Christmas? Really?"

"I'm sorry, Roberta. I need Oberon as an ally and I've had to work hard to earn his trust. I don't know where I stand with your grandfather at the moment. That idiot knight of his was involved in your abduction."

She began to cry in earnest as he held her, trying to comfort her the best he could.

YULE

"Lord Maug's forces have been doing exceptionally well here… here, and here." King Oberon pointed to the map that was laid across the long marble table. Many of the kingdom's advocates stood around it, looking on with nods of approval. Titania glanced up only slightly interested in the proceedings. The red dragon had always been a worthy opponent in battle. She had a few of her own loyal advocates and knights standing near her side. In this particular conflict, her lord husband had not seen fit to ask her assistance. Just as well, he tended to be reckless and brutal. The Fairy Queen didn't care to risk any of her Court if she didn't have to. "It reflects well on you, Charles."

"Thank you, my liege." Charles Tampton inclined his head. He was tall, slim, still in his prime. His fair hair barely dusted with grey. The Advocate of Ridges Hollow was dressed in a pressed suit from the Geotic Realm, rather than the finery of Court. Charles Tampton disliked the politics of Sebastian's Keep and refused to ally himself with either Court. He was only in attendance because his heir was involved in the conflict and he wished to stay abreast of its course.

Queen Titania listened while she started the next line of stitching on her needlework. She was only here because Oberon insisted. He was playing a game, but she didn't know what it was.

"The Yule holiday is coming and I wish to reward my dragon commanders for their good work." Oberon leaned up and regarded those around him, "I mean to host a week of festivities."

"An excellent idea!" Sir Ducan put in near the king's side. He had been a longtime advisor to Titania's husband. He was a solid man, stocky in build with a full ginger beard and hair. Titania sniffed. He was only looking for the spirits to be provided at the crown's expense. Dull drunkard, that's what he was.

King Oberon's eyes fell on his wife with a small twist of his lips; his dark eyes gleaming with delight. Titania felt a quell of apprehension. Her eyes darted to meet her husband's. "Isn't Lord Maug's chosen mate under one of your advocates, my Lady?"

Titania licked her lips before she spoke. She knew what he was speaking of.

It was a bad bit of business and Titania did not approve. Ezra hadn't involved her because he was in a difficult position. He needed the alliance with Ridges Hollow, but also knew that his queen would be displeased with the idea of a human child marrying a dragon. The Fairy Queen had used her shadow maiden in the Geotic Realm to interfere, but the woman had failed, nearly ending her existence in the process.

"Ezra Caleb Parks is in negotiations for the hand of his granddaughter in marriage," she said. "But I know nothing of this mating you speak of."

"Charles?" King Oberon's deep voice inquired.

The Advocate of Ridges Hollow cleared his throat and glanced at Queen Titania with a hint of an apology. "It is true," Charles answered carefully. "Both about the marriage negotiations and the young woman being Lord Maug's chosen mate. She wears his mark."

Oberon's eyes danced with amusement and Titania felt a chill pass through her. Had the dragon really done that? How could Ezra have allowed such a thing to happen?

Oberon smiled at his wife. "Tell your advocate to bring the young woman to court."

"She's a child, Oberon," Titania replied with impatience, her mind working quickly. If the dragon had truly marked this girl, would Oberon work to end her life? The girl was human, it wasn't as if the beast could breed with her. "Ezra does not fully approve of the match. He would rather some time pass–"

"She wears the mating mark of a dragon lord," the Fairy King said in a voice full of humor. It turned Titania's blood to ice. Gods, where would he go with this? "I'd say she is old enough. And it will be a suitable reward for my Lord Dragon to be with his mate at Christmas. In fact, we'll have all the Dragon Lords here with their mates. It'll be a good opportunity for them to get reacquainted."

"I disagree." Titania tightened her jaw. Her finger's crushing the needlework in her lap. She looked around the room and could tell that many would side with her on this issue. Putting that many dragons in one place, let alone the Dragon Lords themselves, was trouble. Oberon knew that. She pressed her lips into a hard line and shook her head.

"Too bad." King Oberon raised his eyebrows. "Really Titania, I'm surprised at you. This will give you an opportunity to bring your pet to court with my leave."

"This isn't about him," Titania said angrily. That was all she needed as well. Oberon hated Ezra. For good reason, she admitted. But if keeping Ezra's granddaughter from court meant the Queen wouldn't see him for a few years, Titania would pay that price for Ezra's sake.

"Heh." King Oberon chuckled and walked away, motioning for a few to follow him out of the large study. Titania watched most of them go, but made a motion for Charles Tampton to stay, with a nod to her own attendants until it was just she and the human.

Titania turned on him with hot angry eyes. "Did you have to tell him they mated?"

"It's the truth, my Lady." Charles rubbed the back of his neck. "Don't ask me to get between you and Oberon in this. Bad enough Ezra is my friend."

"If he's your friend you wouldn't want the girl anywhere near court!"

"Maug will be here," Charles dismissed easily. "And he'll be pleased to see her. Oberon's had him at war for months."

"Along with every other dragon lord." Titania closed her eyes. "Gods, Tampton. Can't you see what Oberon is doing?"

"He's trying to irritate you." Charles raised an eyebrow. "And is doing a fine job of it."

"There's more to it than that." The Fairy Queen pointed a finger at him as she walked away. "Mark my words."

~ ~ ~

"So did you get the word?" Lord Tauc asked without preamble as he walked into Turis's tent on the battle line.

The black dragon, Lord of the North, looked up with a nod. They were running the northern part of the campaign, with Lord Maug's forces holding the west. Tauc was likely in Turis's camp for reinforcements and supplies. They had both received new orders to report to Sebastian's Keep for the Yule Holiday.

Along with every other dragon lord and their mates. Hardly the best news, Turis thought grimly. He got up and indicated to a decanter, offering the red dragon a drink. The winds were howling, and snow blew outside of the tent. Turis used simple sorcery to keep it warm, but Tauc had just flown in through the blizzard.

The red dragon nodded, pulling off his gloves and helmet. His red hair fell into his eyes and he grinned. "Has Oberon lost his wits?" Tauc asked, taking the metal cup from Turis. He drank deep and nodded with approval. "Good stuff. How do you manage to keep so well supplied?"

"Experience." Turis smirked. He had at least two hundred years on his lord brother. Turis indicated for Tauc to follow him deeper into the tent, where it was less likely spies could hear their words.

"That doesn't seem to be doing you any good in this campaign." Tauc rolled his eyes, throwing himself in a chair. "Maug is kicking all our asses. It's embarrassing."

Turis nodded, drawing his eyes back to the map splayed on a small wooden table. It was true. Maug had been fighting fiercely and had pushed the enemy back on three fronts. Oberon should be releasing them, letting them go back to their holdings, rather than forcing them to dance attendance. "Maug's certainly making a name for himself."

"Tell me," Tauc asked, lowering his voice. "What is your mind on this move of the Fairy King?"

Lord Turis picked up the piece that represented Maug on the map and tossed it to Tauc. He nodded at it significantly. "I believe," Turis said archly, "that our fledgling has taken a mate."

"So?" Tauc shrugged as he tossed the piece in the air then caught it again. "He's young and amorous. What of it?"

Lord Turis rubbed two fingers together and then lifted his cup to his lips.

"He told Giet he marked a female." Lord Turis lowered his eyelids. "Do you have an idea why he may have done that?"

"Because he's stupid?"

"Maug's a lot of things, but he's not stupid." Turis walked around the table and took the piece from Tauc's hand. "No, if he marked her, he has a plan. One King Oberon will not approve of. And if it's true, Oberon will try to end his life."

"So Oberon wants us there to start something?" Tauc's lip's twisted. "Thinking one of us will kill Maug? That's the only thing I can think of."

"You noted that he ordered Tsui and Lein to bring their mates?"

Tauc nodded. "He's trying to get an idea of who might be nesting."

"Yellow Tsui's been bonded with his mate for, gods—how many years? I doubt they are even capable." Turis grimaced. "But I don't know how Lein holds his house. His mate may be little more than a bed warmer. He never speaks of her or brings her out," Lord Turis said. "Which is the intelligent thing to do. No, I believe Oberon is up to something bigger. He wants us all there, in one place, under his power, for a reason."

"Do you know for certain if the upstart took a mate?"

Turis shook his head. "I know there is a female he's infatuated with. But if he truly marked her and mated her…?" Lord Turis shrugged. "It's impossible to get intelligence out of Maug's camp. The wolves guard his back. They are too loyal. I've tried planting spies with no success."

"Me too," Tauc admitted. "Your followers aren't so much so."

Turis grinned at the red dragon over his cup. "Yours either."

Tauc laughed at him. Turis smiled. The Dragon Lords had played games for over a thousand years. How better to keep an eye on your rival?

"I think we have to be ready," the older black dragon said. Turis stilled and listened to the howling wind. His black hair hanging across his face for a long moment while he listened to the wind, trying to sense if there was anyone near. When he was satisfied, he straightened and turned to Tauc, and nodded. "Send word to the others. Oberon watches me."

"For good reason," Tauc pointed out. "What about Maug?"

"No," Lord Turis shook his head. "He's intelligent enough to make the right decision when it comes down to it. But I don't want to test his loyalty yet."

"We may have to kill him," Tauc said with a frown. "You know that."

"If it comes to that," Lord Turis agreed. "But I'd rather have him as an ally than an enemy. We'll need his power when we stand against Oberon."

"I still say you overestimate him." Tauc stood up with a stretch. "But we're willing to follow your lead at the moment, Turis. You've earned that right."

Turis nodded, knowing that this Yule at court was likely to be the most danger the Dragon Lords had ever faced before.

~ ~ ~

Christmas at full court. Gods, what could be worse? Maug thought unhappily to himself. He stood off to the side with the other Dragon Lords. He wore his red dress armor and a long red cape. He had made his obedience to King Oberon and Queen Titania earlier. The King had been in good spirits, and the queen had regarded him with open hostility. Probably the two of them were feuding.

Again.

He snorted and shifted the setting of the sword on his hip.

Truly, this was the last place he wanted to be. He wanted to spend the holiday in the Geotic Realm. He hadn't seen Roberta in months. Internet communication was impossible where he had been, so they had relied on parchment and pen. He'd been fighting for months, and they had finally pushed the demons back over the mountains to the west. Maug had made sure it would be a while before they were able to regroup and come back. The dragon longed to see his mate, and he knew Roberta missed him just as much.

But Oberon, in whatever fit of madness, had demanded all seven Dragon Lords to Court, which had brought out dragons of all sorts seeking mates and alliances. With so many dragons, there would be title challenges, while others would jockey for power; everything that went with putting that many dragons in one place. What the hell was Oberon thinking?

"Don't be like that, fledgling," Lord Turis said in a low voice. "I heard that Oberon is especially pleased with you."

Maug turned to Turis, whose black dress armor was more elaborate and ornate than Maug's. Turis was over two hundred and fifty years older than Maug and his build showed it. Only the yellow Tsui was older than Turis out of the Dragon Lords. Turis didn't have a trace of grey in his black hair, something the black dragon could do with magic, but it was more that the Lord of the North was still in his fighting prime. A dragon could easily live to be a thousand if a challenger didn't kill him.

"Lovely," Maug muttered. Oberon's attention was bothersome at best, damned dangerous at worst. Turis chuckled. Maug eyed the black dragon with suspicion. "What do you know?"

"Mm?" The black dragon raised an eyebrow. "If you'd leave your rooms once in a while you'd know a thing or two as well."

"I have no interest in Court gossip. I have my laptop with me and had business in the Geotic Realm that King Oberon has kept me from long enough," Maug said with no humor. "Sebastian's Keep is one of the few places in the Thaumaturgic with an Internet connection. I intend to make as much use of it as I can."

The older dragon rolled his eyes and shook head.

Maug smirked. "I've got my reasons for staying connected to the Geotic."

"Ah yes." The black dragon grinned toothily. "Your human. Did I hear right that you claimed her as a mate?"

Maug closed off his expression. "I'm not sure what you're referring to."

"Is that so?" The black jerked his head. "Is that not your mark?"

"What?" Maug uncrossed his arms and looked sharply in the direction the older dragon indicated. He heart dropped into his stomach. Roberta was walking in with her grandfather. She wore a long, white, high-collared dress, which was cut low at the back, and revealed Maug's brilliant red diamond mating mark across her neck and shoulder blade. He felt both elated and apprehensive. He cast his eyes along the Dragon Lords as they nodded and pointed at Maug's mate. Maug frowned sharply at Turis, who offered a wry eyebrow and a sardonic smile. Maug shoved him aside. "Out of my way."

Turis chuckled as Maug pushed his way through the throng of courtiers towards the step near the side of the royal dais.

King Oberon flicked his dark eyes in his direction. "Ah, Lord Maug, I see you spotted your Yuletide gift. A reward for your outstanding performance in my service."

The dragon's irritation seemed to amuse the monarch. If the Fairy King had truly wanted to reward him, he could have released him to go to his mate. Not wave her around like scented prey in front of every dragon of power in the realm.

"I heard my good Lord Dragon had taken a mate," the king continued, raising his voice and bringing a hush to the hall. Maug shifted uncomfortably. Bad enough that Roberta was here, displaying his mark, but the king had to announce it too? "It's not often one of the great Dragon Lords does such a thing. I wanted to see the child that captured his heart and to see if it was true. Judging by the mark she wears—I'd say it was."

Maug dropped to a knee and inclined his head, trying to both rein in his anger and calculate how to control the situation. The best way was to make sure everyone knew that he wasn't going to tolerate any inference between him and his mate. He raised his eyes to the King's. "It is true, my Lord King," Maug said in a steady voice. "I've taken Roberta Parks as my mate, and once her grandfather Ezra Caleb Parks agrees, we are to be wed."

There was a rise in murmurs at Maug's proclamation. Many of the guests in the large reception hall nudged and pointed in both his direction and Roberta's.

"Marriage is a worthy institution." King Oberon smiled turning to his wife. "Don't you believe so, Titania, my love?"

But the queen turned her head aside. Maug watched the Fairy Queen, realizing that this had more to do with Oberon and Titania's ongoing feud than anything else; likely because Roberta's grandfather had long been a bone of contention between them. Still, Maug cared little for him and his mate being drawn into their game, especially when it would endanger Roberta.

Maug got up and stood in front of Roberta. He took her hand and pressed it to his cheek, closing his eyes for a moment. He took a deep long breath, relishing her scent and touch. She smiled brightly and threw her arms around his neck. He leaned into her shoulder pushing his head against hers. He stepped back and raised her fingers to his lips before he led her away. Ezra Caleb Parks offered him a small nod, and Maug returned it.

Many of the guests craned their heads to get a look at the young woman. He tried to keep his body in front of her and shield her as best he could. He pulled her into a small alcove and took her into his arms, leaning down to taste her lips.

"Don't be mad," Roberta said quietly. "Granddad said King Oberon wanted it to be a surprise."

"I'm not mad at you," he said, casting his dark eyes around. "I just wish Oberon hadn't made such a display of it."

"I missed you," Roberta said. Her fingers ran along his arm. "I really missed you. I wasn't going to say no to a chance to see you."

"Gods, Roberta." Maug drew a deep breath and eyed her with hunger. "You don't even know—"

"But I do!" She laughed and then turned around to find her grandfather. "But I don't know if I should leave Granddad."

Maug leaned down and nosed the top of her head while keeping a sharp watch on those around them. "You belong at my side, not his. You are my mate. He knows that."

Roberta smiled. Maug pushed her hair away from her face and felt his heart melt. It was so black it nearly glowed blue in the light. He ran his hand around her neck and teased her hair. It had grown since he had last seen her. It was longer and framed her lovely blue eyes.

"I think," he said, offering her a lopsided smile, "that I would like a place a little more private, to give you a proper greeting."

Roberta beamed. She leaned forward on her toes and brushed a kiss on his cheek. "I'd like that a lot."

Maug laughed and took her hand, leading her in the direction of his rooms.

~ ~ ~

"My, my..." a yellow female muttered as she stepped closer to Turis. He was watching Maug take his human female out of the hall. He turned away, ready to leave himself. The black dragon had only stayed to see if the rumors were true. When he saw the bright red diamond pattern on her neck and shoulder, he knew for sure. The idiot upstart had indeed bonded with the human girl. It irritated him because now he and the others would have to take great pains to keep her from Oberon's power, which would either work for or against them. Turis shrugged, accepting the situation as it was. For better or worse, it was what they had to work with. "A human?"

"What of it?" he asked, looking down at her. She was a pretty, frail thing. A sharp personality, atypical for her color, and a daughter of Lord Tsui and his mate. Turis never kept an empty bed. He had toyed with the idea of taking her tonight; she was always willing to entertain his interest. But that was until he spotted the lovely Katrin near Maug's mate. Ah, so she had finally returned to the Thaumaturgic Realm. Turis smiled with quiet delight. He'd been too busy with Oberon's campaign in the north to pursue her for the last few months. However, now she was here, he planned to make the most of it.

Turis studied the other dragons in the room. He wasn't the only one that had scented her, hardly a surprise. She'd been nearly in season in the summer. He'd hoped she wouldn't be out by the time he could get back to her. He took a deep breath and smiled. She still smelled of sweet bliss.

Turis dismissed most the other dragons in attendance. Truly, the only ones that could offer any real challenge was his brother dragon lords, with Maug at the top of the list. The red was a bastard in a fight and a damned powerful mage.

Thankfully, the Lord of the West was far more interested in his new bond-mate than the wonderful smelling green. Let that be the idiot's loss.

"What would he want with a human?" The yellow pouted. "You know it's impossible to have hatchlings."

"Lust?" The black smirked. When he first noted Maug angling for the girl, Turis had the same concern. But he knew hatchlings were possible now. If orange Maglin had children with a human, there was little doubt Maug would be able to manage the same when it was time. "She took his mark without dying. The rest is his concern. That is unless you're interested in him? As a second mate perhaps?"

"What?" The yellow turned on him. Her nostrils flared in indignation. "That fledgling?"

"He's a fine catch for any ambitious female." Turis was slowly moving across the room towards the green. She was being plagued with suitors but was so far putting them off. *Smart girl,* he thought. "Still, I am surprised Lord Maug intends to marry a human."

"Lord Maug," the yellow sneered. "A stolen title."

"Fairly won." Turis looked at the yellow askance. "Come now. How do you believe these things are done?"

"Fair nobility," the yellow said, quickly reaching to touch his arm. He frowned at her sharply, and she withdrew it. "By true blood."

"Any dragon has that," Turis dismissed, feeling irritation. She'd learned such nonsense from her sire, who certainly held a far inflated sense of self-importance. As far as Turis was concerned, it was Lord Tsui who held a stolen title—it had been gifted to him, rather than him having to kill for it. "Our numbers are too few to be otherwise. Besides, Lord Maug's blood by his dam ought to be good enough, even for your father. Now, go away. I'm busy."

The yellow paused, trying to see what had caught his attention, and then saw the green. She turned her head back to Turis with a frown, understanding his intention.

"I thought you and I—" she reached out to put a hand on him again. He pushed it away with a snort.

"You thought wrong," he replied as he stepped away from her.

As Turis got closer to the green, the other dragons noticed his approach and moved off. Good. They weren't stupid. Turis would enjoy a fight for her. It would light his blood before he took her to his bed.

The green stiffened. She turned around slowly, and then stepped back. "I'm not interested."

He chuckled and took her trembling hand into his. "Don't be that way," he softly scolded as he raised her fingers to his lips. "Have you forgotten me already?"

"Yes."

Turis smiled with indulgence. Katrin snatched her hand away, her green eyes flashed with heat. "Leave me alone."

"I don't care to," he told her, stepping closer to her side. Gods, he wanted her. Turis grinned, enjoying his happy luck. "Besides, why else would you be here, if not to seek a mate?"

"Because Bobby had to come." The green glanced over her shoulder to where Maug had taken his human female.

"Maug's mate?" he questioned as he glanced in the same direction. True enough, they were friends. He'd known that from before.

"I came so she wouldn't be alone."

"And now, she is with her lord, as it should be."

Katrin glared at him and walked around him toward one of the exits. He followed, watching the other dragons in the room eying her, waiting to make their move. As long as he was close, they wouldn't dare try.

The delightful child frowned. "I have a boyfriend," she said as she kept walking.

"I see no mark."

"Don't be ridiculous."

"If there is no mark then you are not claimed." The black stepped in front of her. He was rewarded with a small shudder as he ran a finger along her jaw. Her eyes clouded with confusion.

"It's not like that!" The green slapped his hand.

He laughed at her. "Oh, but it is." He grabbed her wrist and brought it to his lips, his eyes never leaving hers. "And you know it."

The green paled, shrinking down and shaking her head.

Turis paused, his ice colored eyes flicking around the room. Sizing up his rivals, trying to determine who would make a bid for the green. By the sour looks of many, Katrin had many admirers. *As it should be.* But the strongest always got the female.

Out of all, only the Dragon Lords would present a challenge. Giet was watching, but his posture didn't indicate he had any plans to make a move. Lord Jaka was at Giet's side. While the purple dragon cast a smile in the green's direction, Turis knew he wouldn't try and take her. Tsui was over a thousand if he was a day. He watched with interest, but his equally ancient blue had her fingers gripped tight on his forearm.

That left Lord's Lein and Tauc. Tauc was the next youngest to Maug. A red too, he displayed much of the hotheaded behavior as the Lord of the West, only worse. For having nearly a hundred years on the fledgling, he acted with far less maturity than Maug showed. Tauc looked willing to make a move, but he was going to wait to see if he would have to, perhaps thinking Turis would move off.

Lord Lein had crossed his arms and watched the green with cool calculation. That was far more dangerous than Tauc's open interest. Lein had produced a mate, as he'd been required to; a pretty orange dragon, with hair as bright as the sun. Lord Giet had taken one look at them and laughed. The two black dragons were tight friends. Giet's reaction told Turis that Lein had brought a decoy, unwilling to bring his mate to Sebastian's Keep. Lord Lein was a canny dragon and showed good common sense in that. Only a fool would bring his mate this close to Oberon's power. But it also meant the Lord of the Northwest was free to pursue the green.

Out of the Dragon Lords, Turis was confident in his own power. And he was certain if he wasn't the strongest, he was in the top three. He wouldn't walk away from a fight if it came down to it.

"Leave me alone," Katrin said in a low voice. He stood a little straighter. The other dragons watched with jealous eyes. Except for Lein. He uncrossed his arms and settled his sword on his hip, getting ready to make his move. Playing too hard to get for an audience would lead her into trouble. He leaned down and whispered into her ear.

"It's me or one of the others," he told her softly. "You are endangering yourself with this foolishness. Now stop this game and come with me, silly one. I can protect you."

The girl glanced up at him with frightened green eyes even as they darted around to the others in the room. Katrin wasn't an idiot. It wasn't difficult to see that more than one dragon was itching to take Lord Turis's place at her side. The Lord of the North watched her with admiration. She was truly beautiful. Her long brown curls cascaded down the back of her dark green dress. Her unblemished skin was a warm hue. But it was her green eyes that made her stand out among the other females. They were large, expressive and lovely. He had never seen her true form, and he ached for it. She seemed to be considering her options too. She was the prey, and she was intelligent enough to know it. She trembled harder. Turis smiled and wrapped an arm around her shoulder, half covering her with his cape as he steered her out of the ballroom.

It didn't take long for him to have her alone in one of the patio gardens. Turis knew the girl was aware of his intention. He hadn't tasted her flesh since the summer, and he surprised himself with how much he missed her. He spread his black cape on the ground. She tried to pull away from him, but he took her firmly into his arms, easing her down as he kissed her neck. She gasped, tipped her head back and ran her soft fingers along Turis's neck and under his shirt. Her body arched against him.

Lord Turis nuzzled along her jaw and then paused as he caught the hot scent. He gently turned her face to meet his eyes. She tried to conceal it, but as she responded to his overtures, the barriers slipped away.

"Ah… you are in season then," he said quietly. She shook her head and turned away. Tears leaked from her eyes. Her hands clenched into fists, and she pushed against his chest.

"I'm not," she denied. The black dragon felt a rising tide of blood heat as he kissed her, tasting, dominating. He gripped her body, pulling her close and leaned his head against hers. He closed his eyes and tightened his jaw.

Clever Jaka had found the rest of the spell to force fertility. There were two ways for Turis to learn it. He could study and practice the technique over the course of several months, or he could mark Jaka and roll him in the sheets for it. Since Turis believed he had missed the window of opportunity with green Katrin, he'd opted for study. Since there was no urgency, and he didn't care to make a bond-mate of the Dragon Lord of the Northeast. His plan had been to use the spell the next time Katrin would be in season, five to seven years in the future. He couldn't believe his luck. She had to be close to the end of her two-month heat, though, so he didn't have much time to act.

Turis paused, and considered the risk of invoking such strong magic here, but quickly decided it was worth it. Turis wouldn't be able to draw upon the environment, but his reserves were deep. He took a deep breath, knowing what he had to do to make this work. First, he had to bond with the green, making her his own. Since his plan involved her being the mother of his children, he shouldn't be as concerned with it as he was.

But he'd been wounded deeply by this very thing before. Turis didn't know if he could live through it again. They would be going to war with Oberon soon. Could he really protect a mate? His grey eyes glittered as he considered for a long moment, then nodded.

Yes.

The breeding imperative was too powerful. His race desperately needed children. Even if they won this battle with Oberon, it would be meaningless if there were no children to gift their independence too.

He would force his fertility.

But first, he twined his fingers in her hair and pulled her head back.

"I claim you," he growled softly against her ear.

The girl shook her head. "No—you can't!"

"You are mine."

The black dragon moved his mouth to the girl's collarbone and sank his teeth into her. She screamed and pushed against him, trying to squirm away. Turis held her tight as his venom ran deep inside her. She stiffened and then melted against him, breathing heavily. He licked her wound tenderly and kissed her, watching his black spiked star appear on her skin. For now, it would be a light grey. He would finish this later, in the privacy of his chamber where they would have no chance to be disturbed. Then his mark would glow an ethereal black of a fully consummated mating.

Next, he drew on his internal stores of power, knowing he could draw nothing from the environment in Sebastian's Keep. Using the old words, in a tongue half-forgotten, he whispered the words in her ear. Katrin moaned, tipping her head back. Fire flooded through his body. He had to take her from this place now, or he'd sate his desire there on the damp ground.

"Come now, sweetling." The black dragon nudged her, whispering softly, his voice hoarse with need. Her presence warmed his soul. Frail and afraid, forever abandoned, always alone. Turis vowed to protect her and hoped she could sense that. She would never have to fear again. She was his mate, and he would stand between her and the world. "I will take you to a safe place so you may greet your lord properly."

~ ~ ~

"I should get back to Granddad," Roberta whispered against Maug's chest. He had taken her to his chamber and loved her with reckless abandon. Maug cradled her against him. He shook his head even as he kissed her.

"No," he told her. She started to protest, but he brought a finger to her lips and spoke seriously. "You need to stay with me so I can protect you. If I don't, every male dragon in the Keep will hunt you. Ezra Parks knows this. You can go back to him when the holiday is over."

"I don't understand. Why would anyone be after me?"

Maug watched her face for a moment and then rolled away, stretching his arms above his head. "It's simple," he said. Maug pulled her closer against his chest. "King Oberon, in his madness, has ordered all seven dragon lords here, which has drawn the other dragons who are hoping to elevate themselves. If I don't guard you, one of them will try and take you from me."

"Like I would go with any of them!" Roberta retorted sitting up a little. "Seriously?"

"Yeah, seriously. This is a game they've been playing for thousands of years. Mate stealing is an art form."

"Doesn't mean I'd do it," Roberta scoffed. She slid off the bed and started to pull on her dress. He rolled over to watch her with a half-smile. His red hair ruffled from their lovemaking.

"You think you'd have a choice?" he asked archly, leaning on one arm. Roberta paused with a frown.

He pulled the covers away and stood beside her. "They won't care if you want to or not. They would take you by force and think nothing of it. Their goal is to turn my mark black."

"Turn your mark black?" Her eyebrows furrowed as she touched the side of her neck. He leaned down and kissed her fingers and then ran his tongue along it. Gods, he'd missed her more than he'd let himself admit.

"If you have sex with someone besides me, my mark with go black. The way it was before the first time we—"

"Oh," she said as her face colored. "I guess you would always know then, wouldn't you?"

"Well, it goes both ways," he admitted with a small smile. "If I were untrue to you, it would turn. Dragons are notoriously possessive."

"Wait. You don't trust me?" Roberta stopped with a stern frown.

The dragon blinked at her a few times. *How had she managed to come to that conclusion?* He pulled on a pair of brown pants. "Why would you ask that?"

"You put your mark on me." Roberta's brows drew tightly together. He would laugh at her, but he was wise enough to know she'd probably feed him his stones if he did. Instead, he took her hands and drew her to the edge of the bed and sat down with her.

"I put my mark on you to bond with you. Because I love you," Maug explained. He ran his thumb over her lips tenderly. "Dragons don't mark all their mates. We only do that with those we keep. The ones we want to have children with. When I marked you, I gave you my soul."

Roberta snorted softly and then turned and wrapped her arms around his neck.

"I know. I can feel it," she said. Maug leaned forward and kissed her gently.

"And because of it," Maug said quietly. "You can be used to hurt me. That is the sport with mate stealing, especially a bond-mate. It causes pain and humiliation to the other dragon. I'd rather not risk your safety because some dumb bastard wants to challenge me. You have to understand, mating is all fun and good. But breeding can be deadly."

"I thought dragons weren't fertile that often."

"We aren't, and that's the issue. It's a matter of timing, magic, and a good deal of luck."

"But what does that have to do with me? With us? Can we even have children together?"

"Do you want to?" he asked, feeling his heart still. Gods. That hadn't even occurred to him. What if Roberta didn't desire children? Dragons were hard wired to have hatchlings. It was a genetic imperative they couldn't resist. But no dragon had laid a clutch in so long that many were saying the dragons were going extinct.

"Well, yes," she said. "Eventually. Not now."

Relief flooded through him, and he leaned down to kiss her, nuzzling his lips against her ear. This secret was for her alone. "You are a tremendously powerful mage, my little love." He kissed her ear gently. "Charles's wife is my blood aunt. They have children, and we can too."

She pulled back a little, fixing him with a calculating eye. "How often are you fertile?"

"Eager?" he teased.

"I want to be married first," she retorted, pulling away from him. He grinned. She stepped in front of the mirror and straightened her dress. Maug wrapped his hands around her waist and set his head on top of hers.

"Not for three years," he said. "It'll be my fourth season. Gods, I don't even know what it'll feel like now I have a mate."

"Your fourth?" she asked and then her brows drew together. "Maug, I've never asked you this, but how old are you?"

"Thirty-seven," he said. He touched his lips to her neck, his blood reheating. He wondered how long it would take to get her back out of that dress.

She pushed him away. "You're almost as old as my dad? Seriously?"

Maug laughed.

"You think that's funny?" she said with a snort. "My brother is going to kick your ass! No wonder Granddad has been stalling! You're an old man!"

Maug laughed harder at her dropping to the bed.

"I'm sorry," he said. "But it is funny! I'm barely a hatchling to most of the dragons, nothing more than an unruly upstart. Turis is over three hundred!"

"Maug," she protested. He grinned and got up, grabbing her waist to pull her against him. He smiled and leaned in for a kiss. A sharp knock on the door interrupted them. He rolled his eyes and pulled away from her.

He took the piece of parchment the page handed him and nodded, closing the door.

"Ugh." He made a face as he glanced over the summons. "Oberon."

~ ~ ~

The Lord of the North ran a light finger down his new mate's naked chest, between her breasts and lower. He rolled her under him, feeling renewed heat. Turis hadn't expected that forcing his fertility would have driven him to distraction, but he should have known better. He'd lived through the cycle enough times. But only once before had he been with a female that could truly answer the mating call. He'd all but forgotten how it turned his blood to fire.

She moaned, pressing her body against his, clawing at his back. In the throes of full heat, she had given up her resistance to him. Turis smiled and lost himself in her ardent response. His flesh thrummed with delight. There was no reality other than the taste of his mate. A firm knock on his chamber door yanked him out of his near dream state. He lifted his head, growling low in his throat. The dangerous warning echoed through the stone cut walls. Who would dare? Whoever it was risked death by interrupting a dragon in heat.

"Stay here," he ordered his little mate. Her green eyes widened, but she only pulled the sheet up and watched him get out of bed, pulling on a pair of leather pants he didn't bother to fasten. He wouldn't be wearing them long enough.

He jerked opened the door. "What is it?"

"I am Ezra Caleb Parks—"

Turis cut him off with a gesture. "I know who you are." The dragon glared at Parks's companion, holding back his snarl. It was one of the shadow creatures that inhabited Sebastian's keep. Little wonder Parks had a knight shadowing him. Oberon made no secret of wanting to kill the advocate if the opportunity presented itself. "And I know what that is. I have little interest in Titania's pets. What do you want?"

"You may not have Katrin," Parks said, getting right to the point. "She lives under the protection of Spoons Forge."

"Ah." The dragon arched an eyebrow. "Well, I've already taken and marked her, old man. She's mine now."

"What?" The knight stepped forward, putting a hand on the hilt of his sword. Turis raised his other brow. Did the fool creature think to challenge him? The advocate put a hand on the shadow knight's arm to stay his sword.

"You may not have her," Ezra repeated calmly. "She does not live in this realm. She is not your prey."

"You plan to challenge me for her?" Turis asked. The old man paused and stood a little straighter. "I intend to keep my mate and raise our hatchlings together."

"Hatchlings?" Ezra Parks looked at him aghast.

"Don't tell me you didn't know the bitch was in season?" The black grinned, showing his teeth.

"I want to talk to her."

"No." The dragon offered a dark grin. "She is mine. Now go away."

"I will take this to Oberon," the advocate warned. Turis's lips twisted in scorn. As if he cared what the Fairy King thought.

"You do that," the dragon retorted. "I've done nothing wrong."

~ ~ ~

"Lovely child, your mate," Charles Tampton said as he approached Maug. They stood in one of Oberon's small audience chambers. The stone walls were decorated with bright tapestries from days long gone.

"Don't start," Maug muttered in a low tone. He expected his foster father to get a few digs in about the age difference. But in reality, he was a dragon and wouldn't be considered fully mature for another forty years. "I'd rather you'd got acquainted anywhere but here."

"I can imagine." Charles nodded, motioning for one of the pages with a tray of drinks. He picked one up and motioned to Maug with a raised eyebrow. The red dragon shook his head. He needed to keep his mind clear. Something smelled bad about this.

"Why did you let Oberon do this?" Maug asked testily.

"One doesn't *let* Oberon do anything." Charles brought the drink to his lips. "You know that."

"This whole affair is a bad idea."

"I'm aware of that. Still, little we can do about it now. Ah… here he is."

Oberon entered the room with a few of his knights. He looked around at the small gathering of his inner court circle. The King had summoned all seven dragon lords and their allies, as well as his advisory council. He also had the intelligence to have a full hand of knights in attendance. Likely they would intervene should the dragons start fighting among themselves, which even in a group this small, could easily happen.

"Gentle creatures," the king acknowledged.

Everyone bowed, making room for the monarch to come to the center of the room. He wore his usual black and grey fur, with purple seams. A fine gold crown sat on his head. Maug felt his heart still as the Fairy King pinned his foster father in his gaze.

"So, tell me, Charles," Oberon started. "What do you think of this match your dragon has made?"

Charles shifted uncomfortably. He flicked a glance at Maug, who nodded with a stoic expression. Maug and Charles had already discussed this at length. For all the shit Charles gave him, his foster father was supportive. Charles had voiced his concern that Roberta was human and hatchlings were chancy at best but admitted it was a good alliance with Spoons. It would join their two lands together eventually, to the benefit of the creatures residing in them.

Whose court those lands ended up under, was an open issue. Maug stood in Oberon's court while Roberta's grandfather was firmly in Titania's. Maug knew there had to be a political reason for Oberon to be so interested in his union.

"I've approved it," Charles said, setting his drink down. "It's a matter of record that Ezra and I are in negotiations for the girl's hand."

"Is that right?" Oberon said moving his eyes to the red dragon. "Must be vexing, Lord Dragon, to have to negotiate for your own mate."

"Marriage with the laws of Court and the traditions of dragon mating are two different things, My Lord," Maug answered. He'd already worked out a ready answer. "Regardless of what demands Ezra Caleb Parks makes for the Lady Roberta's hand, she's still my mate."

"Well said." The King walked around the table. He turned to another of the dragon lords, his gaze narrowing on Turis. Maug frowned with curiosity. "Lord Turis has also taken a mate. Had you heard?"

Lord Turis glared at the monarch. Maug frowned. Bringing Turis's intentions to the attention of the others was going to make the other dragons want to pursue her. And that wouldn't amuse the black dragon; not at all.

Ah, Katrin, what mischief have you gotten yourself into? Maug sighed to himself. The black had been determined to claim her, but Maug had hoped the Lord of the North had only been looking for a bed-warmer. If Turis took her for a mate, that would change the situation. Especially when it came to Bradley Parks. Maug ground his jaw unhappily.

"But there is an issue." King Oberon held his hands in the air.

"There is no issue," the black stated flatly. Turis's tone was deep and unyielding. "She's mine."

"Ezra Caleb Parks says otherwise." King Oberon smirked. The black dragon folded his arms and glared balefully at the Fairy King. "He says the green is already spoken for."

Maug jerked his head up. Could Parks be stupid enough to drag Bradley into this? Sure, he was a sturdy knight, but he was *no* match for Turis. Maug would have to interfere before he could let the black dragon murder his mate's brother.

King Oberon shrugged. "I believe we should give the advocate something more important to worry about than a silly green."

The King's eyes fell upon the red dragon.

"What?" Maug asked in a low voice with a hint of challenge. This wasn't good. Maug could go a thousand years before he cared for the King's attention. But Oberon smiled lifting his hands in the air.

"Nothing bad, my Lord Dragon," he said. "I am going to propose that we push the banns through and have your marriage approved. I want you and Roberta Parks wed and part of my court before the end of the holiday."

Maug paused and glanced at Charles, who nodded slightly. Maug inclined his head. "If that is your will, my liege," he said. Maug supposed he should feel some relief, but his stomach twisted with apprehension.

Oberon laughed and ordered drinks to be served to all, then quietly conferred with his advisors on the other side of the room.

Maug stepped closer to Charles and whispered. "What is he up to?"

"Hard to say, but it probably has more to do with Ezra than anything else. Do you know if he and Titania have—"

"I've been too busy with my own affairs, thank you." He knew of Parks's long time affair with the Fairy Queen. A thing that either enraged or amused Oberon, depending on his mood. Today, it seemed he was only going to allow the nuisance. "What's this about Turis?"

"I thought you might know something about that," Charles said with a hint of surprise.

"As I said, I've been entertaining my own affairs. I have no idea what my lord brother has been doing."

"Well, I think it's that green that came with Ezra." Charles shrugged.

Maug made a face and felt his gut twist. Of course it was Katrin. There wasn't another female, other than Tsui's yellow bitch, that Turis had shown any interest in. Maug threw a hostile glare in Turis's direction, but the black was intent on ignoring him. *Bastard.* Did the old black have any idea how old Katrin was? And shit, how was he going to explain this to Roberta?

Charles turned, briefly touching Maug's arm. Maug shook his head and moved in Turis's direction. He planned on asking the Lord of the North a few pointed questions. Turis looked down at him with an arched eyebrow and a small smile. But before he could speak, King Oberon clapped his hands, calling everyone's attention.

"I want the Dragon Lords and their mates at tonight's ball," he said. Maug shifted uncomfortably. They threw dark looks at one another, while the King chuckled with amusement. "You lot are incorrigible. You need to get along if you are to stand against the Western Horde and the Southern Queen."

"We get along fine on the battle line," Turis said. "We just don't care to spend that much time together."

"And you wonder why your numbers are dwindling," the monarch chided with malice. "How else am I to make the formal announcement of Lord Maug's nuptials?"

Maug stepped forward. "We should see if Ezra Caleb Parks will agree first." He wasn't eager to bring Roberta out of his rooms. A few smirks from the other dragon lords made him even more aware that they were waiting for an opportunity to get close to her. Damned Oberon anyway.

"He'll agree to it," King Oberon said in a deceptively soft voice. A voice that meant the king was at his most dangerous. "Or he forfeits the girl's life—to me."

Maug felt a flash of hot anger. He started forward, and a hand gripped his forearm. His head spun around, and he met Turis with a fierce glare.

"Not now," the black dragon advised in a low tone. "Not here."

Maug yanked his arm free and turned around, but King Oberon had left the hall. Maug glared at the black. "He can't threaten my mate."

The other dragon lords nodded, softly murmuring their agreement. Oberon ought to be more careful. Maug may not be a favorite among them, but he was still a dragon lord.

"Oh, calm down." Turis shoved him. Charles came back and handed Maug a cup of spirits. Maug took it and set it aside on the low table. He was in no mood to be placated. "He's not going to touch your mate. Likely he'll hand her life over to you, even if he does take her from the advocate."

"You don't know what he's capable of."

"I know better than you, fledgling," Turis said and then nodded to Charles. Maug frowned, looking between the two of them. He had the feeling there was more going on than either was saying. "But I also know that you're a valuable ally to him. I don't think he'd risk that to get back at his bitch over Parks."

Maug took a deep breath, trying to calm himself.

"I need to speak to Jeffery. Can you stay out of trouble for a few minutes?" Charles took on a pained expression. Maug snorted. "Then we need to get ready for tonight. I am looking forward to spending some time with the Lady Roberta."

"I'll look forward to that as well." Turis lowered his eyes at Maug in a calculating fashion. "Our mates are close friends, after all."

Before Maug had a chance to demand answers from Turis, Old Tsui came forward. "What made you take that bitch, Turis? Trin said there may have been an alliance for us."

"Trin?" Turis asked the elder dragon with curiosity. Maug snorted and shook his head. Turis was being an asshole baiting the old yellow.

"My daughter," Lord Tsui replied drily.

"Oh, that one." Turis shrugged. "I never knew her name."

Maug rolled his eyes and crossed his arms. Oh, he knew Trin. So did Turis. A more backstabbing wicked bitch never lived. Lord Tsui was welcome to keep her. Like Maug and her father, she was a member of Oberon's court, and he'd seen her many times. Maug worked hard to stay out of her way. The female was determined to latch onto the most powerful dragon she could bed. Little wonder she was after Turis. Maug was certain the black could shred most of the other dragon lords without much effort. Turis practically broadcasted his power to warn off challengers. Maug preferred to be subtle and not let anyone get an idea of what he wielded until he had his claws in them.

It had placed him far beneath the yellow's notice, which suited him just fine.

"She'll be very disappointed in you," Lord Tsui said. "Perhaps there could still be an alliance. A second mate, perhaps?"

Lord Turis made a noncommittal sound. Then the old dragon's eyes fell on to Maug. "And you… really?" the yellow said with open disapproval. "A human? Your mother would be devastated."

"Good that she's dead then, isn't it?" Maug offered him a pleasant smile that earned a small chuckle from Turis. Tsui made no more comment and walked away.

"You're incorrigible," Turis told him.

"We all are according to Oberon." Maug tightened his jaw.

"Oberon seems to forget that the Dragon Lords are his allies," Turis turned to Maug, "not his minions."

"Oberon sees no difference between the two. You know that."

"We may have to stand against him," Lord Turis said archly, switching to the tongue of their ancestors. "You know that?"

Maug lowered his eyes and nodded. It was then that Charles came back. He jerked his head, and he and Maug left to get ready for the evening's festivities.

~ ~ ~

Queen Titania listened mournfully to Sir Edwin McGaffy's sad song about lost love. He sat at her feet, playing a lute in her private rose garden. A nearby fountain splashed. It was a tranquil oasis away from the press of court. The song had long been one of her favorites, but this performance had more feeling in it. He had a beautiful voice, but today it seemed filled with such longing. When he finished, she ran her long fingers through his brown curls.

"That was more than lovely, Edwin," she murmured. He turned away and focused on tuning the lute.

"You like that one because it reminds you of Ezra Parks," he said without looking up. "Doesn't it?"

Titania sighed and pushed her long platinum hair over her shoulder. She had never told the knight that she and the advocate were lovers, but it was hardly a secret. Her husband knew of her indiscretions. It was just not considered a topic for polite conversation. Even now, with Ezra in Sebastian's Keep, the Queen longed to go to him but stayed away. Oberon was looking for an excuse to act against him, and her; and her court. Her spouse was always seeking ways to make her less powerful.

"It does," she acknowledged. The way she chose her words made Edwin look up at her with worry. "I'm careful, Eddie, dear."

"You can't be too careful," Edwin admonished in a low tone. But before they could continue, Oberon strode into her patio garden with an arrogant sneer. If only she'd had the luxury of marrying for love. She would have never chosen this oaf.

"Ah, Titania." He eyed Sir Edwin with irritation. "I see you're not busy."

"Never too much for you." She sighed, getting up and going to his side. She leaned down and lightly brushed her lips across his cheek. His lips twisted slightly, but his eyes didn't warm. Titania couldn't decide who hated who more? He or she?

"I want the girl," he said with no preamble.

Titania paused. "You've never asked my permission for a girl before Oberon." She frowned. He laughed, gently pushing her away. Edwin turned to the lute and started to play a light, sad tune in the background.

"No, not for that." He put a hand to his chest. "Not for me. My Lord Dragon's mate. I want her in my court."

"You can't have her," Titania retorted, seeing where he was going with it. He wanted control of Ezra's granddaughter because it would give him some control over Ezra. And eventually, it could bring the whole of Spoons Forge into his court, should her longtime lover go through with his talk of making the girl his heir.

"Why not?" the King asked with humor. "She's the dragon's mate, and he is a member of my court."

"She's still a child, and they're not wed."

"I plan to remedy that." The Fairy King nodded. "I'm waiving the banns and the right to challenge. The dragon has already mated her. The mark is proof of that."

"I care little for your so-called proof. I'll not hand a child into the arms of that foul beast, or your court."

"You'll do it, or I'll have the Advocate of Spoons Forge executed for violating my marriage bed." Oberon lowered his voice with menace. "I will do it tomorrow. Don't try me, Titania."

"Y-you wouldn't!" Titania looked at him aghast. "Why now?"

"Because I've heard the girl is Parks's heir." The king crossed his arms and gazed at her coldly. "Once she's married to the dragon, she's in my court whether you like it or not. Spoons Forge will be too when the advocate dies."

"When you kill him, you mean!"

Oberon shrugged. "You do this. You release the girl and not protest the marriage, and I'll leave the advocate to you until he dies."

Titania started to protest again. Oberon raised his hand.

"Naturally, beloved." He grinned at her. "Until the man dies, naturally. He's only human, after all."

Titania looked at her husband and bit her lip, then turned her back on him. If she could extract this promise from him, it would be worthwhile.

"I'll not protest," Titania said in a small voice, not turning back to him. "You can let your dragon marry the girl."

"Mm," Oberon grunted and turned to leave the garden. Titania closed her eyes, rubbing her fingers against her temples.

But she hadn't promised not to work against it in every other way possible. She turned to Sir Edwin who sat staring at his lute. She went over to him and knelt down.

"Eddie," she said softly.

"I can't believe you just did that," he muttered angrily. "You don't even know Bobby, and you just gave her away."

"Eddie, listen to me," Titania said urgently. "I need you to do something."

He looked at her with large brown eyes.

"I need you to take Roberta Parks away. I know how to free her of the dragon's bite."

"Can you do that?" Edwin's face paled with disbelief. She nodded and pushed her fingers through his hair.

"You remember that woman? Elizabeth? She has Oberon's Mirror. It will break the bond. It can break any spell. Use it on Ezra's granddaughter, and she'll forget the dragon ever existed!"

"The dragon killed her," Edwin said.

"No." Titania smiled. "That puppet of Oberon's saved her. I may have misjudged him. I would have never given him credit for it."

"I'll need to get her away from court." Eddie started to pluck on the lute. "And I don't know that Ezra can know."

"He can't," Titania assured him. "Don't trust him in this. But if you can't… if you can't get her away, you must kill her before she falls under Oberon's power."

"Kill?" The young knight looked at her with a stricken expression. "You want me to kill Bobby?"

"No. I don't." She assured him, leaning forward to press her lips against his forehead. "It is very important that you don't fail. If you do, the girl will have to die."

~ ~ ~

Some coaxing had been involved in getting Roberta to wear the richly colored red dress that Maug had brought to his chamber. He smiled at her as she stayed close to his arm. He had worn his red dress armor. Roberta had chided him, and he relented about wearing the helmet. He accepted that the large ornate piece, shaped very similar to a dragon's head, would have been somewhat out of place at a formal ball.

Still, he wasn't the only dragon dressed for a fight. All seven dragon lords wore dress armor and were heavily armed. Maug wore his long broadsword on his hip.

The first of his brothers to meet his mate was Lord Jaka. The purple dragon's aura bristled around him. In his human guise, he was a slim brown-haired man wearing a rich colored armor of violet. He was handsome and had no trouble with the ladies on his own.

Lord Jaka, however, was not mated, and eyed Maug's mate with appreciation. His eyes lingered on her mark as he reached and drew Roberta's fingers to his lips. Maug was tempted to remove his hand from his wrist for the trespass. The idiot could grow another after a moon or two. But he decided it would upset Roberta. Instead, he sent a small push of power and shoved Jaka back when he lingered too long. Lord Jaka chuckled.

"I remember being as young and impetuous as you." He stood up and eyed Maug with humor. "I still wouldn't have bonded. It makes you vulnerable."

Roberta frowned, raising her chin at the other dragon. But before they could speak they were interrupted by the arrival of Lord Turis and Katrin. Roberta brightened considerably at seeing her friend. She squealed in delight, throwing her arms around the green. Turis's eyes flashed with hot temper, and he stepped forward. Maug knocked him hard on the shoulder, pushing him back.

"Leave them be," Maug growled low in his throat. "My mate is no threat to yours."

Lord Turis tightened his hands at his side and nodded almost imperceptibly. Maug looked at Katrin. Turis had her in a black dress, lightly trimmed in green. Its wide scooping neck displayed the brilliant black mating mark along her shoulder and chest. Maug caught her scent and looked sharply at Turis. Maug frowned when he caught the black's scent as well.

"Well," he muttered. Both Katrin and Turis were in season? How was that even possible?

Lord Turis crossed his arms. "I'll have my hatchlings a year from next spring," he said, confirming what Maug suspected. "When do you suppose you'll have yours?"

"Hatchlings?" Maug mocked in a low voice. Roberta was speaking in an equally low tone to Katrin, likely trying to learn how the green ended up with the black's mark on her. Not that Maug had to ask. She was in season, and Turis wanted her. It was all very simple. He doubted Roberta would understand, though. "This is true love, brother."

Lord Turis narrowed his grey eyes and snorted. "I doubt that, and she doesn't seem that gifted to me."

"Good." Maug's short answer earned him a smile from the black.

"But I know better," Lord Turis continued. "I've watched your career, youngling. You've done nothing that hasn't been carefully calculated. I doubt this is any different."

"I have no idea what you're talking about."

It was then that Lord Tsui made his way in their direction. He had both his mate and his daughter with him. Maug made a gagging noise, and Turis grinned at him.

"Can't say you're wrong," the black agreed and put his hand on his chest. He inclined his head to the old yellow dragon. "Lord Tsui."

"Where is this mate of yours?" Lord Turis stiffened and glanced to where Roberta and Katrin were standing. It caught the ladies' attention. Katrin paled, shrinking back. But Roberta watched the newcomers with polite curiosity. Maug's mate, naive as she was, wasn't intimidated by the raw power coming from them. Maug was certain she could sense it, but it didn't frighten her. And truly, as long as he was by her side, it didn't have to.

"Not much to look at, is she?" Trin said. Maug glanced at the yellow. She was a beautiful dragon, but he preferred his own mate. He supposed if he had to choose between Trin and Katrin, that he would take the green as well. She wasn't a royal bitch. It was then Lord Tsui caught Katrin's scent. He narrowed his eyes and almost moved towards her. Tsui's mate put her hand on his arm as she eyed Turis warily. The black was ready to lash out, should the yellow step any closer. "Ah. Is she in season then? That's clearly all she has to offer."

"You're not so hot yourself," Roberta said, defending her friend. Katrin put a hand on Roberta's arm and whispered urgently to her. Bobby ignored her. Maug smirked, ready to claw the yellow's throat if she took one step towards her.

"Oh, you would be Maug's pet." Trin sneered.

"Lord Maug," Maug corrected icily.

"Lord Maug is our esteemed ally." Lord Tsui turned and inclined his head to the young red dragon. Maug snorted and crossed his arms. Jaka and Tsui were the weakest of the Dragon Lords. The only two Maug was concerned about was Tauc and Lien.

Lord's Giet, Lein, and Tauc took the opportunity to join them, with Lien's quiet mate following behind. An orange dragon, but Maug saw no clear mating mark on her; but that didn't mean she didn't have one, only that it wasn't visible.

Maug shifted to give himself a better angle to move between them and Roberta. He noted that Turis had done the same on the other side. Just as well their mates were in one place. It would be easier to defend them from the others.

"What? A party? And we weren't invited?" Lord Giet smirked, shoving Lord Jaka aside. The purple dragon looked at the black with hot annoyance. It didn't concern Maug. The black Giet and purple Jaka were close friends. They were the most intellectual out of the Dragon Lords and would spend hours drinking wine and expounding the theories of magic and science.

"I am only meeting our Lord brothers most lovely females." Jaka pulled his cape straight.

"Yes." Tauc set a hand on his hip and examined Roberta and Katrin. "This one smells—"

"Mind yourself, Tauc," Lord Turis snapped. Roberta looked back at Katrin, who had flushed with color.

Lord Tauc turned to the side and spoke to Maug. "I'd say she's not the only one that has a hint of something."

"What are you talking about." Trin stepped in front of him. "She's just a human."

Lord Tauc laughed in her face. "As if a female could smell anything," he scoffed. He flicked his dark eyes back to Maug. "But I'd say you could."

"Why don't you take Trin." Maug made a gesture. "She's available."

"I like yours better." Lord Tauc dropped his smile. Maug tightened his stance and put his hand on the hilt of his sword, readying for the challenge.

"As if I'd go with you." Trin sniffed and smiled at Lord Turis. "I want Lord Turis."

The black dragon shrugged. "I have no interest in you, and I have a mate."

"Then I'll kill her first," Trin said with anger. That caught everyone off-guard. Maug tore his eyes away from Tauc as Lord Turis moved blindingly fast, grabbing Trin by the neck. Gods, was Trin that reckless that she would threaten a dragon's mate in front of him and not expect to be killed outright? Lord Tsui stood next to him, putting an urgent hand on Turis's arm.

"She didn't mean anything by it, Lord Turis," the old yellow begged.

"She'll die for it anyway," Turis growled.

Maug heard a squeak from behind and spun around. His eyes widened. Tauc had Roberta against the wall and was leaning over her with a smile. Maug loosed a small energy bolt, shoving the red dragon away from his mate. He loosened his sword and sliced Tauc's left arm off at the elbow with a full swing. Roberta screamed, and Maug drew a deep breath, trying to slow his heart even as he pointed his sword menacingly at the other red. Blood splashed onto the red marble floor. Maug had to rein in the urge to kill him, fighting his instincts to finish the job.

The hall dissolved into chaos and screams as most fled the area.

"I'll gut you next time," Maug warned. Tauc winced, shaking his red hair out of his eyes, and smirked. Maug knew that had taken a lot, considering the pain he had to be in.

"You can try," the Dragon Lord of the East snarled at him.

"All of you, stop this now!" King Oberon roared as he came into the middle of them. Maug stood a little straighter but hadn't sheathed his sword yet. The King shouldn't have been surprised. Violence was the likely result of creating this situation. Maug was equally certain that one, maybe two, of them was going to end up dead before it was over. He just had to make damned sure it wasn't him. The monarch pointed at Maug. "Put that up."

Maug inclined his head and slid the sword into its sheath as Oberon rounded on the other dragon lords.

"I will see all you good dragon lords now!" the King bellowed.

Maug felt his heart stop. Oberon thought he was going to leave his mate? Clearly, he wasn't the only one that felt that way as both he and Turis hung back. But Oberon glared at the two of them. "You will leave your females and follow me!"

Maug frowned and eyed the Fairy King, even as he leaned down to kiss Roberta's cheek. She looked so pale that he worried she was going to be ill.

"It'll only be for a moment," he murmured. Then he fell into step with Turis and followed Oberon out of the hall. Turis didn't even spare a glance in Katrin's direction.

"You'll spoil your mate if you treat her like that," Turis chided.

Maug glared at him. "And you'll not keep yours with the way you treat her."

"Are you threatening me?"

Maug shook his head as they followed King Oberon out of the hall.

REVOLT

"And just what was that display of bad behavior?" King Oberon roared at the seven Dragon Lords. He paced back and forth in the expansive stone throne room, having led them there from the Crimson Ballroom with a growing number of shadow knights and mages falling in behind them. It was seldom used; both monarchs preferred the more open and airy halls on the ground level of the Keep.

The Dragon Lords shifted and watched the Fairy King balefully. It took a few more moments before the three advocates who held voice for the Dragon Lords hurried into the throne room. They all had land that was part of the dragon's territories, and it would be their voice the king heard in matters of law.

Turis glanced at Tauc and smirked. Served him right, the idiot. If he were going to make a move for the other red's female, he shouldn't have had the stupidity to do it under his nose. If anything, Turis thought Maug the fool for not killing him.

"I'm very sorry, my good Lord King," Charles Tampton said as he pushed his pale hair out of his eyes. "I'm certain none of the dragons—"

"It was your dragon that did the most damage!"

"Not as much as I should have." Turis heard Maug mutter.

Tampton threw Maug a scathing look and turned back to the King. "Surely your Majesty understands that by their very nature, dragons aren't—"

"They are at court, and they will behave like civilized creatures!" the King yelled. His outburst made the dragons stir more. Turis wasn't sure what the Fairy King expected from them; they were not going to act like the placid prey creatures his mate seemed so fond of. "They will not try to kill each other at a formal event!"

Maug shoved forward. "I can assure you, my Lord, had I wanted Tauc dead, he would be."

"You wish, upstart," Tauc sneered. He'd wrapped the stump in his cape and was likely using what magic he could to stop the bleeding. Maug fingered his sword, and Turis drew a deep breath to calm himself.

"Enough," Turis said, his deep voice carrying across the stone chamber. He paused and smiled. "Perhaps the Fairy King is right. We shouldn't be fighting among ourselves."

King Oberon narrowed his eyes at Lord Turis. Clearly, the King knew what the dragon lord was getting at. If they weren't fighting among themselves, they were likely to be rebelling against him. Something Oberon had feared for a very long time. For good reason too. It was antics such as this that lead to the Dragon Lords frustration with him.

King Oberon's eyes returned to Maug, not with the hot anger, but with cold calculation. "You will be executed."

Maug straightened to regard the king evenly. His rigid posture and hard countenance betrayed Maug's contempt for the Fairy King. Turis couldn't suppress a small smile. Oberon had done it. There was no chance, from that moment on, that Maug, Dragon Lord of the West, would stand against his brothers in favor of the King.

"No!" Charles Tampton yelled, stepping in front of Oberon. "Maug is my ward and my heir. Did you forget that?"

Oberon looked ready to lash out at the human, and may have too, except the other advocates were gathering their power. Clearly they were ready to stand with Charles Tampton on this. Not surprising, because Charles had never made it a secret that not only was Maug his heir to the Advocacy of Ridges Hollow but that he considered the dragon his son. The man held a genuine affection for the red dragon, and Turis respected him for that. Unlike many, who valued the Dragon Lords for what power they could offer, Charles had given Maug unconditional support without any attachment.

Oberon glanced around the room. He was outnumbered and out powered, and unless he wanted an immediate and open rebellion, he had to retreat and reconsider his strategy.

But still, being Oberon…

"Fine," he sneered. "I'll have him whipped instead. One hundred lashes for his assault on a fellow dragon lord."

If the King thought he was going to divide the dragons by having Maug punished for defending his mate, he was mistaken. Turis's voice wasn't the only one to shout in protest.

"Tauc had it coming!" Giet yelled. "Gods!"

"I'd have gutted him!" Lein retorted.

Which coming from the two who were Tauc's closest friends ought to have said something, but even still…

"It's only a wound," Tauc scorned. "You can't take this seriously."

Oberon stared at them with disbelief that bordered on fury. He pursed his lips. "Fine. The beast gets it for disturbing my event. Is that a good enough reason?"

"Seems petty to me." Lord Turis crossed his arms and looked at the monarch coldly.

"You're one to talk." Oberon glared hotly at him. "Assaulting a woman!"

"The bitch threatened my mate," Turis snarled. "You're lucky Maug got to Tauc first, and you're not cleaning up her mess."

"How can you expect the other creatures to treat you as civilized when you act like this?" the King demanded. But it was Charles Tampton who stepped forward to answer.

"How can you demand they act like prey when they are predators?" he shot back. "You want them for allies as long as they stay on their leash?"

"Yes!" King Oberon raged. The dragons shifted and eyed the monarch warily. "And if they don't, I'll open season on the bastards again, and don't think I won't!"

Oberon made a gesture, and two of his shadow knights took hold of the young red dragon, only to have Maug yank himself away. He threw a belligerent glare at Oberon and walked out of the room the way a Dragon Lord should. Oberon followed after, his face full of raw fury.

Tauc growled low in his throat and turned to Turis with hot anger. "How long are we going to let him get away with this?" he hissed.

"Oberon means to destroy us," Turis agreed. He had seen the hate and fear in Oberon's eyes. It was ruling his judgment. His desire to destroy Maug, who had been his strongest ally, was a clear indication of that. The young dragon had grown too powerful for the Fairy King to risk him continuing to stand with the Dragon Lords. He had been trying to fill their ranks with the likes of Lord Tsui and Jaka, where he could force such confirmations down their gullets.

Turis turned back to the others with a slight nod, drawing them closer. The human advocates were staying together, speaking softly, probably about their own strategy. Turis shifted into the speech of dragon kind. A language that even King Oberon hadn't been able to get a spy or spell to break. "Evacuate your mates and households from Sebastian's Keep. Likely this was Oberon's plan all along. Once they're safe, we'll get Maug and leave."

"And then what?" Lord Jaka asked. "You may be able to hold against the Fairy King, but I can't—"

"We can if we stand together," Turis said pointedly. The blacks, Giet and Lein nodded, and Tauc grimaced.

"Wonderful timing on that idiot wounding me," he complained.

Turis gave him a rough shove as they left the small meeting chamber. "Lucky it was his mate and not mine," Turis growled. "I would have left you dead."

~ ~ ~

Katrin followed Bobby out of the large hall, rubbing her friend's back as she emptied the contents of her stomach in a patch of bushes. Bobby choked back her tears.

"What did he have to do that for?" Bobby gasped between feeling ill and panic-stricken. She had been riding a roller coaster of emotions since Maug had been taken away. She was terrified for him. King Oberon had been so angry.

"He was defending his claim," Katrin told her in a quiet voice.

"But that dragon didn't do anything." Bobby straightened and wiped her mouth.

Katrin bit her lip. "He was going to."

"What? Flirt?"

"Oh, Bobby." Katrin drew a deep breath and then opened her green eyes. "You don't know how dragons are."

"I know you!" Bobby protested. "I know Maug!"

"Bobby," Katrin moaned.

Bobby touched her arm. "And what's going on with you? I thought you and Brad were—"

Katrin shook her head violently, gripping Bobby's arm. "Don't say his name," she said in a hushed whisper, looking about. "It's not safe!"

"Safe?"

"I'm in season." Katrin's leaf-green eyes darted around and then returned to meet Bobby's. "And so is Lord Turis."

"So?"

"So Lord Turis marked me." Katrin bit her lip and glanced at the black star on her chest; it gleamed with a subtle energy that Bobby could sense.

"Oh." Bobby murmured, realizing what Katrin was saying. "So you and that other dragon are going to have kids?"

Katrin's face flushed deep with color, and she dropped her gaze. "Yes."

Bobby drew a deep breath even while she felt a panic of worry; not only for Katrin but for her brother too. Brad was in love with Katrin. He had been for years. When they finally started dating, Bobby figured Kat returned his feelings. Now she didn't know what to think. Was being a dragon really that different? She didn't believe Katrin loved the other dragon, but now she was bonded with him. The way Bobby had bonded to Maug.

Bobby ran her fingers along her neck, touching Maug's mark, and was comforted by it.

"I want children, Bobby." Katrin reached out and touched her arm. She watched her with a solemn expression. "I need to have them. This is the only way I can do it."

"Do you even like that guy?"

"It doesn't matter," a snide voice said. Bobby jerked her head around. The woman that had been bitchy to Katrin in the ballroom was standing here. She was slim; her yellow hair pulled back in a severe style, and her eyes golden yellow. Her regard was open hostility. Bobby grabbed Katrin's hand. "How dare you think you're good enough for a dragon lord?"

Bobby glanced at Katrin, uncertain if the woman meant Katrin or her. Bobby drew in a deep breath and stepped in front of Katrin. "Yeah," Bobby said. "I mated with a dragon lord. I love him, and we're going to be married. What's it to you?"

"You?" the woman snorted. Her hands started to glow with power and Bobby reached for the resources around her in response, but found it walled off from her.

Fuck, she would have to use her own.

"Powerless human cur!" The woman threw a hot bolt of crackling energy at her. Bobby threw up her hands and blocked it and was very nearly ill again.

"No!" Katrin yelled, shoving Bobby aside

"Foolish green commoner!" the woman snarled, hurling a bolt that caught Karin just above the knee; Katrin fell to the ground with a scream. Bobby put herself between Katrin and the hostile woman.

"Stop this!" Bobby said. "What are you doing?"

"I'm going to kill her," the woman sneered. "Get out of my way, or I'll kill you too!"

"No!" Bobby ground out, blocking another attack. Katrin wept behind her and Bobby threw up another shield. She felt another wave of nausea and knew she couldn't keep this up.

It was at that moment the black dragon, the one that had "claimed" Katrin appeared, and he looked murderous.

"Stop this," he ordered, his voice cold, but his face full of raw fury. The woman spun around and paled with terror. "Or do you intend to end your life today, bitch?"

The woman panicked and transformed into a huge yellow dragon, launching herself into the sky to flee. The black dragon watched her flight and tensed as if to pursue her, but Katrin cried out, and his head jerked back to her, his grey eyes glowing with heat.

"Stay back," Bobby ordered, afraid. She tried to throw up another shield, but he swiped it away with a gesture. Bobby cried in pain and dropped to her knees.

"I'm sorry, Lord Turis," Katrin stammered. He snorted and kneeled in front of her, running a hand along her jaw. "Please. Is Bobby okay?"

He flicked his eyes in Bobby's direction and then went back to Katrin. "Maug's mate is fine."

Bobby's body tensed, but then her eyes riveted to Katrin's bleeding thigh. "Katrin," she said. She moved to her side and put her hand on her friend's leg. The man moved to block her, but Katrin put a hand on his shoulder. Bobby used what was left of her reserves to heal Katrin's leg. The wound closed, leaving no bruise. Bobby sat back on her heels and smiled. "Better?"

Katrin nodded, her face still streaked with tears.

Bobby stiffened. A sharp pain seared her back. She screamed, arching. "Maug!"

And then the world turned black.

~ ~ ~

"Bobby?" Katrin sat up as the girl blacked out. The dragon caught Maug's mate before she fell to the ground and watched her draw a shuddering breath. Yes, Tauc had been right about her scent. It wasn't fertility, but power, and she had clearly felt Maug's pain under Oberon's lash. He tightened his jaw. Turis would have preferred the bond to be a little less true. If she could feel him, then Maug would be tied to her just as much, or more.

She could be used against him, Turis thought grimly and had to wonder if Maug had fully understood what he had done. Probably not. This was the thing; unless you lived it, you never truly understood.

Turis had lost a bond-mate years before. It had been Oberon's treachery. He'd been young and idealistic. Turis and his mate had laid their eggs and gone to Court to share the happy news. His mate was dead within hours, and the eggs turned black and cold. Turis had lost a chunk of his soul that day but swore he would have his revenge.

The black dragon hadn't expected to meet another female that would be able to give him hatchlings. His eyes glittered as he watched Katrin. He would have to safeguard her carefully. He had no plan to relive that tragedy.

"This girl," he said. His mate regarded him with frightened eyes. "What do you know about her?"

"She's my best friend."

"That is not what I asked," he rebuked. "Don't try and hide it from me."

His mate frowned and turned her eyes away. He drew in a deep breath. She was young and silly, and he didn't have time for her games.

"Can you walk?" he asked. "I can't carry both of you."

She nodded and got up slowly, still stiff and sore from the injury. He was half tempted to turn to his true form and carry them both off. But he didn't want to tip their hand to Oberon. The Fairy King would already be incensed about the yellow's disobedience; using her true form inside of the Keep was absolutely forbidden. Turis didn't care to start a war with the Fairy King in his own stronghold. War would come soon enough, though.

Turis smiled. The young red would be incensed when he learned his mate was in his arms. There was no end of eyes and quiet gossip as he made his way through the stone halls of the Keep to his rooms. He intended to put Maug's mate in his chambers for now. He would move both the females from Sebastian's Keep to Terra Su Mudan once the others had vacated.

He'd suspected Maug had been vague about the girl's potential for a reason. After seeing her fend off an attack and manage a healing, inside of Sebastian's Keep, Turis was certain there was far more to the human than her red mate had let on. A smirk twisted Turis's lips as he realized the red idiot was going to breed with this human, and how furious the Fairy King would be about that development. And given he was also equally certain Katrin would give him hatchlings in a little over the year? The first dragon to clutch in over forty years? Oh yes, this was going to thwart the fairies plans in a very large way.

Once the three of them were back in his chambers, he set the girl on the bed and looked at her, feeling a light heat in his veins. Yes, power called to power. Turis was already hot from being in season, and he felt a physical reaction as he watched her still face. He leaned close and drew in a deep breath, debating if it would be worth the fight with the red if he were to impregnate his mate? The girl was fertile. Humans were nearly all the time. Maybe Turis should try her—

"Lord Turis!" His mate's voice cut through the fog. He closed his eyes and sat up. Another dragon had claimed and bonded with this female. The only way Turis could be sure to seed her was to mark her, which could shatter her mind and split her soul. Maug would become a mortal enemy, and they would likely die together in combat. Turis nodded and moved away from the bed. He went to where his mate sat in a chair and knelt in front of her. He pulled up her dress, running his fingers along the skin where the wound had been healed.

"How long have you known this girl?" he asked softly.

"A while," Katrin said, offering no other words. He drew in a deep breath and asked his ancestors for self-restraint. He moved his lips to her leg and licked along the inside of her thigh. She tipped her head back and uttered a soft moan.

"You are my mate," he said with soft patience. "And I am your Lord. You will tell me everything you know about her."

Katrin's green eyes darted away and then returned to his. Turis pinned her in his gaze. She nodded.

"Nearly all my life," Katrin replied in a small voice. "I was born in the Geotic Realm but was orphaned. Ezra Parks was my guardian, and he placed me in a family near Bobby's. She is my best friend. You can't ask me to betray her."

"I'm asking no such thing." He ran a finger along her jaw. "She's my lord brother's mate. He's not able to protect her at the moment, but I am. I need Lord Maug as an ally."

He leaned forward and caught her lips with heat. Aroused, he wanted his mate. She wilted and submitted under his attention.

"Come," he stood to take her hand and take her out of the chamber. "Let me love you, and then we must pack to leave this cursed place."

"What about Lord Maug?"

Turis pulled in the immediate fury of hearing his mate speak another dragon's name. It would only frighten her. "Lord Maug will be brought when they can free him," he said. "And then I swear to you, I will return his mate to him."

~ ~ ~

The whip bit into Maug's flesh, tearing the skin from his back. His body beaded with sweat as he forced himself not to cry out. They'd like that, bastard fairies and their fallacious punishment. He supposed he should be grateful. Their whimsical king had wanted him dead.

But he couldn't see a logical reason for it. Maug had stood with Oberon since claiming his title as Dragon Lord. Oberon had not supported his confirmation after Maug had deposed the former Lord of the West, so he'd worked hard for his approval, served in his campaigns. Carried out his agenda. Maug had been careful to stay on the good side of the Fairy King. He wanted his backing. Not for the Dragon Lords, they couldn't care less about the evil little toad. But for the magical creatures living in Ridges Hollow. They either worshiped the Fairy King or shook in fear when he approached. Usually both.

For Maug's long-term goal for Ridges Hollow, he needed the support of the people and creatures there. Many were reluctant to follow a dragon in the first place. So long as Maug had the backing and approval of Oberon, everything would work out the way he needed it to. Without the King's support, it would be problematic.

When the leather bindings were cut away, he dropped to the stone floor of the dimly lit dungeon, breathing heavily. Blood dripped from his back, and he smelled the burn of flesh that had been cut away by the whip. He could heal himself in a day, less if he didn't have to stay in the Keep. Oberon's paranoia over a magical plot kept it tightly shielded and made working magic inside difficult. Only the strongest of mages could manage a spell inside Oberon's barriers. Maug would beg off and go to one of his holdings if it didn't mean leaving Roberta here. It was bad enough that he was being lashed like an animal, but it had left his mate on her own for how many hours in the open court? Had anyone even spoken to her? Maug's best hope was that she had gone back to her grandfather, but he didn't know if Oberon would allow it. The dragon had a feeling the Fairy King had other plans for Maug's mate, and he was certain none of them were good.

"What are you two doing here?" he heard his captors say.

Maug eased himself onto his knees and squinted up to see Lords Giet and Lein. He frowned. The two blacks weren't dressed for court but wore their day-to-day armor.

"We've come to get our brother," Giet said pleasantly. "He'll need those wounds tended. And this is no place for a dragon lord."

Maug snorted. He dropped his head, and his hair fell across his face. Yeah, he supposed not. But it was where Oberon was going to have them all if he got his way. At least, the ones he couldn't control. The ones who were too powerful, too dangerous. The reds—he looked up again—and the blacks.

"He'll be spending the night here." He heard the one with the whip say gruffly.

"His punishment was the lashing," Lein said in a far less friendly voice than Giet's. Even though Giet tended to be more pleasant, he had the worst temper out of the two of them.

"His punishment was given over to me." The man indicated to himself with the end of the whip. "And I says he's not contrite enough for his trespass. So I says he stays here until he is."

"And who are you to order the punishment of a dragon lord?" Lein asked coldly. Their steps came close to Maug. He wished he had the energy to come up with something clever to say. But it was taking everything he had just to stay conscious.

"A human is better than a dragon any day," the guard sneered.

"As if one of Titania's shadow creatures could be called human," Lord Giet mocked. "Maug is ours—and we're taking him."

"You do that, and you'll be under my lash next," the man said. "I'll take it to Oberon hisself!"

The two black dragons lifted Maug from the ground and hauled him up the stairs between them, he ground his jaw against the shock of pain. One of them tossed his red cape over his raw back, and he winced.

"You'll get yourselves in it," he muttered.

Lord Lein shrugged and flicked his dark blue eyes at him. "We are anyway. We've vacated court. You're the last."

"What? Are you insane? Oberon will go crazy."

"Likely." Lord Giet grinned on his other side.

Maug struggled against their hold. "I can't leave. My mate is here!"

"Probably not by now." Giet smiled slyly. "I heard she was taken by Lord Turis. He's probably got her with his mate."

"What!" Hot rage boiled inside Maug. He yanked himself free and pointed a finger. "You had better tell me where they are! Now!"

"Where do you think we're going?" Lein grabbed Maug's arm again, leading him outside. The cold air soothed the dragon's wounds but did little for his temper. Lein frowned at Giet with annoyance. "You had to get him going."

"He looked pathetic," Lord Giet mocked. "I gave him a little motivation to fly."

"I'll give you motivation," Maug snarled. He dropped his human guise and let out a roar, sinking his claws deep into the ground. He launched himself into the air, working his wings furiously, despite the pain it caused. The other two were soon at his side. They nodded to each other and created a portal between them, and then all three dragons disappeared in a flash of bright light.

~ ~ ~

"The dragons have rebelled." King Oberon stood in the center of the throne room, watching each of his nobles with keen eyes. Queen Titania sat behind him on her throne, staring down at her hands, working them in her lap. Charles

Tampton stiffened at Oberon's words. Ezra glanced at him with worry.

There was a slight rise in murmurs as most looked back and forth at each other with concern. The realm was populated with all kinds of magical creatures; pixies, sylphs, griffons, unicorns, just to name a few. There was also the clan kind, animals that held dual forms; foxes, rabbits, bears, and of course, the wolves. The dragons were feared more than any magical creature. For good reason too, even the weakest was usually more powerful and deadly than the typical fairy or wood sprite. Should the dragons wish to make war on the land, it would be terrible.

"But… h-how can this be, my lord?" A young knight from Oberon's court stepped forward. He was painfully innocent, and Charles doubted it had been long since he'd been brought from the Shadowlands to fill Oberon's ranks at court. "The Dragon Lords have long been our allies."

"Dragon's know nothing of loyalty and honor," the King scoffed. "They are showing themselves to be nothing more than the beasts they truly are. I had hoped that by bringing them to court this Christmas they could at least behave themselves."

Charles stepped forward. "What makes you think they rebelled? Just because they didn't stay at court?"

"Because I ordered them here!" King Oberon narrowed his black eyes on the advocate. "And they left without my leave. That, by its very nature, is rebellion."

"They were going to kill one another if they stayed."

"Which only goes to show what foul creatures they are," Oberon bellowed. "And your dragon isn't any better. He could have stayed and stood with me, but he fled with the rest."

"You had him flogged!"

"For good reason!" King Oberon snarled. "These beasts have to be kept in check if they are going to mingle with civilized creatures."

Charles tightened his jaw and worked his hands into fists and released them. He had been shocked when Oberon had tried to order Maug's execution, and failing that, having him whipped for being, well, a dragon. Maug had stood with Oberon for years. He'd never been unfaithful.

He knew the dragons were sure Oberon was their enemy. His old friend Jeremiah Kincaid had believed the same and threw his lot in with the dragons years before. Charles didn't have to make a decision on where he stood. Oberon had done that when he had threatened his son with death.

Ezra seemed uneasy and glanced around the room. Charles flicked his eyes at Queen Titania, but she kept her head down, staring at her hands, another bad sign. She obviously wasn't supporting her royal husband, but for some reason, he had cowed her into silence.

"The Senate of the Advocacy needs to meet," Ezra stepped forward and said calmly.

Oberon turned to the advocate of Spoons Forge. "This is a matter for the Crown."

Charles Tampton let a small smile play on his lips. Of course, Oberon would feel that way. The King didn't want the advocates weighing in on a matter of law.

"How so?" Ezra asked politely.

"They have broken their treaty with my royal house." The King frowned at him. "As such, the treaty is void. There is nothing to rule on."

"Well, actually there is." The advocate from Brooks Range stepped forward, pushing his long black hair over his shoulder. "Especially if you plan to void a legally binding treaty that's been in place for over 300 years. Really, Oberon, you know better than this."

"Stay out of this, Marcus!" Oberon pointed a finger. "I'm opening hunting on these beasts. 500,000 gold plus a title for every dragon head brought to me—and I'll pay 600,000 for the females!"

"You can't… you can't do that!" Titania found her voice behind him. "Oberon! You can't hold every dragon accountable because the Dragon Lords refused to bend under your heel!"

"I can. You know why, Titania, and you have no say in this matter. The original treaty—"

"A treaty you look to void," she snapped. "You can't hold me to something when you refuse to keep your own word!"

Oberon snarled at his Queen with murderous intent before he turned back to the advocate who had spoken against him. "Fine, Marcus," Oberon sneered. "Call the Senate. But I will speak, and I will demand the dissolution of this treaty based on the Dragon Lords treason!"

The King of the Fairy's swept out of the hall with anger. Titania threw a troubled expression in Ezra's direction and then followed her lord. Charles watched them with dark anger.

Ezra put a hand on Charles's shoulder and leaned to speak softly in his ear. "What is going on?"

"I'm not certain," Charles muttered. He drew in a deep breath. The lines in his face etched in worry. "Maug was taken by two of the blacks before I had a chance to speak with him. I don't know where they went."

"Do you know where Roberta is?"

Charles pressed his lips into a firm line and indicated for him to walk with him to his rooms. The knight that shadowed Ezra in the Keep fell into step behind them.

"I don't know," Charles said in a low voice. "I was looking for her after they hauled Maug off. I heard Lord Turis had taken her to his rooms with his new mate. I can only guess when he vacated he took both the girls with him."

"Why would he do that?" Sir Edwin's voice came over Ezra's shoulder. Charles felt a stab of irritation at being interrupted but controlled his temper. "We have to go after her!"

"We don't know where they went," Charles replied, keeping his voice neutral.

"So you say," the knight snapped. "But that dragon is your acting second and heir. I doubt you don't know where he went, or that he hasn't contacted you."

"Maug was likely in no shape to send word," Charles chided, ignoring the fact the knight had just called him a liar, his long years of diplomacy being called upon. "I'm certain the other dragons took him. I'm sure he wouldn't have been able to get out on his own..."

"I thought the Dragon Lords never stood together," the young shadow said with scorn. "Aren't they too busy in their own internal power struggles?"

"So Oberon believes," Charles said with a heavy sigh. "Oberon has done much to harm the dragons as a race. They aren't stupid beasts no matter what the Fairy King believes."

"Just because you're fond of your *pet*," the knight growled. Ezra put a hand on his arm to silence him.

"Pet?" Charles snorted softly. "I'm probably far more his pet than he is mine. He humors me out of affection."

"I need to review the original treaty. There's something in there that Oberon doesn't want attention brought to," Ezra interrupted before his knight could speak again. "Do you know if any of the current dragon lords were the original signers?"

Charles shook his head, and they continued down the long hall. "Lord Tsui was alive, but he wasn't a dragon lord at that time. And I believe Turis and Lein were just hatchlings."

"That will make it easier for Oberon to dissolve," Ezra said. Charles nodded in agreement. "So we'll have to see what else may be in there that will help protect the dragons."

Charles turned to face his friend. "I'll not stand with Oberon over this—and I'm not the only advocate saying that. We believe he's out to exterminate the whole race."

"Good," the knight muttered from behind him.

Charles shot him a scathing look. "You be sure to stand with Oberon when he orders the extermination on the unicorns because they'll be next on his list of creatures to go. Mark my words."

Ezra nodded in agreement, and Charles knew his point was valid. Oberon would move against any magical creature with any amount of power. It would make it easier for him to manipulate and control the rest. He had an idea what this was about. But for now, he would start things in motion and get word to his people.

They were going to war.

~ ~ ~

Bobby stirred against the pillows and opened her eyes slowly. Katrin put a cool hand on her forehead. She had tied her curls back in a ponytail at her neck and was wearing a tight brown leather top that scooped around her shoulders. Bobby sat up and looked around. She was in a large cavern with no windows and a narrow tunnel at one end. The walls were brightly lit by magical torches and had colorful tapestries hanging on them. Bobby was lying on a large four-poster wooden bed. Long sections of shimmering fabric hung around it and could be pulled around for privacy, but for now, they were tied back with bright green cords.

"Where are we?" Bobby asked.

"Are you okay?" Katrin asked. She walked over to a nearby table and poured a glass of water from a decanter. Bobby noted her friend was wearing a pair of tight black pants and high boots. Nothing like the finery they had been wearing before. But somehow, in this place, it seemed natural.

"My head hurts a little," Bobby admitted, taking the glass from her. The water felt cool and soothing on her throat as she gulped it down. Katrin smiled indulgently as Bobby held the glass back to her. "More?"

"Don't drink it so fast. You'll make yourself sick again."

Bobby made a face, but her stomach rebelled. She could still taste the bile in the back of her throat from where she had retched earlier. That reminded her of the last thing she could remember.

"Oh!" Bobby put her feet over the side of the bed. She was still dressed in her red gown, but her feet were bare. "How's your leg?"

"Healed," Katrin said.

Bobby looked around again. "So, what is this place?"

"I'm not sure." Katrin took the glass and set it on a nearby table. "A place Lord Turis said we would be safe. I think the other dragons are here too. A lot of dragons."

"Other dragons?" Bobby spied her shoes at the bottom of the bed and grabbed them, pulling them on her feet.

"I can smell them," Katrin said. "I've heard the calls from outside the cave. I think this used to be an old dragon holding. My dam told me stories about a place like this."

"Your mother?"

Katrin nodded. "A long time ago, dragons used to live together in high mountain holds like this one."

"But they don't now?" Bobby asked, tying the shoe's ribbon around her ankle.

"No." Katrin shook her head. "Dragon's don't get along. They fight and it was decided we shouldn't live together anymore. Our numbers are too low for us to be killing each other."

"That's sad."

"It's for the best," Katrin assured her.

"At least according to good King Oberon and his mate," a deep voice added. Bobby turned to see the dragon that had "claimed" her friend as a 'mate.' He walked in from the long tunnel. She frowned at him, remembering him from the May Day celebration and from the night at the bar with Maug. He pulled off the gloves that matched the black leather armor he was wearing. Bobby had to admit he was good looking. He had fine black hair that was cut short around his face and ears. His features squared off, and his body and muscles seemed more defined than Maug's, and he was taller too. This dragon's eyes were the color of ice, giving him a strong otherworldly appearance. Being a dragon, she shouldn't be surprised.

"But if all you did was fight and hurt each other," Bobby said, standing up. "It kinda makes sense."

He regarded her for a long moment before he spoke. "It wasn't like that. Oberon didn't want all the dragons in one place. It made it too easy for us to unite against him. Too easy to find mates."

"But we do fight," Katrin protested, moving forward.

Bobby realized that Katrin was afraid of the black dragon. Bobby was surprised she was able to tell his color so easily. Or maybe Katrin had mentioned it, but Bobby could almost sense the way it clung to the power he practically breathed. He ran a hand along the side of Katrin's face with tenderness. Katrin dropped her eyes to the side, not looking at him.

"When we have reason to, yes," he agreed. He turned away from her and poured himself a cup of water. "But Oberon used it as an excuse to move us away from each other. But if we don't fight, even if it is with each other, we aren't truly alive."

He nodded to Bobby.

"We have never been fully introduced. I am Turis," he said with a slight incline of his head. "I hold the territories to the far north. Please accept my gratitude for defending my mate."

Bobby frowned. "Katrin's my friend."

"And for healing her. That certainly goes beyond what is expected for a human."

"Why?"

"Because she is a dragon."

"She's still my best friend. Besides, I've got lots of non-human friends."

"And a dragon for a mate," he said in a low voice.

Katrin stood between Bobby and the black dragon. "Lord Turis," she said in an almost pleading voice. "Don't."

His glanced at Katrin and shrugged, then returned his attention to Bobby. "What is your name, girl?"

"Bobby Parks."

"That's a boy's name," he chided.

"She is Lord Maug's Lady Roberta." Katrin put a hand out in front of her. "You can't forget that."

"I'm not going to, but the others are likely to."

"They can't," Katrin started, but he made a dismissive gesture with his hand.

Bobby heard a trumpeting, roar-like sound. Both Katrin and Lord Turis turned around.

Lord Turis nodded. "Took them long enough."

He walked towards the tunnel. Bobby hurried after him, and Katrin chased after her.

They emerged on a high ledge over an ice-covered valley, Katrin put her hand on Bobby to steady her as she stumbled. Her heart was in her throat from vertigo.

"Oh shit," she gasped, stepping back closer to the wall. "It's really high."

"A proper nest for a dragon." Lord Turis nodded in agreement. But that wasn't what she had meant. Looking at the mountainous walls, she saw several other cave openings. There were hundreds of them.

Before she could ask anything, she heard another roar, more low pitched this time, and looked down, spying its source. A large orange colored dragon sat on its haunches, letting out a bellow. Bobby swallowed as she eyed the large creature. She had seen the female who had attacked them turn into a dragon, but before that, she had never seen a dragon in its true form. And the female had been quite a bit smaller than the orange below.

A brilliant flash of light lit the sky, and three dragons' hung there for a moment. Two blacks with a red between them. All three were at least twice the size of the orange. For a moment, Bobby felt real panic. She focused on the red and calm washed over her. She didn't know how she knew, but she did.

"Maug," came the barest whisper.

Lord Turis cast a glance over his shoulder with a wry grin. "The bond is true."

The two blacks wheeled their way to the valley below, but the red struggled. Bobby gasped as the red dragon crumpled around himself and plummeted towards the ground.

"Maug!" Bobby's voice tore from her throat as she nearly bolted off the ledge after him. But she was caught in the strong arms of Lord Turis.

He laughed at her in amusement. "You can't fly, idiot girl," he scolded even as his features shimmered and his form changed into an enormous black dragon. He clutched her tightly in his front claw as his gigantic wings swept, and took off into the air. Bobby squeaked and closed her eyes. Her stomach dropped like a pit. In only half a heartbeat she was on the ground next to where Maug had crashed. The red dragon groaned as Bobby bolted to him and threw her arms around his large snout.

"Are you all right?" she demanded as her eyes welled with tears. The dragon snorted and nudged her, slightly closing his eyes.

"Mm," he sighed. "You smell good…"

Bobby stood up and looked him over. He had lost consciousness. She noted a series of large wounds across his back and wings and shook her head. She leaned against his shoulder, calling upon the healing magic the wolf Larubaba had taught her to work. Bobby was still tired from taking care of Katrin, but she had to do this. She had to take away his pain.

~ ~ ~

Turis shifted back to his human form as the girl pushed herself into a healing trance. He crossed his arms, noting Lein and Giet landing deftly on either side of Maug, craning their long necks to get a look at the girl. Giet drew in a deep breath, sniffing at the air. He turned to Turis, who glanced backward and saw Katrin had stepped behind him. She moved closer, putting a light hand on his arm.

The other dragon lords came out and gathered around the fallen red.

Tauc, in human form, moved closer to Turis. "So, you had the bastard brought here, eh?"

"We need him." Turis nodded with a glance to the red's newly healed arm. "You get one of the shamans to help with that?"

"Yeah." Tauc shrugged, flexing his arm. He raised an eyebrow in Turis's direction. "We don't need him. He's too young to know anything."

"He's a dragon lord." Turis watched as Maug's mate fell unconscious against him. He eyed where Maug's wounds had been, noting she had completely healed him. The girl was indeed powerful. Turis pulled off his cape. He didn't need her catching her death in the cold night air. Likely the child didn't even know how cold it was. "And a powerful one at that, even for his age."

"He's little more than a hatchling." Tauc pointed out. But Turis ignored him, moving forward. True, Maug was painfully young. But Turis hadn't seen a dragon mage that powerful in a very long time. If Maug was this strong now, there was little limit to what he could grow into in a few hundred years. Maug had as much raw power at his call as Turis had now, and that was considerable. The youngling just didn't have the experience to harness it. When he did, Maug was going to stand with the legendary Dragon Lords of old. Turis could see it. As his eyes swept the other dragon lords around him, he knew they did too. A few years ago, these same dragons would have happily turned on Maug, shredding him while he was weak because of it.

But not now. Not when they finally understood what the Fairy King meant to do to them; to all of their kind. Now they knew they needed the likes of Maug to destroy Oberon and his mechanisms against their race.

When he got closer to Maug and the girl, the red dragon opened his dark eyes to slits and growled quietly. Lord Turis chuckled. It was so like the young rogue to go against convention and take a human for a mate.

"Stop that," Turis ordered and didn't hesitate to move towards Maug's mate. He laid his cape over her, tucking it around her shoulders. The girl snored softly against the dragon's bright red skin. "I have no designs on your mate, fledgling."

Maug lifted his head in front of the black's. "You have my gratitude for taking her from Court. Oberon can't know—"

"I didn't do it for you." He jerked his head to where Katrin was standing. "I owe the child a debt of my own.

Just as you owe us for your liberation from the fairy court's justice."

"Justice," Maug sneered as he took on his human guise and held his mate in his arms, still wrapped in Turis's cloak. "Oberon's madness, you mean."

"It's the same thing," Turis said dryly. "You'll both be safe here. The wards are over three thousand years old. Even Oberon doesn't know its location. We've sent a call out for every dragon to come here for their own safety."

"They'll never believe you." Maug shook his head as they walked towards the high mountain cliffs. The other five dragon lords had taken human form and were following. "They'll think it's some sort of trap. Hell, I would."

"Until the first handful are murdered and taken to Oberon as a trophy," Turis agreed. "Then they'll come."

"And what?" Maug asked, turning to him. "We can't hope to stand against Oberon and his armies. You know that, right?"

"I know that we"—Lord Turis indicated around them—"control a good portion of Oberon's armies for him. And that you, in particular, are trusted by those that serve you."

Maug's worried eyes traveled to where Turis's mate stood, and then glanced down at Roberta.

"Why now, Turis? Why do you want to risk war with Oberon now? Don't you understand what you have to lose?"

Turis glanced back to the little green. "Oberon knows I've got hatchlings coming," he said in a low voice. "He'll have my mate murdered. Again."

"What do you mean—again?" Maug looked at him with open shock.

Maug's mate stirred against his bare chest, and Turis pointed. "One of the blues will take you to the cave we've apportioned for you and your mate," Turis said. "Get some sleep. We're going to have a full council in the morning."

Turis walked back to his mate, wrapping an arm around her waist and drawing in her full scent as he closed his eyes.

Yes, this time, Turis would be sure the Fairy King didn't get the opportunity to harm what was his.

~ ~ ~

The seat of the Advocacy, and where the senate met, was deep in the mountains of the far eastern portion of the Kingdom, in the city of Barton's Heights. Oberon had tried, and failed, to have it moved to Sebastian's Keep, but no one was of the mind to give him that much power over any proceeding.

Dissolving the Kingdom's treaty with the dragons had been brought to a vote; not only of the Senate of Advocates, but the representing counsel of all the magical creatures in the realm.

Even the unicorns had argued against the dissolution of the treaty with the dragons. The Senate of the Advocacy, with one hundred and fifty members, had examined the original terms of the treaty. It had given far too much weight to Oberon when it had been drawn up, including a provision that prevented Titania from speaking on the dragon's behalf, effectively silencing her in all matters that had anything to do with them. But from what Charles could remember, it was because the Dragon Lords were desperate to end the endless siege against their race. The original intention was that the dragons would be able to keep their nests safe from the constant threat. It was the only way they thought they could maintain peace with the other creatures of the Thaumaturgic Realm.

Of course, Oberon had extracted a sort of fealty oath from those first seven dragon lords. And had pressed them, and their successors, into his armies to serve in his campaigns, to hold against the western hoard and southern queen. A hand in friendship he had said, even while he sent them to their deaths, defending his kingdom while taking them from their own lands and holds.

But none of the original signatories were alive, and because none of the standing Dragon Lords had come forward to contest Oberon's move to dissolve it, the Senate voided the treaty.

Charles Tampton wasn't sure they weren't right, but he had voted against dissolving the treaty anyway. This act was going to lead to open war with the dragons. Oberon had reinstated the bounties on the dragons already, offering a higher price for females. Charles felt his stomach twist. The females weren't fighters or warriors. If this move wasn't a clear indication of his genocidal tendencies, nothing was.

Charles ordered his people to start packing. There was little doubt which side Ridges Hollow would be on. Maug was his ally, his adopted son, and his heir. He had no intention of siding with the capricious Fairy King over this. He didn't know where Titania's court would fall on the side of the conflict. Oh, the queen would despise it, of course, but she was so against war he doubted she would take a military stand against her husband.

He opened the door to the office he kept in Barton Heights and smiled. "Laru-Baba. I haven't seen you in some time."

"I've been with my pack, trying to talk my sons and daughters out of this madness." She trotted into the office in wolf form and he closed the door behind her. "They are too loyal to that reckless idiot of yours."

"Ours," Charles corrected. He took off his glasses and set them on his desk. "You had as much of a hand in his upbringing as I did."

"Little good it's done. You know he means to breed with that human?"

"If he can," Charles mused, watching the wolf. "But it's not that easy. Just because he thinks he can do it, doesn't mean he'll be able to."

"The girl will be a powerful mage." The wolf shifted into human form and looked at him worriedly. "I don't doubt she'll be able to. But more to the point, if Oberon thought she could breed a dragon, he'd have her executed before she turned another day older."

"Why would he do that?"

She bit her lip and then turned back to him. "Because Oberon's been killing mated dragons since the ink started to dry on that treaty," she answered. "He's worked very carefully and very hard to make sure they would die out. He had hoped to do it 'naturally.' Slowly enough that no one would notice."

"I'd think the dragons would notice if their mates started dying."

"Some did." Laru-baba nodded. "And some were very careful about their mates, and where they kept them. Lord Tsui earned his place as a dragon lord because Oberon hadn't been able to stop him. He wanted Tsui with him where he could watch him. Not long after, Turis was able to breed a clutch, and that's when…"

"When what?" Charles walked around the desk and folded his arms.

"When Oberon used Titania to invoke one of the old spells," she said in a low voice. "No dragon female that lives here, in the Thaumaturgic Realm, will ever conceive a clutch."

Charles wasn't shocked by this; Maug's sire, Mugan, had made Ridges Hollow his home, and had cryptically alluded to the spell, but Charles never learned the details.

"How was Maug's clutch conceived?"

"Mugan was the strongest mage I ever knew. And the Lady Jaylinn was incredibly powerful as well. I may have helped them to negate the spell."

"Titania's spell?"

"She wove it herself, but…" The wolf hesitated, dropping her head, "But I helped the Queen with it."

"Laru-Baba," Charles chided softly.

The wolf shook her head. "I was young and foolish. I didn't understand what it was for until it was too late. Then years later, I thought I could make it right by helping Mugan. But ultimately, that's what got him killed. Helping to raise Maug was my chance to make this right."

They were silent for a long time before the wolf spoke again.

"There is one other thing, the dragon that Lord Turis took as a mate, she was born in the Geotic Realm so the blood curse doesn't apply to her. I have it on good authority that Turis found an ancient spell of the Dragons of Legend and used it to force his fertility. In reality, this action of the Dragon Lords has far more to do with Turis's mating than anything to do with Maug."

"You think she will bear a clutch?"

"Yes," the wolf answered honestly. "The black wouldn't let anyone near her once he marked her, little surprise. Lord

Turis has already lost one bond-mate to Oberon's scheme. I doubt he'll risk another."

"What happened?" Charles asked. This was history he had not been made aware of, but given how events were playing out, he didn't doubt the truth of it.

"Poison," Laru-baba said shortly. "At Court. Not long after Turis won his title, he and his mate had a clutch of eggs. Oberon insisted he and his lady come to the Keep to celebrate. I tried to save her, but my magic was hampered by the wards on the Keep. I begged Oberon to lift them, but he refused. Saying that if she wasn't strong enough to survive, she wasn't fit."

Charles closed his eyes. "And Turis knew this?"

"Oberon said it in front of the Dragon Lords," Laru-baba whispered. "I think that's when they began to plot against him. Lord Turis was too devastated to care at first. But now? With the possibility of another clutch with a new female? Oberon tipped his hand too far by ordering them here because of Lord Maug's new mate. I think Oberon meant to kill her too. Or use her to control Lord Maug. I'm not certain which."

"Oberon probably didn't know himself." Charles went over and picked up his briefcase. "Do you know where they went?"

"There's been a call for the dragons and their allies," Laru-baba said. "But I don't know where they are going. I'm going to try and join them."

"Then you stand with the dragons?" Charles asked.

"Don't be insulting." Laru-baba shifted back to wolf form and trotted next to him as they left his office together. "As you pointed out, I helped raise Lord Maug from a near hatchling. He's the same to me as he is to you."

"Give him my regards," Charles said as she turned way. "And tell him if he needs anything, not to hesitate to ask. Safe travels, Laru-baba."

WAR

The Dragon Lords met in a low-ceilinged cave deep in the cavernous mountain. It was purposefully small, so they had to be in human form to fit. The ancient designers of the holding made most of the chambers this way, which was a curiosity to Maug. It seemed odd for a dragon holding to require them to be in human form to use many of the facilities.

Lord Turis entered. Beside him, a blue carried some maps. A green came from the other direction and handed dispatches to the dragon lords; Maug included. He could only guess theirs, like his, were news from allies of what was going on at Court, and where they stood with the dragons. Maug hadn't had one refusal from his, but Lords Jaka and Tsui hadn't been so fortunate. Because of Oberon's backing for them to be dragon lords, they didn't have such loyal allies. No one believed they were strong enough to stand against the king.

Oberon's desire to replace standing dragon lords with less powerful dragons was the reason Maug's confirmation had been hotly disputed by the Fairy King. He'd been a nineteen-year-old stripling when he'd killed the former Lord of the West, an old black named Telsui. Telsui had killed Maug's maternal grandfather for the title, so the young red felt entirely justified shredding the old bastard to take it back.

The Fairy King had very much opposed him being named the Lord of the West. The Dragon Lords had stood against the King as Maug had won the title fairly, and it wasn't for Oberon to say who had a place in their ranks. Since that day, Maug had worked hard to earn the King's confidence. He thought he had it too.

However, now he had spoken to the others and reviewed many of the things Oberon had done before Maug became a dragon lord, he realized that it wasn't possible to have ever been a true ally of the Fairy King; only a servant. He snarled under his breath. He had always known he couldn't trust the King because of his temper but hadn't realized his hatred of dragon kind ran so deep. Or that he would be so quick to call for Maug's death.

The Lord of the West felt hot resentment towards his peers for keeping this from him for so long. Lord Giet, leader of their council, had spoken to him with quiet words, but it stung that they hadn't entirely trusted him.

"We've got thirty-seven percent of Oberon's standing army in our control," Lord Turis said. "Word has it that all of yours will be coming, Lord Maug?"

Maug looked up from the latest dispatch he was reading and nodded. "Yes," he said. "They had to wait for some of my people from the outer holdings. They should be coming across the pass tomorrow."

"There you go again, thinking so little of us."

Maug turned his head and frowned sharply at the source. Laru-baba trotted into the chamber in wolf form, along with the wolf commander, Still, who was in his human guise. Maug growled low in his throat. "Bitch," he muttered, turning back to Turis. "I stand corrected. My forces will be here today."

"Don't be like that." Laru stepped forward and shifted into human form. The Dragon Lords watched her keenly. "I've news from Court."

"We already know about Oberon's bounties," Lord Lein said. "And about the Senate voting to dissolve the treaty."

"The treaty should have been voided long ago," the wolf told him. "It was Oberon that broke it."

"Can't argue with that," Lord Tauc grunted. "So, what else, wolf?"

"Many of the advocates are working on a new treaty without Oberon's knowledge," she said. "One they hope they can force him to sign. It will be more legally binding than the last."

"He'll never agree to it." Lord Turis frowned at her. "They know that, right? Stupid humans."

"True," she agreed. "But it gives them a reason not to stand with the crown. They need a legal standing to go against Oberon. Also, over half the constabularies are not going to allow the dragon bounty."

Lord Giet rolled his eyes. "Spoons allows no hunting of any sentient creature."

"Speaking of Spoons Forge." The wolf brought her sharp yellow eyes back to Maug. "How is the advocate's granddaughter?"

"My mate?" Maug asked pointedly. He wasn't sure that he trusted Laru-baba with information about Roberta Parks. The wolf had never been comfortable about his mating, and he expected she would campaign to send Roberta back to her grandfather or her family in the Geotic Realm. "She's fine. Stay away from her."

There were soft chuckles around the table. Laru-baba had the insolence to smile at him.

"Sorry, my Lord," she said with no real hint of apology in her tone. "But Ezra Caleb Parks has asked that I continue her training."

"Eventually," Maug replied evenly, flicking his eyes around the table. The other dragon lords had seen Roberta heal him. They knew she had talent, but not how much. Something he didn't care to reveal to them either. "Later."

"No, my Lord." Laru-baba pulled off her gloves. "Now."

"The girl is a mage, isn't she?" Lord Tauc threw a wicked smile in Maug's direction. "We can sense it, you dumb bastard. How stupid do you think we are?"

"Stupid enough," he muttered with no humor. That only seemed to amuse them further.

Laru-baba shrugged. "Even Ezra Parks doesn't know Roberta's true potential."

"The Lady Roberta"—Maug stood and pointed at Laru-baba—"is my chosen bond-mate, wolf. Don't forget that. And she will be my wife as well."

"Unfortunately," Laru-baba's lips twitched, irritating the red dragon further, "her grandfather agrees with you on that point. He's approved your marriage contract."

"Did he?" Lord Turis turned to the wolf with surprise. "Or are you lying about that?"

Laru-baba sighed. "I did my best to talk him out of it."

"Bitch," Maug muttered again glaring at her.

~ ~ ~

Lords Tauc and Turis stood on a high ledge, looking down at the flurry of activity in the cavern below. It was teeming with dragons and allies who had come to aid in their resistance against the crown. The two had been discussing strategies when a movement of bright white caught their eyes.

"Ah." Tauc pointed. "Maug's mate and her pet unicorn."

Turis narrowed his eyes, seeing the girl walking between Laru-baba and the young unicorn that had come with Maug's forces. He had to admit the colt had a lot of courage to come on his own to a dragon holding. Turis shrugged. The unicorns as a whole were standing with the dragons. Enough so Oberon was about ready to put a bounty on them as well. Rumor had it that Titania had raged at him, and he had withdrawn that proposal.

"She's been helpful," Turis said. "But if I were Maug, I wouldn't let her out of the nest. His mark will turn if he's not careful."

Turis noted the entrance of the Dragon Lord of the West at the far end of the cavern. Maug's eyes swept the chamber, fell on his mate, and he went to her. They happily clasped hands and kissed; then she playfully pushed him away.

"A human," Tauc scoffed. "As delicious as she smells, I'd not keep her."

"You're a fool." Turis's lips twisted slightly. "She's fertile, she's female, and she's strong enough to bear the mark of a dragon? Why do you suppose the fledgling claimed her?"

"Because he's young and amorous, as well as stupid. Not that we weren't all that way once."

"There is that," Turis agreed. He watched Maug catch his mate around the waist and pull her to him. The black dragon paused for a moment and then glanced back at Tauc. "He plans to breed with her."

"With a human?" Tauc turned back to him. "Can that be done?"

"It *has* been done." Lord Turis folded his arms, watching the couple. He didn't care to give Tauc the details on orange Maglin and her human mate. If any of the dragons believed the female to be fertile, they would try to kill the advocate to take her. It was the reason for Maug's rage when Turis had visited his aunt. And perhaps, had he not been hunting the green, Turis would have entertained the notion. Maglin was a fine-looking female, and she had a tongue that could keep even a dragon lord in line. She would have made a good mate to any, but her heart belonged to Charles Tampton.

A human she was able to mate with and have children with.

"Old stories. Nest tales told to hatchlings." Tauc made a face. "And even if it's true, with dragons that were far more powerful than that upstart."

"I believe he can do it."

"Perhaps. Maybe. But by the time that day comes, his little human mate will be long dead."

"What of the other dragon females that have come," Turis asked, changing the subject slightly. "Any in season?"

"No," Tauc answered. "Most are being canny about the time of their next season. Some to trap a mate, others to put them off."

"Typical," Turis murmured. If a dragon female held any power, the last thing she wanted was for a male to claim her. If she wasn't strong, she was desperate for the same.

That brought his own mate to mind, and he frowned. She had complied with every demand he made, as she should. Even though she wasn't one of the powerful ones, she had resisted mating strongly. Turis knew she would run given the opportunity. Being bonded to her, he knew it was her intention. Turis wasn't of a mind offering her one.

"What of your mate?" Tauc asked. "She's in season."

"What of it?"

Lord Tauc put his hands up slightly. "It's obvious you're in season as well."

Turis nodded. "I've made no secret of it. Our hatchlings will be born a year from spring, so there is little point, other than sport, for any to pursue her."

"Ancestors." The red rolled his eyes. "No one is going to challenge you for her. But the point is, we need more than just one female nesting."

"I know." Turis drew in a deep breath and watched Maug and his mate. "Maug's mate is fertile. Human's always are."

"There are three males in season other than you. They aren't strong enough to take him. But you are."

"Their bond is true," Lord Turis said thoughtfully. "And her cooperation is necessary for breeding to work."

Tauc grinned. "I wondered what was stopping you."

Lord Turis smiled. He'd honestly considered it. "If any of us touch her, Maug would fight until he killed us or died."

"And I'll tell you again," Tauc said, pushing his red hair from his eyes, "we don't need him."

"We do," Turis disagreed. "We need that spell from Jeremiah Kincaid. When it's time, we need all our combined power and cooperation to cast it. Maug's too talented a mage for us to lose."

"Turis, if you believe you can seed that human, you should."

"I'd rather try something else first," Turis mused. "I've learned how to force my fertility. It can be done to another."

"How?"

Turis arched an eyebrow with a small smirk.

Tauc looked slightly ill. "Ugh."

"It's no time to be squeamish, Tauc." Turis grinned and turned his attention back to the mated pair below. "I'd do the same to you."

"I'd claw your stones off first," Tauc snarled as he turned away. Turis watched him go. Folding his arms across his chest, he watched Maug's antics with his human mate from above. Maug would likely feel the same about it as Tauc. He also knew that the process wasn't going to be easy, and for it to work, the younger red dragon would have to feel his bite.

Maug certainly wouldn't thank him for it, and there would be a steep price to be paid by the black. He would be able to force Maug's fertility, but Turis would be bound to him for life, just as he was with the green Katrin. Turis did not relish the idea of making the hotheaded red a bond-mate, but their circumstances were too dire for him not to try.

~ ~ ~

Maug didn't want to return to his mate until he'd washed the blood off his body and armor. He'd come from a hard skirmish at Slorns Pass. Oberon's troops had tried to ambush a supply train coming in from the western camps. Maug had attacked from the air with claws, fangs, and bolts of energy. Still and his wolf pack had come around them on the ground.

Not one of Oberon's allies lived through the attack. It had been bloody and brutal and Maug wanted to clean up and put the violence aside. Roberta saw the result of the war in the wounded and maimed as they returned to the holding of Terra Su Mudan. She was working with Laru-baba, honing her skills as a healer. Maug felt a deep bite of guilt that she had to get her training this way.

Maybe Laru-baba was right. Maybe Roberta should go home to her family, but he couldn't be sure she would be safe there. Oberon had set spies on Ezra Caleb Parks, and Maug was certain that Oberon knew where her family lived. He probably hadn't killed them because he was waiting for Roberta to return home.

He went to an inner grotto, far off the beaten path, to try and re-center himself. He pulled off his clothes and slipped into the steaming pool of water with a sigh. He was as tight as an overstrung lute and the water felt divine. He sank to his chin and forced himself to relax.

Tomorrow, there would be another battle. He was longing for the day when they could take it directly to Sebastian's Keep. They may not be able to kill Oberon and his bitch Queen, but they could destroy their allies and cut them off from their power.

"Maug."

He opened his eyes to see Turis standing at the water's edge. He was covered in nearly as much blood as Maug had been. Maug acknowledged him with a small nod and stepped out of the water. It was time he found his mate anyway. He grabbed a towel and started to dry himself, turning his back on the other dragon as he wrapped it around his waist. He turned to leave.

"Wait."

Maug paused but did not turn around. The black set a hand on his shoulder. Maug drew his brows together; his bloodlust churned in his gut at smelling Turis so close. Little wonder, he'd just come in from a fight, and was still agitated and on an adrenaline high from the battle. The scent of fresh blood was nearly enough to set him off to find another enemy to devour.

"What is it?" Maug asked. Turis's lips were close to his ear. He closed his eyes, feeling his breath on his skin.

"I have a gift for you."

Maug frowned. "What—"

Turis hit him hard from behind, knocking him to the floor, and pinning him with his vice-like arms. Maug tried to throw up a defense, but Turis blocked his ability to shield. Before he could whisper another spell, Maug felt a sharp stab of pain in his lower back. He arched, hissing in pain.

The black's venom sank into him. He became weaker, unable to pull away. Turis's fingers moved to Maug's crotch to fondle him.

"What are you doing?" Maug moaned, panting hard.

"You'll hurt yourself if you struggle," the older black told him. Maug shuddered as a hot, wanton need surged through him. Turis licked the wound and played his fingers across Maug's body. He felt the tingle of magic and knew the black dragon was dragging him into a spell. He tried to resist, but it was no use. Maug turned and met Turis's lips. Turis cupped his jaw, leaning down to dominate him, demanding his submission.

"I don't want this." Maug pulled his lips away and tipped his head back. Turis moved his lips to his neck and pushed against him roughly.

"Don't lie," Turis chided.

Maug felt the bond tighten and moaned. He *did* want it. "I have a mate."

Turis's pulled back slightly and met his eyes. "I told you, it's a gift."

Maug couldn't resist. He was drowning in an oblivion of need. Turis sank his flesh into Maug with one smooth movement and worked against him. It wasn't long before they were deep in the throes of mating. Once sated, Turis rolled away from him, panting and drenched in sweat. Maug was covered in blood from the kill Turis hadn't washed away. He pulled away and sat up, glaring at the black dragon.

"I'll kill you for this, Turis." Maug spat as he moved to the water to wash again.

Turis leaned up on his elbow and regarded the younger dragon with a smirk. "Not likely." The older dragon grabbed his pants and started to put them on.

Maug's back burned hot from the bite, and he swallowed hard. Gods, it was probably true. The young dragon didn't know if he would be able to harm Turis after he had forced the bond with him.

Maug snarled as he grabbed his clothes. "If you believe this bought you loyalty, you are sorely mistaken."

"It was necessary." Turis moved to stand next to Maug. He reached out and set a hand on Maug's neck. The younger dragon didn't flinch away. There was no point now. Maug knew that Turis wasn't going to attack him again. He'd gotten what he was after. "This is an old spell, and it took some time for me to master. We don't have the luxury of time for you to learn it on your own."

Turis's lips twitched as he caught a scent of something. Maug stiffened, feeling the subtle change and began to sweat. He stepped back, putting a hand to his head as he felt a flood of heat rolling through his veins. He refocused his eyes on Turis in hot anger. "What they hell did you do to me?"

"You already know the answer to that," Turis said with a nod. "Now, go find your mate."

"I'm in season?" Maug tightened his jaw. "Damn you, Turis!"

"Go. Find. *Your.* Mate."

The black dragon turned and walked out of the spring-fed grotto. Maug closed his eyes and pressed his head against the cold stone of the wall. Now he saw what the bastard had done. He'd heard rumors of the spell to force fertility, and Turis obviously knew how to do it. Likely that was how he had impregnated Katrin. But Maug wasn't aware that it was possible to force another's.

And if he could, why him? Why not one of the others? Maug closed his eyes, feeling the tide of need well up in him. He pulled his pants and boots on, leaving the rest of his clothes and armor behind. As much as he didn't want to, he had to find his mate.

Now.

Roberta wasn't in their chamber. He tightened his hands into fists. Damn her. He'd told her to stay in his nest. He closed his eyes, trying to calm himself. It was his mating need feeding his anger. She wasn't going to be cloistered away like a dragon female, and Maug wouldn't expect her to do that. He couldn't be angry with her. Not now. Not ever.

He lifted his nose slightly. If he could catch her scent, he'd be able to find her. Roberta, being human, was most often fertile. Compared to dragons, she would nearly always be in season. He caught her scent, and it sent a hot bolt from his head to his crotch. He groaned, turning to go and find her.

He found her with Laru-baba and that pain in the ass unicorn, counting supplies in a lower chamber. His sudden appearance startled them. Roberta smiled, although the wolf eyed him with suspicion. Little wonder, her senses were as keen as any dragon. She knew his intent before he even walked in.

He tried to smile but felt like he was failing miserably as he went to take his mate's hand. Even her touch made him weak. He didn't think he'd be able to take her back to the chamber. His eyes flicked around the room. It would be good enough.

"Is something wrong?" Roberta asked. He swallowed hard and licked his lips.

"Laru-baba, take the unicorn and go away," Maug ordered softly, not taking his eyes from his mate. Roberta laughed and tried to pull away, but he held his hand tightly on her wrist.

"But we're busy right now," Farni protested.

"Now," Maug whispered hoarsely, even as he moved closer to Roberta. She looked at him with wide-eyed concern, running a hand along the side of his face. The wolf shooed the lad out of the room, and the door closed with a click. Maug moved his mouth to cover Roberta's, and she squirmed under him.

"Maug," she protested. "We can't. Not here!"

"Yes," he murmured, moving his lips to her neck, licking it and pulling at her shirt. "Here. Now. I can't wait."

She tried to squirm away from him. He gripped her tighter, his dark eyes smoldering with need. "Maug, anyone could walk in!"

"I'll kill them if they do," Maug growled, running his tongue along his mating mark. The need to mate was a raw living thing. Ten thousand years of his ancestors howled in his blood.

Damned Turis!

Roberta sighed and stopped struggling, and he eased her on a pile of soft furs. Her gentle hands came up around his shoulders, pulling him closer. He started to pull at the ties of her trousers and then stilled, meeting her eyes.

"It's time, Roberta," he whispered, running a hand along her face. "I need you to help with this."

"I don't understand." Roberta drew her eyebrows together. He nodded. This was going to be difficult. They should have been able to wait until she was older, more experienced in her power. He paused; the same could be said for him.

"I'm in season. It's time for us to try," he said, closing his eyes and touching her lips with his own. "It's time for us to try to have children."

"Now? Are you sure that's a good idea?" There was no fear, just concern, love. And great good gods, did he love her.

He nodded slowly. "Now," he confirmed. "I'm sorry. But it has to be now. Think of it like healing. Do you trust me?"

"Yes," she whispered, and Maug felt the familiar touch of her magic wash over him. He took it and drew it into his own spell, even as he worked to discard the rest of her clothes, along with his own.

"Good," he moaned as he enfolded her fingers into his. "You'll need to share your magic so we can make this work."

~ ~ ~

Black Turis walked into the storage room with Larubaba. He looked over to where Maug was laying on top of his mate. They were both sleeping soundly, but he could sense the hue of pungent magic around them, the smell of sex thick in the air. Turis's star pattern was flat black against Maug's lower back.

"You did that?" Laru-baba demanded with a low growl of anger. He flicked his eyes in the direction of the wolf. He didn't need to answer that. He turned and walked out of the storage chamber with the wolf right behind him. "Why Lord Turis? Why would you bond my Lord Maug to you?"

"Don't question me, wolf," he growled back, but she stepped in front of him and looked at him with real worry in her bright yellow eyes.

"He's young and impetuous," she said. "But he was willing to stand with the Dragon Lords. There was no need to force such a bond!"

"That's not the reason," Lord Turis said scornfully. "Maug has proven his loyalty."

"Then why?" the wolf almost howled. "He is happy with that damned girl. He doesn't need you!"

"I have no intention of keeping him." Turis laughed as he continued to walk through the lower levels of the hold.

"Please." She stopped him by putting a light hand on his arm. "Please explain this to me. You have to understand. When my Lord's dam died, she entrusted his care to me. Me! I can't see him hurt!"

Turis stopped and considered the wolf's words for a moment. That added information on Maug's background that he hadn't known before. Maug's mother, the Lady Jaylinn, had been one of the most powerful dragons he had ever known, male or female. Had she been male she could easily have been a dragon lord herself. Maug's sire hadn't been a dragon lord either; not because Mugan couldn't, but because the black dragon mage thought it would be irritating and bothersome. His only interest was females and mastering strange magics. Turis had more than one fond memory of the old rogue.

Mugan tricked the canny Jaylinn with the use of a spell and then bound her to him with his bite. She had taken care not to be trapped as anyone's mate. Her time of fertility had been one of the best-kept secrets in the realm. Being a mate was a role that she found beneath her—until the black caught her. Turis grinned. Mugan had been pleased with that one. Especially since it near incensed the Dragon Lords to have the lovely Jaylinn claimed by nothing more than a common rogue.

They had one clutch together, the last Turis had ever heard of being hatched. Not long after, Oberon used trickery to poison Mugan. Lord Turis was sure the Fairy King was alarmed by the birth of the clutch and wanted to ensure that no more would be born to them. The beloved Jaylinn didn't last an hour after her bond-mate died. It had been a shattering blow to their race. The fiery tempered red female had been one of their most loved; there wasn't a dragon that didn't keen at her loss.

Rumor had it at the time that the clutch had been murdered after their parents's death. It was years later when word came of a hot-tempered red being raised by the Advocate of Ridges Hollow. It wasn't difficult to see he'd come from the clutch of Jaylinn and Mugan. And later, when Maug was nineteen-years-old, he challenged old Lord Telsui for the title of Lord of the West. They had scoffed at the fledgling upstart for having the stones to take on the dragon lord.

Until Maug shredded Telsui's barrier and tore out his beating heart.

It was then they took more critical stock in the dragon who had earned the right to stand in their midst. Giet was the first of their number to challenge Maug, being Telsui's son. But Maug had flattened the black dragon, using magics that were outside of what any of them had learned when they were young. Many attributed them to Charles Tampton's tutelage. But if the old wolf shaman had a paw in his upbringing, it was more likely that his early training in magic had come from her. Little wonder the arrogant bastard knew so many different kinds of magic outside of the draconic. Laru's power and skill were legendary in the Thaumaturgic Realm. And if the Lady Jaylinn had entrusted the care of her hatchling to the wolf, Turis owed her a small amount of respect for that.

"We need the hatchlings," he answered in a low voice. "I helped him do something he was planning to do anyway."

The wolf turned her head back to the chamber and then at Turis. "This is madness. We are in the middle of a war," the wolf growled. "Now is not the time—"

"Now *is* the time." Turis frowned at the wolf. "We need every hatchling we can get. And if we've got to get them out of that boy and a wretched human girl, we're going to do it."

~ ~ ~

"This is getting out of hand, Ezra." The advocate of Spoons Forge looked up upon hearing Titania's voice at the door of his office. He smiled and got up to walk across the floor.

"Titania," he said. "You should have sent word you were coming. I would have had the cooks prepare one of your favorites for dinner."

"Oberon doesn't know I've left court." Titania pulled off her cloak and cast it over the tall chair opposite his desk. She pinned him with a sharp glare. "Do you know where those cursed dragons are?"

He watched her with a careful expression. "How would I know that?"

Titania pressed her lips into a frown. "Your granddaughter is with them. Come now, Ezra. You have to have some idea."

"I'm working very hard to stay out of this conflict." He inclined his head. "At your request, I may add."

Titania turned and sat in the chair opposite his desk and settled her skirt, refusing to look at him. "We cannot have rebellion in the kingdom."

"Most of the dragon's holdings aren't in the kingdom," Ezra pointed out. "And Oberon dissolved the treaty."

"For good reason."

Ezra frowned. "Why are you siding with him, Titania?"

"Maybe… maybe because he's right?" Titania lifted her chin defiantly.

Ezra offered a small, sad smile. "Not likely." He raised an eyebrow. "Come now, love. Who do you suppose you're talking to?"

"Because the only way the dragons can hope to win is by killing Oberon." Titania twisted her fingers in her lap.

"That would take a bit of work, wouldn't it?" Ezra laughed at her. "I don't know how they possibly could. You are both immortal. Forever tied to the land."

"It is possible," she whispered. He leaned back on his desk to regard her. "They could find out how."

"What are you talking about? There's no possibility—"

"But there is," Titania stood and put both her hands on his chest and leaned forward. She drew in a deep breath, realizing she would be tipping her hand, but she trusted her lover enough to let him know. "But if they kill Oberon, I'll die too."

Ezra Caleb Parks blinked at the Fairy Queen. Then he closed off his expression and put his hands over hers. "I don't want to know anything about this. You should know, my loyalty is not clear. I do not support Oberon in this. If I could, I'd find a way to end his pathetic life myself."

"Don't say that!" Titania started to tear up. "Do you know what… what could happen to our world if we're not here?"

"You're not gods, Titania. The fact you need human advocates to maintain stability is proof of that."

"A convenience," she said, pulling away from him. "But we could do something different."

"Is that so?" he asked.

Titania bit her lip. Even she wasn't sure of that. No one could be. But the queen wasn't trying to play him for a fool. She had come to try and offer him help. "I need to know where the dragons are. We have to stop them before there are more!"

"More dragons?"

"Yes," she hissed angrily. "They are breeding!"

"Everyone has the right to a family," he said in a cold voice. "I heard about what hand you played in Oberon's madness from Charles. What right do the two of you have to play God with a race?"

"They are only ones that can destroy us!" She pounded her fist on his desk. "Damn it, Ezra! If you love me, you will support me in this!"

"Of course I love you," he chided. "But that doesn't mean I can't see you for what you are. So the dragons will have their hatchlings? If you were wise, you would be making them your allies, not your enemies."

"Not when they have the kind of power they do!" Titania got up and paced around the office. "Oberon suspects that your granddaughter may be able to bear dragon seed, you know. He means for her to die. I could protect her for you, Ezra."

"Nothing you could do will protect her from Oberon once he's made up his mind."

"There are ways," Titania dropped her voice. Ezra froze and shook his head. "If she didn't live."

"No!" he said with horror. "Not that. Not ever."

"It would work, Ezra." Titania came to his side and put her hand on his arm. "Not only would you be able to keep her; she wouldn't be able to have children!"

"Or a life, a family, nothing. You would make her a shadow?" He pushed Titania away with anger.

"There's no shame in it!" Titania's eyes flashed.

"After they've had their lives," Ezra said. "Given the freely offered choice, yes, that's one thing. But to murder my kin for your agenda?"

"It's not like that!" Titania raised her voice shrilly. "You should be pleased that I would offer her such an honor. The other is that she'll just be dead!"

"Better dead than that!" Ezra yelled back.

"That could be arranged."

"Only if you find her." Ezra tightened his jaw. "And I don't think that's going to happen."

"Edwin's searching for her." Titania lifted her head. "And he will find her. He's spent enough time with her that he can sense her power. If she uses any strong spell and ties to the land for power, he will know, and he will find her."

"Eddie is a good lad. I hope he's got enough sense to know what you're up to."

"Sir Edwin serves at my pleasure. As do you." Titania pressed her lips into a firm line. "So. If you want your granddaughter to live, you will tell me where the dragons are. And I'll have Sir Edwin return her to you."

"You forget," Ezra moved around his desk wearily. "I don't know where they are."

"Then you had best find out." Titania grabbed her cloak and walked out of the office. "You know how to contact me."

~ ~ ~

Not one of the humans or magical creatures Maug encountered at Ridges Hollow seemed particularly surprised to see him. Ridges had pulled away from the kingdom and stood with half a dozen others in open revolt over the dissolution of the treaty with the Dragon Lords. And truly, Charles Tampton hadn't disinherited him. He was still his heir and acting second. If anything, Maug felt guilty about forcing Charles to be on the Thaumaturgic Realm and away from his family more than he liked. Maug resolved to make it up to him when this was over.

Maug knocked once on Charles office door before he let himself in. Charles offered him with a wide smile. "Maug!"

Charles got up and crossed the room to greet him with a quick hug. The older man set both of his hands on Maug's neck and smiled with affection. "Oberon's not managed to collect your ears yet, eh?"

"Very funny." Maug smirked, pulling away and closing the large wooden door behind him. Then, the young dragon went to the bar and poured himself a drink.

"Make yourself at home," Charles said drily. He went back to his desk and turned the piece of parchment he had been reading over; a move the dragon didn't miss. Something Charles didn't care for him to see?

"Don't worry," Maug said smoothly. He walked over and snatched the parchment from the desk, scanning it quickly. "I will."

"Maug!" Charles protested. "That's personal!"

"Ugh." Maug frowned, feeling a little panic as he read the dispatch from the advocate of Spoons Forge. He took another drink from his glass, then narrowed his eyes. "How much of this is true?"

"All of it I would assume," Charles told him. "There's no reason for Ezra to lie."

"Gods." Maug tossed it back at the desk and scowled at Charles. "This is not good."

"Why?" Charles asked with a shrug. "The girl isn't ready to invoke a spell that would trigger that sort of…"

Maug looked at him dispassionately and took another drink.

Charles frowned at him. "Damn it, Maug!"

"It wasn't my fault," the dragon muttered. "And here I was coming to tell you that you were going to be a grandfather."

"That is not funny!" Charles colored hotly, getting up to pace. "I thought you weren't going to be fertile for a few years?"

"Things change," Maug replied. "I also came to see what we could do about getting Roberta and I wed."

Charles put up his hands and shook his head. "You are in the middle of a war. This isn't the time for you to be—"

"My hatchlings will be born legitimate." Maug frowned at Charles. "I don't believe that's too unreasonable a request. Parks approved the contract, right?"

"Where do you suppose you could get married?" Charles asked. "There is nowhere in the Thaumaturgic Realm that you'd be able to do the sealing ceremony without that knight of Titania's being able to find you. Hell, you'll be lucky if he hasn't tracked her already."

Maug nodded. "She's a danger to the others. We'll have to move her away from the holding."

"And put her where?"

Maug raised his eyes slowly and smiled at Charles. "I believe it may be time for Roberta to return home to the Geotic Realm."

"If she goes home to her family, Oberon will find her for sure," Charles argued.

"That's why"—Maug grinned, looking at his foster father—"I believe it's time for you to go back and spend some time with Maggie and the kids."

"But," Charles protested. "What about Ridges Hollow? Who–"

"I'll take over here." Maug nodded with a hint of finality. "It's not like it would come as a surprise."

"But then Oberon would know where you are and target you." Charles frowned, but Maug only grinned.

"Oh?" The red dragon cocked his head to one side and smirked. "He's very welcome to try."

~ ~ ~

They were all listening to the latest news in council and Turis, admittedly, wasn't paying much attention. That was until Maug cleared his throat.

"I'm moving my mate from the holding," he said. Turis lifted his head with a frown.

"That's a bad idea," he said to the red dragon, who regarded him with belligerence. "No one's going to touch her now that she's clutching, and you know it. Don't be an ass. She's safer here."

"Like I trust any of you rotten bastards," Maug retorted. There were soft chuckles around the table. Turis knew there was some truth in what the young dragon was saying. Since it had become known she was clutching, there was interest in her from some that hadn't turned a head in her direction before. But still, Maug's mate was safer at the heavily warded dragon holding. "But that's not the issue. She's being tracked by one of the shadow knights. Her grandfather sent word through Charles."

"Going to Ridges Hollow alone was ill-advised," Turis said coldly. He hadn't known Maug had done it until after he'd come and gone. There were too many opportunities for being captured and trapped when they went out on their own.

"Oh, well, then you're going to love this." Maug smirked at him. "I'm going back to Ridges Hollow to resume my duties as Charles's second."

"What?" Lord Giet said with a frown. "No. We need you here."

"It doesn't matter where I am. I can launch and coordinate the assaults just as well from Ridges Hollow as here."

"Except that you're exposed." Tauc shook his head. "It's a foolish, arrogant thing to do. Better to stay where Oberon isn't likely to find you than stand out there with a target on you."

"Better me with a target than leading Oberon's forces here because they can track my mate. Besides, if he knows where I am, he'll work on getting at me, thereby freeing you to do more here."

"Not a bad plan," Tsui mused. "However, it leaves your mate exposed, and we need her hatchlings."

"I didn't say my mate would be with me, you old fool." Maug snorted. "I'm just not leaving her here."

"I don't like it," Turis said. "It wouldn't be good for any of us if you were captured."

"You should have thought of that before you bit me," Maug said. That earned a few chuckles from the others. Turis tightened his jaw. There was some truth to that. Maug could be used against him both physically and magically now they had bonded. Thankfully, the red hadn't returned the favor so they weren't as tightly tied as they could have been. But he still didn't relish the idea of the young dragon falling into Oberon's hands.

After the meeting had finished, Maug came to him personally. He liked Maug's next suggestion even less.

"Your mate should go with Roberta," he said in a low voice.

"No!" Lord Turis grabbed Maug by the neck and snarled. Maug smirked and removed his hand, keeping hold of his wrist as he pulled it down slowly. Then he leaned close to Turis ear.

"This location could already be compromised," he said. "That knight would have been able to track the magic from when Roberta and I bred."

Turis shoved him away. "Doesn't mean I want my mate with you," he snapped.

"They won't be with me. Weren't you listening? I mean to send Roberta back to the Geotic Realm."

"Oh, an even finer idea," Turis mocked.

"Which is another reason I want Katrin to go with her." Maug's eyes flashed angrily. "This is your doing, Turis. If you hadn't forced my fertility, this location would be secure."

"Damn you." Turis scowled. "You blame me?"

"Yes!" Maug said angrily. "I could keep my mate with me if not for you. But now I have to send her away. You said you owed her, Turis. There's not much that can harm a dragon on the Geotic Realm, and you know it. That's not so true for a human. And Katrin is in danger here as well. Do you really want to risk your mate and unborn hatchlings?"

Turis glared hotly at Maug. The young red pushed his hair away from his face and lifted his head defiantly. "And Oberon can't touch them there. His magic doesn't cross. He won't be able to find them."

Lord Turis felt cold steal over his limbs as he turned and walked away from the dragon. Damn him for being right. If he truly wanted to keep his mate, his hatchlings, safe from Oberon, he'd have to send her away. And likely the red dragon had a safe place in mind. Turis didn't believe there was any deception involved. He turned and walked away from Maug without another word.

When he got to the chamber he shared with Katrin, he found her sharpening weapons. She looked up at him without a smile. He sighed. He may not have been her ideal mate, but he didn't believe he was that bad. Turis liked to think that eventually, she wouldn't fear him as much as she did.

"Come here," he said softly, holding out his hand. She put down the sword and moved to his side. He ran a light finger along her jaw. He nodded to himself. It would only be for a little bit. "This place is no longer safe."

"What are you going to do with me?" she whispered.

"You will go with Maug's mate to a secure location," he told her. The little green dragon regarded him with surprise.

"You're sending me away?" she asked with dismay. He smiled gently with a small shrug.

"For a bit," he replied as he leaned down to take her lips with his own. "Until I find a safe hatching ground. Then I'll come for you. Do you understand? You are not free."

"I understand," she whispered.

He nodded. "Good," he grunted as he pulled her towards the bed. "Now, come and bid your lord a proper farewell."

SHATTERED

There were two ways to travel between the Thaumaturgic Realm to Geotic, a crossing or a gate. Really, they were both "gates," but one was solid and permanent. Each Advocacy in the Thaumaturgic had a permanent crossing. Spoons Forge had a crossing that came out in a park, not far from Bobby's house in Geneva. That was no accident. It made going back and forth to see her grandfather easier for her family. No special abilities or magic were needed. You only had to step through.

A true gate was a spell and another thing entirely. It took a lot of powerful magic. Farni, the unicorn, couldn't gate on his own, and neither could Bobby or Katrin. Bobby knew her grandfather could, but it was exhausting, and he usually napped for hours afterward.

So when Maug told them to get ready, that they were going to use a gate directly, she had paused. This wasn't a portal, where you stepped through to the other side in the same realm. Those were tricky too, but she had been working on them herself. Laru-baba assured her she would be using portals before the beginning of summer.

What shocked her was how childishly easy Maug made gating seem. Laru-baba offered to help, and he rebuked her with a smirk.

There was a moment of disorientation that made many ill when gating, and then they appeared in a high-walled garden. Bobby turned to see an older style three-story brick house. She blinked a few times in the bright sunlight, suitably impressed. "Where are we?"

"This is where Charles lives with his family in the Geotic Realm," Maug told her.

"Not so much of the family at the moment." Bobby turned to the source of the voice and smiled. She remembered Charles Tampton from her visits to Sebastian's Keep. "Right now, it's just Maggie and I. I've sent the kids to stay with relatives."

"Charles." Maug shook his hand and gave him a quick hug, while the others held back. Katrin stood shyly next to Bobby and Farni, who were taking everything in with eager eyes.

"Didn't have any trouble getting through my wards?" Charles asked.

"You took them down first." Maug made a face. "Don't try and humor me."

"Heh." The gentleman chuckled, holding his hand out to Bobby. "We met in Sebastian's Keep. I'm looking forward to getting to know you better. I've been friends with your grandfather for years."

"How is my granddad?"

"Worried about you," he said. He put his hand on top of Farni's head and smiled at him kindly. "And I've heard nothing but good things about this lad."

"Not from me you haven't," Maug muttered.

"Maug's mean to me," Farni complained to the older man.

Charles laughed and tousled his hair. "Me too," he conspired with the young unicorn. Maug snorted behind him. Charles put a hand to his chest, inclining his head. "Lady Laru, you look well."

"Mm." Laru-baba frowned. "I still don't approve of you spending time in this hellish place, Charles."

"Of course not." He grinned and then turned his attention to Katrin. "And you must be Katrin?"

"My mate thanks you for your hospitality, Advocate," Katrin said in a quiet voice.

Bobby bit her lip. "How far is this from my house?" Bobby asked, looking first at Maug and then at Laru-baba. "From Geneva?"

Charles shook his head and glanced at Maug, who drew in a deep breath and brought Bobby's fingers to his lips. "Far enough," he said. "We talked about this, sweet. Oberon is sure to be watching your family. You can't risk going home."

Bobby felt a pang of disappointment. She hadn't seen her parents in weeks. She even missed butt-head Brad.

"Let's go inside." Charles intervened. "Maggie's got dinner ready and will be vexed if it gets cold."

~ ~ ~

True to the red dragon's warning, the holding at Terra Su Mudan was soon under siege. Not by Oberon's forces as they had expected, but by Queen Titania's shadow knights. Turis wondered if the Fairy King was aware of the Queen making a move against them. From his experience with the royal pair, he doubted it.

But because of the warning, they had moved the noncombatants to a safer holding in the south, and were waiting for the forces when they came through the pass.

The wards on Terra Su Mudan would never fall, but they could be sieged and not be able to get supplies. As much as it pained Turis to leave this place, he knew it would not be breached, and their people were safer elsewhere.

The dragons and griffons took a heavy toll on Titania's fighters from the sky. The wolves and mountain lions tore into those they couldn't reach in the wooded trail. It didn't take much effort, and the forces were routed and retreating.

Still, the shadow knights and their allies wounded and killed three dragons before pulling back. Turis licked the blood off his claws even while he sat and watched the pass, hoping for another round at them. He knew it was best the dragons retreated as well, but he longed to tear flesh for their impudence at challenging them.

Word had it that Maug wasn't fairing much better at Ridges Hollow, but he was holding up; and that was against Oberon's hardened warriors, rather than Titania's court pets. The black dragon snarled softly under his breath. They had to find the way to kill Oberon—and soon.

Jeremiah Kincaid had best find that spell. Turis tightened his jaws in frustration. They were running out of time.

Oberon and his wife had secured their immortality by a blood pact with the dragons. It had been their magic and blood that had granted the fairies the gift of never ending life. But because the Dragon Lords didn't entirely trust Oberon, they had laid a hook in the spell. There was a sister spell to the original that could shatter Oberon and Titania leaching hold on the magical reservoirs of the land to stay young.

Turis didn't know exactly when the pair went mad, or why. Whether it was living too long, fearing death, or the constant wild energies of the realm that had addled their minds.

The advocates had stepped forward to help with the land, countering the flow of disruptive energies. Oberon, in his madness, had replaced more powerful mages with candidates of less talent; leading to a backlash of power that cycled the immortals into deeper insanity.

There was a time when Oberon and Titania's intentions had been good. But that time had long gone.

Turis learned of the spell to break their immortality from Mugan. He had foreseen this war coming. Young Jeremiah Kincaid had been close to Mugan and had been Charles Tampton's previous heir. All this long before Maug had come out of the shell.

What many didn't know was that Jeremiah had been bound to the old black in much the same way Mugan's son was now bonded to Turis. Turis hadn't made it his business to know the extent of their relationship, but he knew that Mugan's death had shattered the human's soul. The only thing Jeremiah lived for after the black died was avenging Mugan's death.

Turis set his head down in thought. Charles Tampton had confirmed that Jeremiah wasn't dead. He was living somewhere in the Geotic Realm, having fled there years ago, but Turis hadn't heard from him again.

He needed to find Jeremiah, and he needed to find that spell. It would take the power of all seven dragon lords to invoke it and kill Oberon. Once that spell was cast, the Fairy King and his tyrannical rule would turn to dust.

Then the real trouble would start. The beasts from the north and the monsters from the south were sure to swarm their borders, eager to take possession of the magical power of the land. The dragons needed a plan ready to hold against them. Turis had been speaking secretly with the advocates, warning them that they intended for Oberon to die. They had to be ready to deal with the backlash of power that Oberon's death would cause. The black dragon hoped that the humans who held the raw power of the Thaumaturgic Realm in check were up to the task.

If they weren't, they were all doomed.

"Too easy." Lord Giet landed next to him and hissed. "It's a trap." The younger black dragon was furious.

Lord Turis drew in a long breath and nodded. "I agree. We need to move."

"We've already started," Giet told him. "I came for you."

"Send word to Maug where we've gone to," Turis ordered.

Giet snickered. "Why? He'll find us eventually."

Turis lashed out, slamming Giet's head hard into the ground with his long powerful dragon arm. "We stand together. And don't forget, Giet, he's the only one that knows where my mate and our future eggs are."

"You have a very bad temper." Giet got up slowly, eyeing him with his ears flat against his head. "And you're getting worse. You had best bring her back soon."

"Let's go," is all Lord Turis said as he pushed himself hard into the air.

~ ~ ~

After a few days of wandering around the large house, Bobby went to find Charles and looked at him earnestly. "I'm bored," she said.

He laughed and handed her a book. She tossed it aside as she threw herself on the couch. "Come on, Charles."

"Well," Charles said, watching her with amusement. "What do you want to do?"

"I want to go home," she said, sitting up hopefully. "I miss my folks; even my brother. I've got other friends too. If I can't be with Maug, I'd rather be there."

"How long has it been since you were home? Since Yule, right?"

"Just before Christmas," she agreed. "I'm sure Granddad told them there was trouble. Can I at least call them to say I'm okay? Maybe Granddad told them I was here."

"Ezra doesn't know you're here," Charles told her. She cocked her head to one side in surprise. Charles and her granddad were good friends and strong allies, which was probably why Ezra Parks had agreed to the marriage contract between her and Maug. She couldn't see him agreeing had it been any other dragon.

"Didn't you tell him?"

"He wouldn't want me to," Charles assured her. He got up from his desk and walked around it to join her on the couch. "This is a very complicated situation, Bobby. There are a lot of politics involved. He can't take sides."

"What do you mean? The dragons are right. Granddad ought to know that!"

"Do you know what the war is about?" Charles asked her with a raised eyebrow.

"Yes. King Oberon wants the dragons dead. He's trying to stop them from having baby dragons."

She colored, realizing her particular role in that part. Honestly, she knew she was pregnant, but didn't know what she would have. Would it be a baby? Or a little dragon? Maug didn't know either. He said he had never learned the specifics of it. He promised he would be here when it was time. And he promised they would live together forever.

Why was forever always so far away?

"Bobby?" Katrin put her head in the office. She was ashen and shaking. Her long brown hair loose, falling around her shoulders. "Bobby, there's something wrong. I think I'm going to be sick."

"I doubt that." Charles got up, put his hands on Katrin's cheeks and smiled. "It has been awhile, I admit, but I think it's time."

"But I'm not ready!" The young green dragon was panicking. "And my mate, he said he'd find a safe place."

"I'm certain he's looking," Charles assured her in a gentle voice. He walked the two of them to the hall and bellowed. "Maggie!" Then he turned back to Katrin with a kind smile. "Don't worry, sweet. We knew this was going to happen. We're ready. For both of you when it comes to it."

Katrin stared at him with terror in her green eyes while Maggie hurried down the stairs. She took one look at the girl and nodded, then went to her side, pushing Charles away.

"Oh, there's a good girl," Maggie told her soothingly. "It's fine. Don't you worry, all right?"

"But I'm not ready," Katrin continued to panic. She spoke over her shoulder to Bobby. "Don't… don't leave me alone. Okay?"

"I won't." Bobby turned from Charles even as Maggie lead the two of them toward the basement stairs. Bobby paused, watching Charles as he went to his study window. He opened it and called down to the garden, where Larubaba was sunning herself in wolf form.

"Laru-baba," he called out pleasantly. "The green is laying."

"She's late," Bobby heard Laru-baba say. "I hope Maug's mate has better manners about this."

Bobby looked at Charles with a stricken expression.

"Laying?" she asked.

"Well, yes, dragons lay eggs. Didn't you know that?"

Bobby didn't have time to process it before she heard her name being called. She hurried to where Maggie had taken Katrin, making her way down the narrow basement steps and into a room that was warm and inviting. There was a wide soft bed, a chair, carpets, and tapestries from the Thaumaturgic Realm hanging on the walls. The one that caught her attention was a red banner with a diamond shaped pattern emblazoned on it. She recognized it as the same pattern on her neck.

"Bobby." Katrin sniffled. Bobby went to her side and took her friend's hand.

"It'll be fine," she said, biting her lip. Maggie Tampton and Laru-baba hurried about the room. She could feel the wolf shaman weaving magic as she spoke in soft tones to Katrin in a language she didn't know. Kat seemed to understand, and she nodded before she turned her head into the pillow.

The hours passed quickly and it wasn't long before Katrin was still, drenched in sweat.

"Oh, wow," Bobby whispered, examining the six small glistening eggs laying around the cushions later. They were practically glowing with color and were warm to the touch. They were just a bit smaller than regular chicken eggs. She looked down to where Katrin was sleeping. Her hair was still damp from the effort of having made… these.

Bobby glanced back and forth between Laru-baba and Maggie Tampton as they wrapped the eggs in small pieces of blankets and towels. Maggie had an electric blanket warming from underneath. Laru-baba inspected it and nodded her wolf head with satisfaction.

"Looks like you've done this before," the wolf said to Maggie. Charles's raised an eyebrow.

"Hardly the first magical creature to take refuge in this house, as you well know," she quipped. "And I doubt she'll be the last. It's her I'm more worried about."

Bobby felt herself color. "I'm not going to do that!"

"Of course not." The wolf lay down and eyed the six eggs Katrin had produced. "You're a human. I doubt we can expect half as many as this."

"Ack!" Bobby squeaked, jumping up. "You're joking! Laru-baba, don't make fun of me!"

"Hush," Maggie frowned as Katrin stirred, then motioned for Bobby to follow her out and up the stairs. "She's right. Charles and I think you'll probably have only one egg, three at most."

"Eggs?" Bobby felt her stomach tighten. "I'm… I'm going to have eggs? But they're so small!"

"They do grow." Maggie's lips twitched. Bobby felt her chest go tight. She hadn't really thought about it until that moment. She had supposed she was going to have a baby. Not eggs. Not baby dragons?

Bobby swallowed, feeling a light sweat on the back of her neck. What did Bobby know about dragons?

"I… I don't know what to do." Bobby looked at the older woman with wide eyes, her breath catching. "W-what am I going to do with three baby dragons?"

"They may not be dragons." Maggie laughed lightly as she put some water in the kettle. "Hasn't anyone spoken to you about this?"

"No!"

"Holy mother. What is that idiot boy doing?" Maggie rolled her eyes and pulled out a kitchen chair for Bobby to sit on. She pointed to it, and Bobby sank into it slowly, feeling like her legs were going numb. "Listen, for you, this is a little more problematic. You see, a dragon usually has five or six in her first clutch. After that, she'll likely have around ten to twelve. The first clutch is always smaller."

Bobby felt numb with shock.

"How can they have so many? There aren't that many dragons. If they have that many eggs at a time, why aren't there more?"

"There can be a lot of complications," the older woman said. "And we don't have clutches often. It's rare for bonded mates to be fertile at the same time. Cycles are anywhere from five to seven years apart, and then males are only in season for two weeks, while a female's lasts two months. After that, the life of a hatchling is dangerous. They are prone to illness, predators, accidents."

"They die?" Bobby felt like the blood was draining from her face.

Maggie got up as the kettle started to whistle.

"When humans and magical creatures breed, children aren't often viable," Maggie said. "Honestly, what is Maug even thinking? Your eggs may not even hatch."

"Not hatch?" Bobby swallowed. First, she'd feared having eggs, and now she was being told that they may not live? She looked at Maggie Tampton with a horrified expression.

Maggie pulled two cups from the cupboard and set them on the table, filling them with steaming water. She pushed a box of different flavored teas in Bobby's direction. Bobby sat stock still in the chair, not touching the box.

"So my children will be half dragon and half human?"

"No." Maggie shook her head. "You and Maug will breed true. You know that I am a dragon?"

"You're his aunt?" Bobby bit her lip.

"Yes, my sister was his dam," Maggie confirmed. "I didn't know a thing about him until he was nearly grown. That's how I met Charles."

"But you and Charles are married. And I've seen pictures of your kids on the walls. Did you adopt?"

Maggie dropped a tea bag into the hot water and lowered her voice. "Human males are fertile all the time," Maggie said. "I did not know this at first. Charles said it would be safer for me to live here, in the Geotic Realm. I've not been back to the Thaumaturgic in over twenty years. For us to have children, there was a good deal of magic involved, but because it was here, I could conceive."

"I don't understand…"

"The first time I was in season, after we married, I had three eggs, and none of them hatched. We tried again five years later, and I laid three eggs again. This time, I had a daughter and a son. The last didn't hatch."

"Are they dragons?" Bobby asked.

"Mostly," Maggie said. "My son Daniel appears human but carries dragon blood. Still, he's never taken dragon form."

"What about your daughter?"

"Victoria." Maggie smiled. "Vicky has a true form. She is a full dragon."

"Oh, God." Bobby started to panic again. "Then I could have a dragon?"

"Your mate is a dragon, Roberta Parks. What did you expect?"

"A baby!" she wailed. "When Laru-baba told me I was pregnant, I thought I was having a baby. A human baby—in nine months!"

"Six weeks to lay," Maggie corrected. "A year to hatch."

"A year?" Bobby looked at her bleakly. "A year? I won't know if my… my eggs will… will even hatch—for a year? And then I won't know what's going to come out?"

Maggie moved out of her chair to hold her. Bobby cried on her shoulder. "Oh god, oh god, oh god," Bobby sobbed. "I… I really want my mom!"

~ ~ ~

"They'll come over the pass here and"—Maug paused, pointing at the map with four of his commanders—"here."

"We've got intelligence that they're going to make a move over here." One of the wolves pointed. "I think we need to redeploy to cover for it."

Maug nodded. "We've got villages in that area. Have they evacuated?"

"Yesterday," Maug's wolf commander, Still, confirmed. It was then that Lords Turis and Tauc came walking in without so much as a knock. The wolves shifted to their true forms with a snarl, snapping their jaws at the intruders. Maug grinned.

"They're welcome," he told the wolves. "Even if they weren't invited. Go on. We'll finish this later."

The wolves slunk around the dragons with a low growl. Tauc looked down at them with a wry grin of amusement. Turis frowned and closed the door after the wolves left.

"You should have called," Maug said as he rolled up the map. "I could have had a nice dinner ready for you. A drink?"

"Shut up." Turis glared at him with a dark expression. "Where is my mate?"

"Safe enough," Maug retorted irritably. "Gods. Don't you have a war to run or something?"

Turis flicked his dark eyes in Tauc's direction. "She's clutched. I can sense it. I want her back. Now."

"Well, sorry," Maug said, pushing himself around the small table by the two. "I'd like to have my mate too. But it doesn't make any difference. They're better off where they are."

Turis grabbed him by the shirt and yanked him, snarling in his face. Maug frowned and struggled to pull away. But the black held him firm as he shook him.

"No!" Turis said in a rough low tone. "I need to get her back. I need her and the eggs where I can—"

"I know," Maug groaned, turning his head away. The young red dragon felt the heady heat of need for his own mate daily. Being apart from her was an agony that tore at his soul. Still, he knew this was for the best. Damned Turis, he ought to know it too. Maug shook his head and pushed the black dragon more gently. This time, he released his grip on him. Maug glanced back over to where Tauc was watching them with a sardonic grin. "And what the hell are you here for?"

"Amusement mostly." The other red shrugged. "Plus, it's getting too dangerous for us to travel alone. We're all not all as stupid and reckless as you."

"It's a sad day when dragon lords have to travel in pairs." Maug smiled sadly. "And it proves the females are better off where they are—with Charles—in the Geotic

Realm. He and his mate will guard them like their own, you know that."

"I don't get over there much myself," Red Tauc told him, walking over to where Maug had a steaming fruit beverage in a wooden decanter. It was a wolf favorite, and Maug found it tolerable. Lord Tauc lifted it to his nose and sniffed. With a shrug, he poured himself a cup. "Why don't the three of us take a little trip? Then Lord Turis can do what he needs to with his mate and stop beating us bloody every time he has a fit of temper."

"Shame on you," Maug mocked and then whipped his head back as Lord Turis lashed out at him. Maug growled low in his throat, ready to turn and launch himself at the black dragon, but Tauc shoved himself between the two.

"This is also why I am here." He smirked, shoving the two backward. "If we leave the two of you alone, one of you will end up dead."

"Your affection is touching," Maug sneered, pushing his hand irritably through his bright red hair.

"We need both of you bastards alive." Tauc lowered his eyelids over his dark eyes to regard Maug with amusement. "Too bad though. I'd love to see Turis take you apart."

"You wish." Maug stood up and lifted his chin with a jerk.

Turis stared at him coldly for a long moment. "We're wasting time," he said. "Take us to where you've hidden them, or I will kill you."

"Don't threaten me," Maug said. But Turis was quicker than Maug expected and grabbed him by the back of the neck, pulling his face inches from his own. Maug braced his arms against his chest and watched his expression warily, feeling a tightening in his stomach. Ugh, why had Turis bonded to him? Out of all the dragon lords, he had to be the biggest pain in the ass.

"Don't try and pretend with me," Turis said softly, raising an eyebrow. "You need your mate as much as I need mine. You think I can't feel it?"

Turis leaned close and blew a soft breath in Maug's ear, causing equal amounts of panic and need in the young dragon.

"Stop it," he whispered hoarsely, trying to pull away.

Turis released him. "Get ready," the older dragon ordered. "We're leaving tonight."

~ ~ ~

Maggie Tampton convinced Charles that Bobby was homesick and miserable. The prospect of having eggs and not a baby terrified her enough that the dragon believed she really did need her mother. Charles relented and sent a car for the Parkses. Oberon would have spies watching the family, but if they came here, Charles believed he could protect them.

Bobby wept between her mom and dad for nearly an hour before she spoke. Then she told them in a low voice what had happened. They were already aware of the marriage arrangement but knew nothing about the war raging between the dragons and the kingdom.

They were shocked when Bobby told them she was pregnant. Her mother frowned, and her father sighed and rubbed the temple of his nose.

"I was worried about this, Bobby." Her mother tucked a lock of her daughter's hair away from her face. "But Ezra said you wouldn't be able to get pregnant."

"They shouldn't have been able to," Charles said. He nodded to Bobby. "I'd like to speak with your parents alone, Roberta. Can you see if Katrin needs anything?"

"Yeah," Bobby hugged her mother tightly and then walked into the hall, closing the study door behind her. Brad was standing in the hall, arms folded against his chest as he leaned against the wall.

"What the hell is going on?" he asked quietly. "First, you and Kat don't come back at Christmas. Then when you do show up, you don't come home, and I'm told that my girlfriend has 'eggs.' And you're pregnant too? Maug said that wasn't a thing that could happen. If it was a risk, why didn't you make him wear a condom?"

Bobby burst into tears and threw her arms around her brother, sobbing against him. He sighed and hugged her, kissing the top of her head.

"So, what?" he asked after a little bit. "Is Maug going to marry you now, or what?"

"Mm-hm." Bobby nodded, pushing away roughly, shoving the tears away from her face. "But there's this war."

"Well, too bad. He needs to get his shit together."

"He wants to," Bobby told him. They walked to the basement stairs together but were interrupted by Farni, who burst through the door, panicking.

"She's gone!" he said. "Katrin's gone! Only her eggs are left! She's been kidnaped!"

"What?" Bobby exclaimed. They ran down the stairs. When they got down there, only Laru-baba and Maggie were in the small room, gathering the eggs and counting them.

"All six are here," Maggie said. "I don't believe anyone took her. They would have taken the eggs too."

"I don't smell anyone else either," Laru-baba agreed. She glanced up. "Oh, hello, Bradley."

"Uh, hi," Brad said uncomfortably. "What's this about Kat?"

"She must have left on her own," Maggie said, even while the little unicorn shook his head vehemently. Tears streaked from his wide blue eyes.

"She wouldn't leave her eggs," he protested.

Bobby bit her lip. She glanced at Brad and knelt next to the young unicorn. "Farni," she said. "You know, Katrin has been really sad. She's not happy with that dragon. I think she ran away."

Brad grunted, and Bobby stood up to look at her brother. "She wasn't happy," Bobby said in a low voice. "She loved you. She told me she did."

He tightened his jaw and turned his face away. Bobby knew he was dying inside. Katrin was to him what Maug was to her.

"But to just leave her eggs?" Farni said with a horrific whisper. "Bobby, you don't understand. That's not the way things work!"

"Roberta is correct," Laru-baba said with a decisive nod. "The girl has been miserable. Dragon females will run if they are not satisfied with their mate. But she can't believe Lord Turis will let this go!"

"Who's Lord Turis?" Brad asked.

Bobby bit her lip and looked back and forth between them. "The father of the eggs."

She didn't want to call the black dragon Katrin's mate because he really wasn't. How could he be if Kat didn't love him? "Maybe she thought if he had the eggs he wouldn't care…"

"If he were a green or yellow, perhaps." Laru-baba turned her head towards Bobby sharply. "But not a black, and certainly not a dragon lord. He'll be furious."

"Maybe he won't know—" She gasped, feeling a sharp stab of pain in her stomach.

"Roberta?" Laru-baba came over and nosed her. Brad caught her in his arms before she keeled over and dropped to the floor.

"Bobby!" he said sharply. Bobby felt another stab of pain, it cut off her ability to speak.

Laru-baba sniffed. "One's late the other early." She snapped at the air. "Can't these girls do anything in the proper order?"

"She's human." Maggie took Bobby, pulled her towards the bed and eased her down. "There is no proper order."

"What's going on?" Brad demanded, hurrying to Bobby's side. She started to pant and gasp for air.

"Nothing you need be part of." The wolf changed into human form and pushed both he and Farni out of the basement room. "Go and tell Charles it has started."

"Bobby's going to have her eggs?" Farni's face glowed with excitement.

"Looks that way," the wolf said, closing the door behind them. "Now go."

~ ~ ~

"She's coming home," James Parks told Charles, pacing the office while Tabitha Parks sat on the loveseat with a deep scowl. He paused and set a hand on his wife's shoulder. "I don't care what you say. Bobby belongs at home with us."

"I don't necessarily disagree," Charles said. He put his fingers together against his mouth. "But there are dangers involved. Your daughter is wanted by the Fairy Kingdom. King Oberon means for her to die."

"Dragons and fairies," Tabitha Parks pressed her lips together. "Ghost knights and unicorns; it's insane. My daughter is in pain, and in trouble. She disappears for weeks, and you want me to what— leave her here?"

"It would be for the best," Charles Tampton said.

Mrs. Parks shook her head vehemently. "No, no, absolutely not." She glared back and forth between the two men. "It's not going to happen."

"Mrs. Parks," Charles drew in a deep breath but was interrupted by a knock on the study door. It was Maggie coming in with a tray of coffee. She smiled politely at the Parkses and set the large tray down on the low table.

"Has Charles mucked things up yet?" she quipped.

"Maggie."

His wife arched an eyebrow at him and turned back to the Parks. "I apologize for everything he's said up to now. The man's an idiot. He's no better than that red he raised."

James and Tabitha Parks were unhappy enough about the situation and Maug. Charles didn't need his wife making it more difficult. Maggie steadfastly refused to pay him any attention as she poured coffee for the Parkses and herself, ignoring him. He cleared his throat. "I'd like some coffee too."

"Get it yourself," she told him over her shoulder. She motioned for James Parks to sit. "This is certainly a fine mess."

"It is," Tabitha Parks said as she threw a frown in Charles direction. "And frankly, I don't know what to do about it."

"Maug and Roberta will get married," Charles said soothingly. "It's what they want."

"And I'm sure people want ice water in hell," Tabitha scoffed. "But my daughter will not be marrying a wanted criminal from a fantasy land!"

"Marriage is not a reasonable option at the moment," Maggie agreed. "Besides the fact that she's human, he's a dragon, and they are both far too young."

"Maug is nearly forty," Charles said.

"He's what?" James Parks exploded.

Maggie sniffed. "Little more than a fledgling." She smiled at the Parkses. "It's always been like this. Charles is forever defending the idiot. I could see what he saw in the cute little tyke."

"He's forty years old?" Tabitha eyed Maggie. "How could you know him as a child? You don't look more than thirty-five."

"Why, thank you." Maggie put down her coffee. She flashed a smile at Charles who rolled his eyes. "I'm holding up amazingly well for my age. But listen, this is important. Bobby has just laid her eggs."

Tabitha Parks drew her brows together. "What do you mean?"

"Her eggs," Maggie repeated. "Two; very good looking and healthy. Still, I can tell them from Katrin's. They're a bit smaller, and the color is a tad off."

"I'm confused," Mr. Parks said. "Eggs?"

"Dragons lay eggs," Charles explained. "Maug is a dragon."

"Hold on," Tabitha Parks said, holding up a finger. "Are you telling me Bobby isn't pregnant anymore?"

"Well, not technically, I suppose." Charles frowned. He had never thought about it that way. A dragon dam was considered to be nesting until the eggs had hatched. But that could just be his thinking, having mated with a dragon.

"Well then." Bobby's mother set the coffee cup down with a nod. "This makes things easier. The dragon can have the eggs, and we can take our daughter home."

"You can't do that," Charles said. "She can't abandon her eggs. They won't thrive!"

"Well, maybe they shouldn't." Tabitha Parks colored. "You said it yourself, the two of them aren't ready to have children."

"But it's happened now!" Charles raised his voice. He threw an annoyed look at his wife. "You could help you know!"

"Bobby needs her family, Charles. At least until Maug can return for her." Maggie flicked her eyes at him. "But I agree, she can't abandon the eggs. We'll have to come up with a workable solution."

"They're eggs," Tabitha Parks said. "Put them in an incubator or something."

"They are your grandchildren," Maggie pointed out. James Parks paused, the color draining from his face. "You do realize that? Those eggs, they are your daughter's children."

The Parkses turned to each other and then Tabitha nodded slowly. "All right, we'll take the eggs home too. We can use a heating pad or, I don't know, something."

"That's for the best," Maggie said. "At least until Maug's finished with this war."

"I can't believe you agree with them!" Charles yelled at his wife.

"They're right!" she retorted indignantly. "Laru and I discussed this. It'll be for the best if we let Bobby Parks get back to her life."

"Except that Oberon is looking to end it," Charles retorted. "Really Maggie. You know better than this."

"And you should cut off all contact with the Thaumaturgic Realm," Maggie said. "You shouldn't have anything to do with Ezra Parks either. You don't know who he's loyal to."

"C'mon," James Parks said. "That's my dad you're talking about. He's not—"

"Ezra Caleb Parks is a pain in the—"

"Maglin!" Charles raised his voice. "That's enough!"

Maggie closed her mouth and looked at her husband with an arched eyebrow.

Charles paused at his desk for a long moment before sitting next to his wife. "There is more trouble going on than you realize." He put a hand on her knee.

"Laru told me, Charles." Maggie pursed her lips. "I think she's right. Bobby needs to go home and forget about the Thaumaturgic Realm for a while."

"My wife is a romantic," Charles said to the Parkses. It was then they heard the shattering explosion from the front hall. Charles threw up a shield as the study door gave way, sending splinters of wood in every direction.

~ ~ ~

"Mm, Eddie," the little unicorn yawned, sitting up. He had been sleeping on the end of the bed when Sir Edwin McGaffy slipped into the basement room. Edwin had been patiently waiting for the Parkses to be contacted about the whereabouts of their daughter. He was rewarded when a car arrived to take them away. The only problem was that he wasn't the only watcher.

"What are you doing here?"

Eddie knelt at the edge of the bed and indicated to Bobby. He wore the daily combat armor from the Thaumaturgic Realm. The Knight shifted his sword around so he could be more stable on the floor. Farni was a sweet creature. Kind and loving. Eddie didn't like lying to him, so he only told him part of the truth. "I've come for Bobby. It's too dangerous for her, Farni. Oberon's forces have been watching the Parks. They'll be making a move soon."

Farni sat up and opened his eyes a little wider.

"We have to tell the advocate!" Farni said. "They can't come here now, Eddie! We just got the eggs!"

"I can't worry about the eggs," the knight sighed. Eggs, with a dragon, it was best to leave them to die. "I just need to get Bobby out of here. Now come on."

"No!" Farni's blue eyes flashed with angry heat. "I guess I understand getting Bobby away, she could get hurt. But I can't, I won't leave her eggs! They're her babies, Eddie!"

"With the Dragon," Eddie said in a cold voice. He shook his head. "No Farni. Leave the eggs and come on."

"You go." Farni watched as Eddie stood, lifted Bobby into his arms, and started out of the room. "I'll stay here. I won't abandon them the way I was."

"Farni, you'll die if you stay here." He started to move out of the room. He had to get Bobby out and didn't have time to argue with the unicorn. "Oberon has left orders that no one lives. Even your shield won't be able to stand that."

Farni shimmered into his white colt form and knelt beside the pot where the eggs were sitting. The little unicorn tapped into his power and set a shield. "Take care of Bobby, okay?"

"Yeah," the knight nodded as he carried the unconscious girl out of the room. "Don't worry. I won't let anything happen to her. I promise."

Sir Edwin went quietly up the stairs, stepping around Bradley Parks prone body in the hall. The idiot shouldn't have challenged him. He didn't like the idea of killing Roberta's brother, but even if he survived the wounds Eddie dealt, Oberon's knights would finish the job. The wolf lay next to him, bleeding as well. Too bad her senses couldn't smell a shadow. They were both allies of the dragon and had to die.

Edwin slipped out a side door and then created a portal. He stepped away without another soul seeing him.

~ ~ ~

The three dragons appeared in Charles's back garden, the way Maug often did. Only this time, the house was engulfed in flames. Turis and Tauc shifted form and took to flight; they were high in the air in a heartbeat. That being the strategic position. Maug's heart froze in his chest before he ran headlong into the flames.

He met resistance on the inside in the form of Oberon's Knights. He knew they were the Fairy King's by their brightly displayed standard on their shields and capes. Maug launched an attack against them, turning five to dust. He heard shouts from the study and ran towards it.

Maug saw the remains of Charles's tattered shield and the bodies of a few knights laying around. He saw with horrified dismay that Roberta's parents lay dead next to each other, half burned with their eyes rolled in the back of their heads. Only years on the battlefield made him not blanch at the sight.

Two Knights advanced on Charles's downed form. Maug snarled and threw two hot bolts of energy. They screamed, disappearing into red dust.

He hurried over to Charles and put his hand on his chest, feeling the overwhelming pain of loss run over him. There wasn't a spark of life left in Charles Tampton.

A small movement caught his attention. He turned and saw his aunt trying to crawl to where her husband lay. Maug leapt over the burning chair and pushed it aside to roll her over, taking her into his arms.

Maggie Tampton opened her eyes to small slits and smiled weakly. She lifted her hand, ran it across his face and then gave it a little slap. Maug pressed the bloody hand against his cheek and kissed it, feeling her pain as if it was his own.

"You little idiot," she whispered.

"I'm sorry, Aunt Maggie," he whispered. "I shouldn't have brought them here."

"Not that." His aunt coughed. "The girl."

"Don't scold me." He snorted, pushing her brown hair away from her face. "I love her."

"Mm." The older woman closed her eyes. "I can die knowing you're not going to be alone."

"No," he begged. He shook her a little. "I need you! I need Charles! You both can't—"

But it was too late. Her spirit slipped from the bonds of flesh. Maug let out a quiet keen as he buried his head against her neck. He held her for a long moment before carrying her to Charles and laying her by his side. He looked at the two of them, feeling like a part of his soul had been torn out. They were the only parents he had known.

He stood. He'd have time for grief later. First, he had to find his mate. He shoved past the door. There were flames everywhere still. Then he saw Laru-baba in the hall with a shield around her. When he got closer, he saw a human male was on the ground beside her. He narrowed his eyes, it was Bradley Parks.

It only took a small tweak of magic to break the wolf's shield. And that was only because she had entrusted him with the 'key' to do it if she was ever unconscious. When he knelt, he saw that Bradley Parks was bleeding from a large wound in the side. He pushed Laru-baba's shoulder. The woman was in wolf form, and far more powerful in that state. She moaned and opened her eyes.

"What are you doing here?" She sighed as she struggled to her feet. She was wounded too. "It's dangerous."

"What the hell happened?"

"Before Oberon's forces got here," she answered. "That Knight of Titania's appeared. He and Bradley argued. I tried to tell Bradley it wasn't smart to argue with a man who had a sword."

"Damn it," Maug muttered. "Where's Roberta?"

"I'm not sure." The wolf shook her head even as she invoked a healing trance for the human. "I left her in the basement with the eggs and Farni."

The basement! Maug jerked his head up. The house was going to cave in soon. "You two get out of here," he said.

"I'll get Charles—"

"Don't bother," he muttered as he got up and started for the basement door. He heard the wolf's words of sympathy, but didn't have time for them. He had to get to his mate before he lost her too. Even thinking of that possibility made his heart tighten.

He had to jump down over the last few missing steps to the basement, and pushed his way into the lower room. He'd spent enough time healing in its heavily warded interior. Charles's house had long been one of the places his enemies hadn't been able to find him. His Aunt Maggie's scathing wit and soothing touch had always welcomed him home.

But the room wasn't the warm and pleasant interior it had been, but rather a burned-out hole. Maug felt his stomach turn. He was too late. The room had been opened to the outside far enough that he could see the sky. Turis and Tauc stood in his way. He pushed forward, certain he wasn't going to like what he found.

"He's been holding the shield," Tauc said in a low voice. Maug's eyes widened with dismay. Farni was holding a shield the color of clear bright metal. The unicorn's eyes were glazed over, his white body drenched with sweat. Oberon's forces must have thrown an incredible amount of power at the lad, but he had held firm.

Unfortunately, Maug's mate wasn't under the shield with him.

"We cleared Oberon's knights out," Tauc continued in a low voice. "But the unicorn won't break his shield."

Maug's turned to where Lord Turis pushed against the shield with his own power. Farni just as stubbornly refused to give way. Maug shook his head in confusion until he saw the tiny treasures the unicorn was guarding. His eyes widened, and he felt another jolt of panic.

"Stop that." He shoved Turis away. "If you break the shield, you could hurt the eggs!"

"I need them!" Turis looked furious. "And that little bastard won't give them up."

"He's been protecting them, you ass!"

Maug knelt at the edge of the shield, getting as close to the boy as he could. "Farni," he said in a low, gentle tone. "It's all right now. Drop your shield. It's Maug."

It was three heartbeats before the boy seemed to refocus. Maug smiled and held up his hands. "Are those my eggs?"

"They're Bobby's eggs too," the unicorn whispered. "I have to keep them safe for her."

"And you've done a fine job."

Turis growled from behind him. It was only going to be a moment before the black launched another assault on the shield.

"Where's my mate, Farni? What happened to Roberta?"

"Eddie," the unicorn whispered in a heartbroken voice. "Eddie took her. But… he left the eggs to die. He—"

"But you didn't let that happen," Maug interrupted. He felt the shield falter a little. The boy was exhausted. "Come on. Let's get the eggs somewhere safe and then we'll go and find Roberta."

"I… I can help?" Farni raised his large blue eyes to the dragon.

Maug nodded. "I think you've earned that right."

The shield dropped, and the boy sagged. Maug grabbed him and held him. Turis moved at blinding speed to collect the eggs.

Maug suppressed a growl. "Don't get attached to them."

Turis flicked an eye in his direction. "They need to stay warm," he said. "They have a better chance together."

Maug nodded. He frowned at Tauc, who was eyeing the unicorn with a hint of appreciation.

"He's not lunch," Maug snapped at him.

The other red dragon laughed as they made their way out.

~ ~ ~

The dragon eggs glistened brightly in the sand-filled cauldron near the fire. Laru-baba had a light shield around them. Lord Turis nodded but wasn't satisfied with the situation. He understood why they had to return to Ridges Hollow though, rather than the safe-haven where the rest of the dragons and their allies were hiding.

With the Advocate of Ridges Hollow dead, Maug had to suppress the wild magic of the constabulary. The young dragon had been trained and raised to be Charles Tampton's heir. With Tampton's death, Maug had a responsibility. Turis wasn't sure how the human Senate of Advocates were going to feel about having a dragon in their midst. Especially at a time when the dragons were at open war with the Crown.

But if Maug could get control of Ridges Hollow, he would be a fully confirmed advocate in the Senate. That could go a long way in promoting the future stability of their race. It would make it even more difficult for Oberon to continue with his genocidal plans against them if he were acting against one of their advocates.

And as such, Maug had to be here, making the preparations. The young dragon had been furious that he wasn't able to return to the Geotic Realm to search for his missing mate. It was only when Turis explained that their eggs still thrived that the young red calmed down enough to push ahead with the plans to meld his power with the land. If the woman had died, so too would her eggs.

Ground quakes and lightning storms had started when Charles Tampton died. His power had kept the wild magic 'compliant,' but with the bindings gone, it was rebelling. Maug had been gone for the last three days, trying to take control of the rogue power.

The weather slowly returned to normal; the ground shakes became fewer and fewer. It was clear the red dragon had been able to do something, but until he came back, Turis couldn't be sure of the final outcome.

He moved out of the chamber where the wolf was tending the eggs. At the moment, he was inclined to trust her with them. And the little unicorn was sleeping soundly in the bed next to Maug's mate's brother. As infuriated as he had been with the little beast for not letting him near his eggs, he understood that it was only due to his brave and stubborn intervention that they had survived at all. For that, Turis would be in the unicorn's debt forever. It was good that the boy was an innocent and guileless creature. Most would be calculating how to make use of a dragon, especially a dragon lord. The unicorn's only plea was to ask if he could stay with the eggs and help keep them safe. A boon Turis was more than willing to make.

When he got down to the main hall, he saw Lord Tauc reviewing dispatches from their brethren.

"Anything?" Turis asked.

"Our Court informants say Oberon is incensed with the murder of Charles Tampton," Tauc said, leafing through the parchments. "You'd think the bastard had an affection for the man."

"More likely he didn't want Maug to get his power." Lord Turis drew a deep breath. "Oberon was always very careful with Charles Tampton. Ridges Hollow is a strategic piece of ground, and Tampton was an incredibly powerful mage."

"Too bad for him."

"Too bad for all of us," said another voice.

They turned their heads as Lord Maug pulled off his travel cloak. He looked paler than he had before. Likely he hadn't eaten in days. Turis would see the young dragon did soon.

"You've secured the land?" Tauc asked.

Maug shrugged carelessly. "Best I could. I don't have the kind of control Charles had. It'll hold for now. And hopefully, it'll be good enough for the other advocates."

"Hope you've studied up on your law." Tauc smirked.

Lord Turis whacked Tauc's shoulder as he went by. "That's your next task," Turis told Maug. "You have to take the exam."

"Gods." Maug dropped in the nearest chair. "No. I'm going to find Roberta."

"The girl can wait."

"I don't want to make her wait." Maug started for his cloak. "I've had enough of this. I'm going after her. She's got to be devastated. Her parents were murdered—and you expect me to stay here?"

"Yes, I do." Lord Turis scowled and walked around in front of him. "And how many days is it since you've eaten?"

"I don't know," Maug retorted. "I don't care."

"You'll care because I'll make you." Turis pointed a finger at Maug's chest. "I told you, upstart. We need you alive."

"I don't give a damn what you need." Maug's dark eyes flashed. "All I want is to find my mate and hatch my eggs."

"Lord Maug has a point," Tauc said with a shrug. Turis threw him an annoyed glare. "Who knows where this girl is, and she is a dragon mother at this point. We can't leave her in the hands of our enemies."

"Don't say things like that," Maug muttered bitterly. "I worry when you agree with me."

"Nice." Tauc raised an eyebrow Turis's direction. "And you bonded with this little bastard?"

"It was the right thing to do at the time," Turis stated. Maug threw him a look of hot belligerence, and the black dragon relented. "I understand, I do. I want my mate back as well. The unicorn said she disappeared before Oberon's forces appeared. Likely she ran away and has no idea what happened."

Maug's searched Turis's eyes, but then the young red shook his head. "I'm going," he said with finality and grabbed his cloak, heading for the door. But before he got there, he dropped to his knees with a sharp cry of pain. Turis felt the all too familiar bite of agony through their bond and hurried to Maug's side. The younger dragon gulped for air, his hand clenched to his chest. Turis grabbed Maug's face, forcing him to meet his eyes and saw stark devastation. Turis pulled Maug towards him. "Check the eggs," Turis rasped, feeling himself being pulled into the pool of Maug's pain.

Tauc didn't gainsay him. Likely he already knew, as Turis did, that Maug's eggs were turning black and cold.

Maug started to shake in his arms. The older dragon closed his eyes and pulled Maug's head to his shoulder. "Don't drown in it. Don't let the emptiness pull you in."

Lord Tauc's hard step sounded across the stone floor. He knelt beside them and shook his head.

"They're dead," Lord Turis said flatly.

Tauc shook his head again. "No, they're fine. The wolf is coming."

Turis looked at the other red dragon, confused, but before he could ask more the wolf trotted in and approached Maug. The young red dragon didn't move, his breathing was rapid and shallow. She narrowed her eyes and licked his nose. Maug didn't even protest at her show of affection. Instead, he went nearly limp in Turis's arms.

"Your bond with the girl has been broken," she told Maug in a tone full of sympathy. Turis felt his chest constrict, knowing that could mean only one thing.

"She's dead?" Turis whispered in a stricken voice. Lord Turis was all too familiar with that horror. He had sworn he would never feel it again. But the wolf shook her head.

"She is not dead. The eggs are thriving." The wolf turned her attention to Maug and poked him hard with her nose. Still he did not react. "Do you understand me, Maug? Your mate is not dead."

He turned his head away, leaning his face into Turis's chest. Laru-baba took her human form and nodded to Turis.

"On your feet, Lord Turis. Get him up to bed," she ordered. "I want him with those eggs, so he doesn't despair and suicide."

Turis nodded, not even feeling irritation towards the wolf. In fact, he was grateful for it. He motioned for Tauc to help him lift the young dragon and take him to where he could see his eggs.

~ ~ ~

Katrin watched the mating mark on the back of Bobby's neck and shoulder change from a brilliant red to a faded, washed out light grey. She frowned, looking up at Eddie and shaking her head, not understanding.

The mirror they had used vanished in a flash of light. Eddie regarded the other woman with impatience. "I thought you said the mark would disappear?"

Elizabeth Cho, like the knight, was a shadow creature. Katrin had seen Eddie take Bobby from the house when she had determined that she couldn't run. It wasn't just leaving the eggs she had so desperately wanted, her soul ached at the idea of never seeing Lord Turis again. Eddie talked her out of returning. He told her they had to protect Bobby. That Oberon was determined to kill her.

Katrin turned her leaf-green eyes on Eddie. "What are you talking about?"

"The mirror takes memories away," Eddie said. "It should have made her forget the dragon and erase the mark. So what happened, Lady Elizabeth?"

"This magic is too strong. It destroyed my mirror," the woman said crossing her arms. "But I believe the bond is broken. We'll see if she remembers him when she wakes."

Katrin swallowed, closing her eyes. "Bobby loves Maug! Why would you do that to her?"

"We talked about this," Eddie snapped at her. "It's the only way to keep her safe from Oberon. My Queen wants her dead too! What do you expect me to do?"

"I don't know," Katrin said as she ran her fingers through Bobby's short black hair. "Something."

Eddie jerked his head. "Oberon killed her entire family."

Katrin nodded. She had cried so many tears that she didn't have any left. Not only for Bobby's mom and dad, but for Brad too. All of them had been slaughtered by the knights.

"Ezra is trying to stay out of the war. You're not going back, right? You said you wanted to be free of the black dragon."

"I do." Katrin felt like her heart was being pulled out of her chest. But she knew her eggs would be safe. She trusted the wolf woman to get them back to Lord Turis. The green dragon knew she would never truly be a fit mate for a dragon lord anyway. He didn't love her. He only wanted her for the offspring she could give him. He would be angry enough to murder her if he found her. "You're right, this is better. But it seems wrong."

"Sometimes there isn't a right answer," Eddie said wearily. "Sometimes there is just a less wrong one. Look, I'll help you two go somewhere they can't find you. Far from here."

"I can help with that." Elizabeth Cho put in. "Thaddeus too. We will be your allies. There is much you can help us with as well."

"What are you going to do?" Katrin asked Eddie.

"I've got to get back to Court and tell the Queen I lost her," he said. "I'll come back and make sure she's safe later."

"All right," Katrin said. Eddie nodded and shimmered away.

Katrin turned to Elizabeth. She didn't fully trust her. This woman had tried to steal Bobby before. Katrin thought Lord Maug had killed her, but she had managed to stay alive.

"Where did you get that mirror?" Katrin asked.

"Oberon's Mirror? It was a gift from my Lady," Elizabeth said. "Sir Edwin and I serve the same."

"The Fairies are dangerous," Katrin said. "You don't know how they are."

"They're only as dangerous as I allow them to be," Elizabeth said. "They don't hold much power here. We're free enough. They will help if we ask, but they cannot directly interfere."

"You didn't mention that to Eddie," Katrin said.

"Eddie is too idealistic." Elizabeth went to the window and looked out. "It's a great day for us, Katrin. You are a dragon. That is a grand thing to be. You and I will be of great help to each other. We will go where these other dragons can't find us."

Katrin didn't say anything. She wasn't positive that there was any place she could hide from Lord Turis should he decide to hunt her down. But she wouldn't be coming into season for another five years. Katrin didn't believe the black would come after her until he thought it might be possible for her to bear him another clutch. By then, the one she had left should have hatched and the little ones just fledglings. Perhaps he would be satisfied with them.

Her eyes travelled to where Bobby was sleeping quietly on the small cot. If Bobby was alive and safe, even if she didn't remember her mate, her magic would still work. And the mark hadn't totally faded. Light as it was, Bobby still wore the mating mark of a dragon. Perhaps one day, after the war was over, she would be able to return to her dragon mate.

But for now, they were safe from both dragon and fairy vengeance. Katrin silently swore she would do anything she could to make sure that Bobby stayed that way.

INTERLUDE

Maug knew Lord Turis had been watching him for some days now. Not that the younger dragon cared. He had ceased caring about anything once the bond with his chosen mate had shattered.

Roberta had been a part of him. She was the bright spot in his soul. Without her, the world was cast in a pallor of grey and hollow emptiness. She was his joy. It was more than love. He longed to close his eyes and never wake. Even their eggs couldn't coax a smile out of him, although they thrived in the black iron cauldron near the fire.

"It means my Lord's mate lives," Laru-baba told him repeatedly. Maug turned his lifeless eyes away. If he couldn't feel her soul breathe into his, then his life had lost all meaning.

"You were tightly bonded." Turis leaned against the doorframe, looking at Maug from across the room. Maug was prone on the bed, not caring if he never got up again. "More than you let on."

"Like I'd let you bastards know anything," Maug muttered bitterly, turning his face away. He heard Turis's heavy sigh, and the door closed. The red dragon thought Turis had left, but when he felt a weight on the bed, Maug turned to look at the black dragon. His ice colored eyes stared right at him. Turis's straight black hair fell into his face. Without meaning to, Maug reached out and ran his fingers through it with a soft moan. "Its like Roberta's."

"You've got to stop this," Turis said in a low, deep voice. "You're practically willing yourself to die."

"Who says I'm not?"

Turis hand shot to Maug's throat. "I don't care for you to die," the black said softly. His touch was light but firm. Maug eyed him, wondering if the black would do him the favor of choking the life out of him. "And you're torturing me with your foolishness."

"You should have thought of that before you bit me." Maug pulled away with resentment and got out of the bed. "This is your fault, Turis. If you had left alone, Roberta could have stayed with me in Terra Su Mudan!"

"Where are you going?" Turis asked, quickly blocking his path to the door.

"Away from you. Away from Laru-baba. Away from those damned eggs!"

Maug didn't even see the blow coming. Turis hit him hard enough to drive him to the floor with a bright blossom of pain along his jaw. Maug growled as the black dragon stood over him and pointed a hard finger.

"Now you listen to me, you ungrateful little prick. Your eggs are everything. Without them, you have no future!"

Maug drew himself back to his feet and tried to pull power, but his path to it was blocked. "What are you doing?" Maug demanded, knowing he didn't have the resources for a full fight with the black.

Turis's lips twitched as he ran his pale eyes along Maug's face and nodded. "I've lost a bond-mate before," the black said, shoving Maug back on the bed. Turis pinned him on the bed and looked down at his face. Maug struggled against him, but he was weak from days of no eating or sleeping. "You think I don't know what you're going though? But you're not only a dragon, you are a dragon lord. Perhaps you should act like one."

Maug clenched his teeth and tried to pull away, but Turis had him firmly pinned. Turis put his lips to Maug's ear and teased it with his tongue.

"Don't," Maug rasped out, struggling. Turis ignored him and moved his lips along Maug's neck, running his hands along his muscled shoulders to his taut stomach and slipped his fingers inside his trousers. "Turis… stop."

Maug's fingers bit into Turis's shoulders, trying to push him away. He didn't care to do that with the black dragon. Bad enough he had forced him before and he wore Turis's mating mark on his lower back. He didn't want it to glow with ethereal color from copulation again.

"No, fledgling," Turis whispered as he ran a tongue along his neck, making Maug shudder with pleasure and arch against him. "You need to re-bond."

"I need to die," Maug groaned, closing his eyes.

"No." Turis leaned against him, and Maug felt his body heat.

Yes, that was the problem. He had that bond with the black, and his soul was howling for its mate; Turis's touch burned him with hot need. "You may feel like she's dead, but she's not. Your eggs live."

"It's a trick." Maug despaired. "Laru-baba did something to keep them alive."

"I'm sure the wolf wishes she was capable of such a thing." Turis ran a thumb along Maug's lip. His grey eyes never faltered, and he regarded Maug seriously. "But it's not possible. If either you or the female died, so would the clutch. It's the way it's always been and the way it'll always be."

Maug closed his eyes and swallowed. "I don't believe Roberta would betray me. She wouldn't."

The black looked at him with pity and pressed his lips hard against Maug's, parting them to taste him. Maug moaned, surrendering himself to the rise in mating heat. He couldn't stop. Turis held his bond by marking him earlier. That bite, along with the magic Turis infused in their first forced mating, triggered the red dragon's fertility. Even thinking of Roberta's touch drove Maug further into oblivion. Turis deftly played against his body, divesting both of their clothes.

When the black dragon entered him, Maug snarled. Without realizing what he was doing, he sank his teeth deep into Turis's muscled bicep. The black dragon hissed with pain even as he continued his hot rhythm against him. Maug felt his venom sink deep into the black's arm, and Turis shuddered hard against him.

After they were spent, Maug licked Turis arm. His bright red mating mark was bleeding out against Turis's skin. He sighed against Turis chest.

"Gods," Maug muttered, thinking of the stupidity of what the two had done. He'd tied himself tighter to the older black than he had been before. Maug felt his arrogant presence moving into the hole that had been hollowed out when Roberta had been yanked away.

"It was necessary." Turis nosed the top of his head and moved his lips to his ear. Maug gasped, feeling the need rise in him again. "We need you upstart. We need your hatchlings."

"I…" Maug felt the tears he hadn't allowed burn his eyes. They streamed down his face, and he shook with raw emotion. Turis held him while his body rocked with sobs. "I need my mate."

"I know." Turis nodded, lifting Maug's face and forcing him to meet his eyes. He pushed a tear away with a thumb while he held his face. There was no reproach for Maug's weakness, just quiet understanding.

ABOUT THE AUTHOR:

Kyleen Valleaux writes because it's cheaper than therapy. She works as a telecom mercenary and takes the stress out on fictional characters. Never one to back down from a writing challenge, she will go without food or sleep to get the stories written. Her family and friends have adjusted to her complete withdrawal from the human race each year during the month of November. She resides in Michigan with three big German Shepherd Dogs, and a millennial.

Please check out Kyleen's other series, Chronicles of the Garlon T'zen. The first book, "Manor Town," is available now.

Connect with Kyleen online!
https://twitter.com/kyleen66
https://www.facebook.com/kyleenvalleaux

If you like Urban Fantasy, you will love R.R. Virdi's Grave Report and Books of Winter!

R. R. VIRDI
DRAGON AWARD NOMINATED AUTHOR

"I believe R.R. Virdi belongs with other Urban Fantasy greats like Jim Butcher. The Grave Report is sure to go far and only pick up more fans with each successful novel. I can't wait to see where R.R. Virdi will take us next." -- A Drop Of Ink Reviews

E.A. Copen's Judah Black will keep you turning every page!

When a werewolf is murdered on a supernatural reservation, Judah Black is thrust into a world of secrets and lies. After her son disappears, Judah will stop at nothing to save him. But it may already be too late. He's not the first kid to go missing on the reservation, and with flesh eating monsters about, time is running out.

Available on Amazon!

www.ingramcontent.com/pod-product-compliance
Lightning Source LLC
Chambersburg PA
CBHW070756190726
48292CB00002B/549